Living Parallel is the first of **Alexandr Kliment**'s books to appear in English. Born in 1929, Kliment is the author of four novels, two story collections, two children's books, and a volume of poetry, as well as several plays, radio plays, and screenplays. From 1970 to 1989, his work was banned in Czechoslovakia, and he was not allowed to continue working as an editor, columnist, and dramaturg. The original Czech *Living Parallel* was published by three different emigré publishers, including 68 Publishers in Toronto, and it was one of the first novels to be published in Czechoslovakia after the Velvet Revolution. Kliment lives in Prague.

Robert Wechsler, the translator, is the author of *Performing Without a Stage: The Art of Literary Translation* (1998) and has been editing Catbird's Czech and German literature in translation since 1988. This is his first book-length translation.

Ivan Klíma, author of the Foreword, is a well-known Czech novelist, story writer, and playwright, and former president of Czech PEN. Many of his novels and story collections have appeared in English; his latest book is the novel *No Saints or Angels*, translated by Gerald Turner.

Living Parallel

a novel by
Alexandr Kliment

translated from the Czech by
Robert Wechsler

foreword by
Ivan Klíma

Catbird Press
A Garrigue Book

Translation of: *Nuda v Čechách* © 1977 Alexandr Kliment

First English-language edition. A different translation of the first
chapter appeared in *Daylight in Nightclub Inferno: Czech Fiction from
the Post-Kundera Generation* (Catbird, 1997).

CATBIRD PRESS, 16 Windsor Road, North Haven, CT 06473
800-360-2391; catbird@pipeline.com; www.catbirdpress.com

Our books are distributed to the trade by Independent Publishers
Group

Library of Congress Cataloging-in-Publication

Kliment, Alexandr, 1929-
   [Nuda v Cechach. English]
   Living parallel : a novel / by Alexandr Kliment ; translated from
the Czech by Robert Wechsler ; foreword by Ivan Klima.
    p. cm.
   "A Garrigue book."
   ISBN 0-945774-51-6 (hardcover : alk. paper)
   I. Wechsler, Robert, 1954-   . II. Title.
PG5039.21.L53 N813 2001
891.8'6354--dc21

                     2001005980

Foreword by Ivan Klíma

Alexandr Kliment, born in January 1929, belongs to the Czech literary generation of Milan Kundera, Pavel Kohout, Ludvík Vaculík, Josef Škvorecký and, although a bit younger, Václav Havel. He belongs to that part of the generation, along with Škvorecký and Havel, who never fell for the enticing promises of the Communist regime. In his works we cannot find any libations to the regime, which so few managed to see through at first. Like the protagonist of this novel, Kliment managed to stand his ground and, therefore, in the fifties he was pushed aside, condemned to do routine work for a textbook publisher. After the Soviet occupation of 1968, Kliment was one of the authors prohibited from publishing his work, and so he made his living as a hotel porter and a proof-reader.

His first novel, *Marie* (1960), stirred up a furious reaction from the official critics not because he wrote about political issues, but because his novel made no reference to communism at all: like all of Kliment's fiction, it dealt with people's feelings, with relationships, with the pain that follows disillusionment, pain that our nearest and dearest hand on to us. Even then, what was most amazing and disconcerting about his fiction was its imagery, which differed so markedly from what the official doctrine, socialist realism, required.

Living Parallel appeared nearly twenty years later. It is the work of a mature writer, whose vision and depiction of the world had become refined and distinctively original. Many years later, I recalled that the novel's theme was love and murder in our country during the period of our youth – that is, in the fifties and sixties. However, this book – like the rest of Kliment's notably polyphonic fiction – had other themes and motifs, of which one of the most significant was the problem of emigration. Should a man who cannot find the opportunity to realize his ideas, to freely develop his talents or personality, remain in a country where a totalitarian regime takes a club to everyone's creativity and individuality? This was a theme most of us took an interest in. I dealt with it in one of my shorter works, where I had the protagonist summarize all the arguments pro and con. His response to the question, Why stay?, was: I don't know.

Kliment's protagonist, the architect Mikuláš Svoboda, at first glance an impractical and not particularly defiant aesthete, but at the same time a man willfully searching for a way to live honorably and to at least build relationships with people (since he cannot build buildings according to his conceptions), responds not in words, but in action. The entire story is devoted to explaining, to justifying his response. The novel alternates between present and past, pro and con, and it might be said that on the one side (I go) the arguments are relatively rational, and that on the other side (I stay) the arguments are more emotional, even irrational, especially the protagonist's relationship with the countryside, with his native land, and with its capital city, Prague.

I recently reread the novel, more than twenty years after it was written, at which time, coincidentally, I was preparing a study of Prague, and for the first time I appreciated how impressively, with what deep feeling for and understanding of its atmosphere and its traditions this writer managed to interpolate Prague into the tissue of his story, into the life of his protagonist. *Living Parallel* is not only a story about people's lives a couple of decades ago, about their loves and about their suffering, which ends for one in a lover's embrace, but for others in an insane asylum, an illegally dug grave, and a suicidal escape from the stifling constrictions of an extortionate system; it is also a story about Prague and about the Czech countryside, about its splendor and about how it too suffered, about what it took to survive all the violence perpetrated against it. It is a story about how interwoven our lives are with our country and its landscape. We are tethered to them. Whereas even the most powerful, dramatic occurrences fade over time, inside of us the landscape in which they occurred remains unchanged.

Kliment's way of telling a story is very special and original. It consists of a continuous alternation of motifs: he jumps from intensely told episodes to lyrical passages about the countryside, and then on to reflections about beauty, ecology, and baroque architecture. He even tries to render dramatic moments in images that defuse their drama, to render drama with the remoteness of a dream. I can now appreciate that Kliment's singular way of telling a story has influenced the best Czech fiction writers of the next generation, including Daniela Hodrová, Jáchym Topol, and Zuzana Brabcová. This only confirmed my conviction that Kliment is one of the most interesting and thought-provoking of modern Czech authors.

translated by Robert Wechsler

Translator's Preface

I was attracted to Alexandr Kliment's novel *Living Parallel* primarily by the beauty and complexity of its prose and by a partial identification with the narrator-protagonist, who lives a similarly internal, aesthetically-oriented life (however, I am fortunate enough to have my internal and professional life intersect rather than, like the protagonist's, run parallel). But the novel's beautiful prose is not the sort I could ever imagine writing myself; it is primarily lyrical and sad, and I tend toward the rational and humorous. I felt less an affinity with the novel than a desire to experience it from within, by interpreting it closely and writing it myself, and thereby expanding my stylistic repertoire. I also wanted to share the novel's beauty with those who could not read the book in Czech.

I quickly discovered that some of the most exciting aspects of Kliment's prose could not be consistently reproduced in English, particularly his mastery of word order. Czech word order is much more flexible than English because, like Latin, it is an inflected language, with gender and numerous cases that allow words to relate to one another in almost any order. Kliment takes full advantage of this flexibility without giving up much in the way of clarity and without seeming stilted. To try to replicate this in English would make an already difficult novel impossible to read.

But it is hard to ignore something that contributes so much to the special quality of Kliment's prose. My decision was to force the English sentence structure a little here and there, but only a lot when it was important to capture a heightened poetic moment, a crescendo of plot, character, image, or language. Also, in many instances where a sentence ends with a particularly important word or phrase, especially at the end of an important paragraph, often the last paragraph of a chapter or scene, I did what I could to end the sentence with an equivalent word or phrase.

These sorts of decisions are more common in poetry, where there is more heightening of effect. I approached *Living Parallel* the same way I would a poem, trying to make the prose rhythmical, the images fresh, the effects equivalent. To do this, I had to decide at each point what quality was most important to preserve, unless I could find a way of capturing everything at once. Usually, the overall effect won out, and I chose rhythm and other sound considerations over exact meaning. Also, I tried hard to keep the images as striking as the author's.

The more difficult a work is to translate into a particular language, the fewer the elements a translator can bring into his language. (Although translations tend to be more difficult the more complex the writing is, very simple writing has its own difficulties.) I usually give a translation a rough percentage. For example, I feel that I was able to capture 85% of *Living Parallel*. The translations of Milan Kundera's Czech novels are 95% (in fact, many feel that his works read better in English than in Czech); those of Bohumil Hrabal's novels and stories are, like Kliment's, around 85%.

The more difficult it is to fully capture the original work, the more a translator feels obligated to make up for what is lost by doing things the author would do, but in different places. Here is an example, which appears on page 172: "Next

to you I am at home. With silent ardor, I belong with you and
nowhere else. You are being admired and your sleep knows it.
You smile just a bit, you're already beginning to wake. A soft
ripple goes through your body, your left breast loses its center
of gravity and slowly pours down upon my hip. Is gravity
plucking you from your sleep? But all you do is sigh, you like
to sigh, you know something about yourself, there's a dream
that's deserting you and you're stretching yourself into the
bliss of a slumber that, today, will not be alarmed by the
diurnal clamor of your alarm clock."

I reproduced the entire paragraph because if I had reproduced only the last clause, which is what I will talk about,
part of it would have made no sense at all, and even as is,
there is a whole host of images and words behind this clause
(for example, the phrase I translate as "am at home" resonates
throughout the novel – a major theme is being at home, and
the prospect of leaving it; in another book, I might translate
the same phrase less literally, perhaps as "feel just right.")

In the last clause of this paragraph, the Czech for "alarm
clock" is literally "waker," the thing that wakes us. There's
nothing alarming in a Czech alarm clock. The clause reads,
literally, "today it [i.e., your slumber] will not be alarmed by
the plain clanging of the waker." In Czech, the future helper,
"will" in English, is also the first syllable of the paragraph's
final word, "waker," and they are only four words apart. So
there is an odd sort of repetition, with a root expanding into
a completely different sort of word, yet one that is also
temporal, that lets us know that the future day is now the
present. This can't be done in English, at least not without a
lot of padding, which would ruin the easy effect.

Throughout the novel, Kliment makes us see common
things and events in a fresh light. Unable to replicate the
Czech word play in this sentence, I found the chance to play

with another word and to show something common in a fresh light, only not at a place where the author had done so. We don't hear the alarm in "alarm clock" anymore; it's just something that wakes us up, more often than not with non-alarming music or with news that alarms us in a different way. So I replaced the original's repetition of the future helper with the repetition of "alarm." It's a different repetition, but it works just as well, and it's the sort of thing the author does throughout the novel, only not here.

You may have also noticed that I translated the word "plain" as "diurnal". The word, *civilní*, which means "civil, ordinary, plain," is another word that resonates throughout the novel, particularly with respect to one character, who happens to be the slumbering woman's ex-husband. But in English it has to be translated as "plain," because the ex-husband works for the Czech equivalent of the KGB: he is a "plainclothes-man," but also a civil, ordinary man, another good man caught in a bind. Kliment repeats this word very often, and some-times it just doesn't work in English, so sometimes I chose to leave it out or used another English word, so that the reso-nance was lost. With this sort of repetition, it's not each specific instance that matters so much as the accumulation of usage, which increases the emotional depth of words, phrases, and images. In this instance, because I didn't feel "plain" would work, I chose a word that further accentuates the temporal aspect of the clause, is striking in a Klimentian manner, and sounds good in the context (sound was also behind my choice of "clamor").

American readers take for granted that their translators will go to great pains to get such difficult sentences "right." But this is not the case throughout the world. In most of the world, literary translators, such as the narrator's ex-wife in *Living Parallel*, are trying to make a living off their translations (here in the U.S., most literary translators are professors), and since payment is low and the deadlines often tight, literary translators often simplify, they often flatten away some of the difficulties, in order to be efficient. In the German translation of *Living Parallel*, which I often turned to when I had a question about meaning or interpretation, the translators, Alexandra and Gerhard Baumrucker, simply skipped many of the most difficult phrases, sentences, even entire paragraphs (it's also possible, but highly unlikely, that the translators' editor made these deletions). It is wonderful that the Germans translate so much more literature than we do, but it is sad that it is often done to the detriment of the literature. Yes, most of it is still there, but some of the most beautiful and important passages of the novel have been sacrificed.

One thing I should alert you to is the fact that I am not fluent in Czech. Having edited numerous English translations of Czech fiction and poetry and translated numerous stories and poems, I have an excellent feel, or intuition, both for Czech and for English translations of it. However, since I have not lived in the Czech Republic, my knowledge of the language is purely literary. I would never think of translating a writer who puts a great deal of emphasis on colloquial Czech, such as Jáchym Topol; Kliment is a relatively formal writer.

I tell you this not only to give fair notice, but also to emphasize that literary translation is less a linguistic exercise than a literary exercise. It is more important that the translator be fluent in understanding and intepreting literature and be able to write extremely well in his own language, than that he be fluent in the language of the original. Literary translation is much more about judgment than about knowledge. Although my translation is most likely peppered with little mistakes, I don't feel than any of them will make a difference to the English reader's appreciation or understanding of the novel. If I did not think that the reader's experience of the novel was far more important than getting every little detail just right (which is, in any event, not desirable, because you give up too much of the original work's artistry to achieve this level of literal fidelity), I would not have done the translation.

In addition, I had some very helpful, knowledgeable people to lean on. I would like to thank the experienced translator, and friend, Peter Kussi for answering so many of my questions, and the author and his daughter-in-law, Eva Klimentová, herself a translator from English into Czech, for answering my questions and pointing out my mistakes. I would also like to thank Trudy Balch for her helpful feedback on my manuscript, Elena Lappin for introducing me to Kliment's work, and Andrée Collier for her translation of this novel's first chapter in Elena's anthology, *Daylight in Nightclub Inferno*.

Remember as you read this novel that it is the poetic first-person narrative of an aesthetic man who in the novel's present is trying to make the most difficult decision of his life. The author does not depend on the suspense of the plot or the growth of the characters, but rather works by the music of the prose and by the accumulation and resonance of the phrases and images. In fact, there is only one character: the narrator. Everyone else appears only in terms of the narrator's thoughts and memories, and does not lead a separate existence.

Try reading the novel aloud; it's meant for that. If you let *Living Parallel* take you where and how it wants you to go, you will have an incredible reading experience. If you try to impose on it your expectations about fiction, you are sure to be disappointed.

Characters, Place Names, and Pronunciation

This page and the next contain the pronunciation of and information about the novel's major characters and locations. If you like to read aloud or be able to say what you read, this will help a lot.

This page can be used as a bookmark, for easier reference. Simply cut along the line, or fold the page each way a couple of times, and rip the bookmark out.

If this book is yours, don't hesitate to mutilate it, no matter what your teachers said. If it's a library's, please leave the bookmark for others to use.

The pronunciations are approximate and informal, as close as possible without lengthy explanation. The order of the characters is roughly that of their appearance in the novel.

MIKULÁŠ SVOBODA *Meek'-oo-lawsh Svoh'-boh-dah* (architect and narrator-protagonist; his first name is the saint who in English is known as Nicholas, and there is a Prague church with his name, which is often referred to in this novel; his last name means "freedom" in the social rather than personal sense, but is also a common Czech name)

OLGA *Ohl'-gah* (painter; Mikuláš's long-time love interest)

JARMILA *Jar'-meh-lah* (translator; Mikuláš's ex-wife)

ŠTĚPÁN *Shtyay'-pahn* (priest and Mikuláš's old friend; he lives in **Hrádek** *Hrah'-dake*, a town in southern **Moravia** *Moh'-rah-vee-ah*, the central part of Czechoslovakia)

BÉDA *Bay'-dah* (Mikuláš's younger brother)

VÁCLAV *Vah'-tslahv* (horseman and Olga's first husband; also the name of the Czech king known in English as Wenceslaus, and a common Czech name, as in President Havel)

KORMUND *Core'-moond* (architect and old friend of Mikuláš'; this is his last name; his wife is **Květa Kormundová** *Kvyet'-ah Core'-moon-doh-vah*; květa means "flower" and is a common Czech name; their children are twin boys, **Petr** *Peh'-ter* and **Pavel** *Pah'-vel*, Peter and Paul)

DR. RYCHTA *Reekh'-tah* (effectively, Mikuláš's boss)

UNCLE BOLESLAV *Bohl'-ah-slav* (Mikuláš's uncle, who lives on a farm near **Beroun** *Bay'-roh-oon*, a town just southwest of Prague, where Mikuláš's project is to be built)

MILÁDKA *Mee'-lahd-kah* (luggagette at central train station and Mikuláš's lover, who lives in the **Žižkov** *Zheezh'-kohv* section of Prague, a working-class area just east of the train station)

VĚRKA *Vyer'-kah* (Kormund's housekeeper and lover)

Placenames

Malá Strana *Mahl'-ah Strah'-nah* (the west side of the **Vltava** *Vil'-tah-vah* river, at the base of the Castle Hill; it means the "small side" but is often translated as Lesser Quarter or Little Town (as opposed to the Old Town), but since all of the choices sound awful, I have chosen to leave it in Czech)

Vrtbovský Garden *Vert'-bohv-ski* (public garden in Malá Strana where Olga lives; it faces the Church of St. Mikuláš, the largest church in Malá Strana)

Čertovka Canal *Chair'-tove-kah* (canal that runs along the Vltava River in Malá Strana; **The Kampa** *Kahm'-pah* is an island between the canal and the river)

Letná Hill *Leht'-nah* (hill to the east of the Castle hill, on which Stalin Monument was built)

Landscape

As I walked across Charles Bridge, I was feeling good, downright festive. I hadn't felt like this for a long time. I gave myself up to the feeling. The bell of St. Vitus', in the Prague Castle, was just beginning to strike five o'clock in the afternoon. The bell's voice, aristocratic, royal, imperial, spread down across the roofs of Malá Strana, all the way down to the banks of the Vltava, and settled on its dark gray surface. And on me too it settled, in me too it rang.

It was growing dark. Autumn, nearly winter. It was lightly drizzling. Nineteen sixty-seven. In two weeks, just before Christmas, I would turn forty. Not long ago it had made me sick to acknowledge this. Now, however, I had the same impression I had had many years before, that everything lies before me. It was not just an impression. I found the drizzling pleasant.

I stood exposing my face to the breeze and to the light sprinkle of the rain, and I believe I was smiling blissfully. Several people looked at me. It's possible that among the turning heads were statues on the bridge. I wouldn't be surprised. After all, we have said a thing or two to one another, my good, aged saints. Even stone can feel someone walking by with resolute steps, someone carrying within him a good decision. Such a man walks well, lightly, festively.

It was plain and simple. I go to the end of the bridge, and then I walk along the Kampa, and in the Vrtbovský Garden I greet the dampened profiles of the Braun statues and then say to Olga:

"Olga, here I am. I will go away with you."

I ran down the steps to the Kampa. The curves of the baroque façades shaped in me a mood of harmonious ornament. The wind propelled toward me the last leaves from the locust, plane, and linden trees. With the help of a bamboo pole, a beige figure right out of a Jan Neruda tale was lighting the gas streetlamps. I watched him for a while. My city, which I would soon forsake, has its little miracles, its everyday liturgy. I stood piously, as at a ceremony.

Inside each glassed-in, cast-iron lantern hangs a white, circular mantle, and there a gas flame flickers. You pull on a ring below the lamp, the gas spreads around the rim of the filament, the lantern flares up and hums quietly, singingly. The bright register of an organ. How many times when I was a boy did I shinny up a Malá Strana lamppost so that I too could light a gas lantern and it could shine for me alone! But what I did was senseless, because I always lit them in the afternoon. By evening they were already lit.

Driven by the flow of the Kampa's Čertovka Canal, the millwheel turns with just as little sense as the world. For a moment I stood and listened to the water sloshing and gurgling through the wooden slats of the wheel. Long ago the mill was a place for grinding. Now it is some sort of warehouse. At such a lovely spot, there should be a pretty dwelling or a pleasant tavern, but I won't get worked up over it.

I stopped outside a forecourt of the Church of St. Mary Under the Chain. The romanesque cathedral burned down in the Hussite Wars. Like everything else, it burned down for nothing. All that remained were two square stone gothic towers and a portal. They restored the church in the baroque style, and its large courtyard allows the viewer a good, airy distance. Go inside! Growing in the forecourt, whose upper regions are demarcated by the buildings of the Knights of Malta, is a bed of hydrangeas. The wonderfully ancient rainfall has soaked the huge, flowered heads of pastel panicles well beyond their prime. Every year I have come to this forecourt to pick a bouquet of autumn hydrangeas. This year I forgot. I will pick a single hydrangea and bring it to Olga.

I always pick the hydrangeas before the first frost comes. I dry them until papery and they last the entire year in a vase without water. Many times, ten times perhaps, Jarmila was with me when I picked them. I am amazed at how vivid are the sentimental memories of a long past love. But I must look ahead. Hydrangeas grow elsewhere in Europe. The memories I can bring along.

The forecourt is carefully swept by the sexton's wife, whose age is beyond estimation. I recall the woman from my childhood: tiny and bent. She had the face of a countess. She swept the forecourt during the First, the so-called Bourgeois Republic, and she swept it when the Germans occupied Prague during the war. After the war, two or three years of problematic democracy, and now we've had nearly twenty years of the communist regime and she goes on smiling just like the time I said:

"It is so nice, the way you tend the hydrangeas."

"All I did was plant them," she said. "These flowers are tended by our Lord God. It is He who gives them rain and sunlight, and you will come again next year to pick some."

This time I picked a single hydrangea for Olga and said to myself: Olga, I am picking it for you and I am picking it now without thinking of Jarmila.

From a nearby home for the blind came the sound of piano music. I looked toward, I gazed at, the music, I let my imagination go, and I and my single hydrangea went off to the Vrtbovský Garden.

Before ringing at the door of Olga's studio, I greeted the Braun statues on the terrace. I was resolved, and that was that. It was almost dark now, but in the distance, in the fog illuminated by the final reflections of the sun, still beautifully unmistakable, was a full view of the Old Town's spires. They say there are a hundred.

One of the statues smiled at me. Was it only one? Yes, it was Miládka who smiled at me. That short, pointy nose and that chin shaped affectionately like a filly's reminds me of her face, and the silhouette of her body, equally baroque. Her powerful body, lavishly curved, yet with delicate limbs and the most slender of fingers. I will go say farewell to Miládka at Prague Central Station. Olga is different, Olga is tall and slender, nearly as tall as me.

Jarmila was small, tiny, but why am I talking like this – was? Why do I tell myself that she was tiny, as if a toy? Jarmila still after all invariably is, on her own in what is still after all this city. Only for me has she become the past that I have already begun to forget, and will until I've forgotten completely. Not that completely. Several fossilized gestures will remain, largely aesthetic in content, and from time to time I will gratefully return to her in the gallery of my memories.

I must also say farewell to Jarmila, calmly and amicably. I will not flee, I will not run away from anything, at least not from myself or the shades of my loves. I am only going abroad.

But I keep standing here immobile, a statue among statues, sharing their calmness and even their most calm resolve: We statues will remain standing and you will go. You will first go across the terrace, you will climb the steps to the garden cottage, and you will ring at Olga's door. Everything will play out precisely as you've imagined.

The door opened. I was dazzled by the light. Olga held out her hand. Despite the light I found her hand and took it, and for an instant I saw Olga upside down. It wasn't something crazy or inconceivable; it was just that at that moment my heart stopped, and a distinct wave of warm air from the studio, thoroughly saturated with the smell of turpentine, poppyseed oil, and beeswax, grasped my anticipation and turned my stomach just as upside down as her. I could hear water thrumming its way through the gutters overhead.

So does love arise.

A moment's flip-flopped sight, and forever we are different.

The first time I saw Olga was every bit as intense. Of course, it had its prelude. Or perhaps I'm exaggerating a bit. Nothing really happened. Just the recording of my feelings about the landscape through which a train was passing. Once I wrote you, Olga, that you, dear, are my landscape.

Nowadays such trains don't run anymore, they don't puff and wheeze along anymore, nor do they whistle. Nowadays express trains whizz back and forth, powered by oil or electricity. I will take such an express train to Paris with Olga.

We are going just before Christmas. The day before or the day after my fortieth birthday. I hope there'll be snow on the line between Beroun and Zdice. I would like that. I will be sitting across from Olga, by the window, but at the same time I will be standing on the snow-covered mountain above Knížkovice and I will be watching the train there in the distance traveling westward. It pierces my heart, as always, when I see a train traveling through a landscape, yes, dear Olga, even a train more technologically advanced.

I am standing on a snow-covered field, and something is pulling away from me. I am pulling away, and I see someone standing on that field. Something, someone is relinquishing it.

It makes me sad. I would much rather be in the forest at Svatá and then further on, at Křivoklát. I'd be better off there, even this evening in the autumn rain. Should I turn right around and go to the station?

Don't worry, Olga, my decision is firm. I am already sitting with you in your studio, and in a few weeks I will be sitting with you on the Paris express. I hope that we will be sitting by the window.

Right away I'll show you that, thank goodness, I have all my papers and they're all in order. By the way, don't you think it's comical, and that after a thousand years or so no one will willingly believe, that traveling from one European country to another European country could be such an enormous problem, and for me such a fateful decision?

I have not chosen between East and West. I have chosen between myself and Olga. It is a personal matter. Nevertheless I must cross the border between East and West, and I know that I will enter another world. Reds are everywhere – I smile, of course, but to some extent, geographically speaking, it may be said scrupulously that, on the whole, from here all the way back to the Pacific the world is substantially red, and from here to the Atlantic the world is problematically white. Our Lord God and several presidents set their hearts on the dividing line going precisely and without any sort of shading along our finely forested border. But why get worked up over it.

It was across those forested hillsides that people used to escape to the West and be shot at. Then up went a continuous barbwire fence, and they had to dream up very complicated ways of getting themselves out. Now it is simpler. Government offices are just moderately tiresome, and by lining up for a bit, everything may, on the whole, be easily arranged. So, for example, I will travel to Paris on the basis of a personal invitation certifying that I will be provided for during my stay. Out there, you can't change Czech crowns into dollars. But my acquaintances understand, of course, that they won't have to give me breakfast. It's a mere formality. Even the official from whom I requested an exit permit understands that the invitation is just a matter of form. All I had to do was show her the stamp on the French envelope. She didn't even want to look the letter over. But my plan to stay out there, that nobody can know, that would not be taken so liberally. If someone were to denounce me, they would shoot me at the border, from the train. But nobody knows, except Olga.

My friends and I have discussed emigration a great deal over the past twenty years. It was one of the principal themes of our endless and hopeless discussions. To stay? To leave? Which is better? Which is worse? To lose home and gain freedom? And it goes without saying that we also explored the question the other way around: but what is freedom and where is home?

We were definitely not active opponents of the Czechoslovak communist regime. But neither were we Communists, that is, party members, and that made our lives rather difficult. The moral and pragmatic burdens of such a life led many people to seriously consider going abroad. For me, however, such a step never seemed real. Very simply, I was never attracted to anywhere else.

When Olga told me that she was going abroad for good, I grieved. At the same time, I was afraid that, out of principle, she would still want to discuss her departure, that she hadn't absolutely decided, and that I wouldn't have anything to add to all those endless discussions. But Olga had firmly and unequivocally decided. If she had felt any uncertainty, it's not something she would have even brought up.

Olga paints with the same utter certainty and mastery. If I were a painter, I would long and doubtfully circle around my conceptions. Olga is different. For her there is no space between conception and spot of color, not even room for a slip of paper; there's just her graceful gesture. I don't recall her spoiling a single canvas during the twenty years I've known her. She experiences her paintings in advance, to perfection, and she composes out of her imagination with the same casual ease I bring to cracking eggs.

"It's marvelous how I enjoy my work," she would say. "You can't imagine how I love getting up in the morning."

I don't recall ever loving to get up in the morning. I've only ever liked getting up Sundays and holidays, and even then it's been quite a while. And yes, there were my student days. Of course Olga, she walks down the corridor, bolts down some eggs, sets up her easel, and starts right in. Some people are lucky. But why get worked up over it.

Me, every morning I have to clock myself in or check in with the guard at the entrance, using the pencil attached to the spine of his attendance book. It's hard to say that I'm actually bored. I'm good at losing myself in my work; it comes handily, but not at all like hers. A Marxist philosopher would say that I am completely free, because I comprehend my boredom. I comprehend that I have to make a living. I am careful with my money, I have a decent spatial imagination and I draw easily. And of course I don't grumble. Architecture is a good calling, but I haven't been successful at crossing the border from the region of drudgery to the world of creation. I don't get to take shots at the goal. I carefully fulfill the assigned tasks and compliantly place apartment units in pre-designated holes on pre-determined plots of land.

I have not managed to implement any of my own projects. Between me and implementation, between my projects and buildings, there are always so many obstacles I am unable to surmount.

Between me and Olga, finally, there are no obstacles. Because I was able to decide with such certainty. Between us there is only time, spread before us like a continent. That time is behind us – our youth – but I have the feeling that the most important time still lies before me.

Olga has been present in my imagination from the first moment I saw her. To me, her image turned upside down. In me, it became fixed forever like my native landscape. And by the way, Olga, don't you recall my telling you that you, dear, are my landscape?

So first the prelude, but nothing really happened. I simply observed the landscape and the train approaching me through it. What occurred twenty years ago was not actually an occurrence. I simply saw Olga for the first time. Although it was a bright afternoon, the tow of the blue spectrum of night colors carried me with it like the incoming tide, like the outgoing tide. An overwhelming feeling cast me onto a foreign land, which for two decades I have explored in my thoughts, and it dragged me down to unknown depths of my imagination. The old Czech proverb goes: Love is born in the eye and descends to the heart.

The year nineteen hundred and forty-seven, late summer. I have been studying architecture for two years. Still full of hope and enthusiasm. Before the beginning of the winter semester I am going to see Štěpán at the Hrádek rectory.

My mother was a deeply pious Catholic. God's in his Heaven and all's well with the world, is what I inherited from her. With all the naïveté of childhood and with all the searching of adolescence, I enjoyed looking after this inheritance, but one day I had to bid it farewell. When I stopped believing, I found a good friend. He was a Catholic priest.

Štěpán did not try to win me over, he did not challenge my doubts. From the landscape of childhood, which was biblical and liturgical, he lovingly led me into the landscape of adulthood, which is plain and aesthetic. As if the Lord God, to whom I'd said farewell, wanted to reward me for the depth of my childhood piety by placing in my path an angel, who said: Don't be afraid of being on your own.

Štěpán served in a country rectory near the southern Czech border. I hitchhiked there. I sat in the back of a pickup truck that was carrying baskets full of apples. An apple-scented journey through the landscape, that was the prelude.

A warm breeze. Indian summer ruled over the bright, contrasting colors: red, gold, green, and blue. In vain I tried to count the fishponds that reflected the sky and the low, painfully white farmhouses. Lanes along embankments marched by. Here and there teams of horses slowly strutted down them. Gliding above a wayside cross a stork, perhaps an angel.

A young man still very much enjoys visiting cemeteries and pondering death as if a distant, promising prospect of the future. Do you remember? There is a church in a southern village called Brloh. On a limestone plaque in the wall of the church, carved in empire cursive, are the lines:

> Have mercy on me,
> At least you, my friends,
> For I have been touched by the hand of the Lord.

Back then, when I was carried away by the scent of apples, I was touched by the warm hand of the landscape, and the thought of death was pleasant. Surely I wanted to be buried here, alongside the road, or there at the foot of that church which after hundreds of years had taken on the likeness of a person of both genders. Slender stone shafts, a swelling, always pregnant dome. Czech romanesque and Czech baroque. But a twenty-year-old architecture student thought: what? Czech baroque and Czech romanesque? Yes, but better romanesque and baroque in the Czech lands.

Bodies lowered into graves in a land with tradition do not lie in nothingness. They lie in history and they are history themselves. Stone walls overgrown with briars, spirea, and elderberries, bones for whom no one is alive to pick flowers anymore. The names on their tombstones washed away by rain, but I am with you, my friends. Now and forever ours is the kingdom of the landscape, amen. You see, Olga, what we will have forsaken.

But back then I didn't know this, I was just looking out over the southern Czech landscape, the plains, from the back of a pickup truck. The scent of apples was intoxicating me like incense when as a child I went to church. I wanted to make a blessing, but with what words and with what gestures? And so I observed.

This is the kingdom of my landscape: She rules with kindness and does not incite the fabrication of colossal myths. Silently and imperceptibly, as only trees can, she towers over her own horizon in the form of solitary lindens, and from their compressed rings is carved a Madonna in the image of the mother of God, based on a painting, the painting of a beloved woman, based on a feeling.

Peaceful, as if painted once and for always. A delicate smile on slender lips. A landscape with lyrical disregard of European dogmas, which nevertheless define her, but in her own way and with a provincial charm, whose deficiencies are transformed into the mystery of character. Chastely, beneath scarlet and cobalt, gold-lined drapery, which so much resembles clouds, and beneath clouds that so much resemble the drapery of gothic statues, she appeals to the longing to rest on her hills with their graceful names: Džbány, Libín, Bula, Čihadlo, Klet', Mahelník. I have in me a relief map of the time I've spent with these most special of words, and it has been the beautiful destiny of their names to fall on these small, isolated, unchanging hills and mountains. I have in me, Olga, a relief map of your body, which my fingers had not yet grazed. Nor yet had my fingertips minded. I was passing through the landscape.

And through that landscape rides a train. In the distance it is still tiny. Don't toys forever remain a part of the way you view objects? And from a distance, aren't you yourself a speck of a toy from the engineer's point of view, as he watches from his smoking, approaching locomotive? You have to intersect. Converge. Who or what will get there first? Him and his train? Me and my truck?

If the railway barrier were to have fallen just a second later, or if the driver of my tumbledown truck were to have gotten out of it just the tiniest bit more speed – and it certainly wasn't for not trying, every nut and bolt of it shook – we wouldn't have had to stop so short at the crossing, and the apples and I would have made it to the other side. Perhaps all I would have done is look round and wave to the engineer, and everything would be different. I would not be sitting here with you now in your studio, once again intoxicated by the smell of evaporating turpentine, poppyseed oil, and beeswax. I love that smell.

"Olga," I said, "that picture on the easel is upside down."

"You're right," said Olga, and she went to the easel and turned it rightside up. "I look at a picture upside down to see if its elements are in their right places."

"Yes, I understand that," I said.

"Why don't you become a painter?" Olga asked. "You observe like a painter. I think that, as a painter, what you see, you experience. Light, shadow, spots of color you add in and take away, and then there is the miracle: preserving a round world in a rectangle. I don't know of a greater pleasure or a greater freedom. Between the painter's conception and the picture there are no obstacles. Between project and building lies an entire mountain."

Between project and building lies the societal regime and an entire mountain of bricks. Or as you say, Olga, patron and material. And I would like to level that mountain of bricks a bit and square things a bit with that society, but I don't have what it takes. It would only get me worked up. Would I like to paint? Yes. Certainly. Perhaps. Possibly. I don't know. I don't believe I have the talent. And what is talent without certainty? Pointless ambition.

"But Mikuláš," said Olga, "I like you just as you are, not any other way. What I need is a normal person. Two painters under one roof, cheek to cheek, would make this place a great big asylum."

"So you think I'm a normal person," I said. "Through and through. Thanks a bunch."

"Be thankful!" said Olga. "It's your greatest talent and art, and my certainty. I'm afraid of people something's always gotten into."

It's true, Olga, nothing's gotten into me for a long time now, but I don't know if that is any sort of art, to cut myself off, to break away, to be all on my own. It's been a long time now since I shed all ambition and consigned my talents to reverie. The most important thing by far is for me to go to a forest, walk through it, along forgotten paths, my hands in my pockets, and study the architecture of branch and blade. I no

longer strive. I live a plain life and I have only one require-
ment: that my life be aesthetic.

The world I live in is ugly. Banality, kitsch, and decay
engulf city, village, and field. Doesn't it seem to you that we
reside in a dust heap? But fortunately I know some paths and
unbuilt spaces where I feel fine, and that's enough. The Old
Town, Malá Strana up to the Castle, architecture that gardens
disembody. The deserted deer parks around Křivoklát Castle.
The kingdom of the southern Czech landscape. A good book,
a good painting, a bit of music and a bit of wine.

On my walks I have often wondered whether the freedom I found has flattened into indifference. Sometimes it
seems that I'm merging with the architecture of branch and
blade's beautiful indifference. And the apathy of snow that
rustles as it thickly falls, this too you must know. Often I let
myself fall in step with the music of the snow, but because I
am a pedestrian, I return home. Then I take a book to bed, a
love story, always a most plain and simple one: between the
eternal me and the eternal you lies an invincible piece of
dying body.

Olga smiled at me. What is more beautiful than this: a
smile you've known for twenty years, always just as dear. The
lamp's glow reflected in her eyes, which were now dark blue,
like spots of amethyst. In the gutters the rain thrummed
sonorously, like a harpsichord, and a gust of wind made the
window panes tremble. Papers' dog-ears shuddered. And
through her windows came the draft of the blue spectrum of
night colors, like then, although then it was a bright afternoon.

We are stopped before the barrier, the pickup truck, the
baskets full of apples, and me amidst their scent. The truck
still jerks and twitches, and one of the apples feels like rolling
off onto the oily floor. I catch the apple and hold it in my

hand. Meanwhile the train passes between the barriers, and whistles. Three short and one long. I wave and the engineer salutes. As, of course, he should. This custom is reproduced even in the world of toys: before the station stands the stationmaster in a blue uniform, watching the local go by. He is holding a red flag, as is fitting.

Back then, they still had train cars with open platforms. I liked to stand on those platforms and lean against the rail. I felt like I was on a balcony that was passing with you through the landscape. Now, possibly forever, we are enclosed inside the car. They say it's safer, considering the greater speed. But I won't get worked up over it.

The old-time train clickety-clacked quite slowly down the track. On the platform of the final car stood Olga. I did not yet know her name, but she must long ago have had a place in my field of vision, like a nearby mountain whose name too I surely do not know.

Although fortunate to be seated there in the abstract, late-afternoon landscape, enthused with what I observe and intoxicated with the concrete bliss of the apples' scented cloud as it carnally couples with the shadowy smoke of the passing locomotive, I am in despair. In a quandary. Quick, what should I do? Cry out? Jump from the truck and throw my body in front of the train? Run off after it?

What do you do at such a hopeless moment full of such good fortune? You throw the apple you happen to have in your hand, and you follow its arc.

Of course, it is possible to calculate it – the speed of the train and the arc of the apple – but it would require a complex equation, and I have the feeling someone solved it long ago.

Olga smiles, possibly at me, possibly at the flying apple, and she catches the apple with both her hands, like a ball. I will forever remember her smile, her face, and the spot of violet in her eye.

It is still a bright afternoon. The smoke of the locomotive idles about the entire area, ephemeral but thick. The undulating dusk of the acrid eclipse is broken by a ray of sunlight, which becomes vividly fixed in my vision.

And then the barriers go up. It's so normal. The pickup truck wiggles its hips before the crossing, and I jump down onto the tracks and watch the receding train. You are standing on the platform in a long white dress. The train is going off with you; that is not so normal.

If I had been photographed at that very moment, the picture would likely have caught my gesture. I would love to take a look at it. A hand reaching? A person in motion? A figure struck with awe? A body frozen in astonishment? A man on his knees, ear to the rail? Does the law of the resonance of a material reaching one's ears along a rail include the pit-pat of your heart?

Idle thoughts: it's far away already. All I can see now is a little box in the middle of rails receding to their vanishing point, then nothing but a dot at the base of an elongated pear of smoke. It's behind me now, even if, as I watch the disappearing object, it is before me now and forever. And I know that it is the beginning of something, a beginning so perfect it encompasses its end. And I know that I will return to the beginning again and again, and that it will always astonish me anew, like every time shift: it's autumn again and time to turn on the heat; it's dawn again, and you can see I'm no longer asleep; the first snow has fallen now and the last has melted; my hair is going gray, have you noticed, Olga?

For another moment I remained standing between the rails. I stand there to this day and you ride off carefree as the Lord God on a wheelbarrow. Please, grant me one wish: let's ride to France together. Relieve me of my memories and lead me not into the temptation of loving the image of your receding figure more than your approaching age.

In the gravel beside the tracks, like a tropical chapel, stood the white cube of an electrical transformer. In the hot, trembling air, in the intense sunlight, it seemed as imaginary as you. The transformer hummed. Even the gleaming rails vibrated like strings – seeming to have not the nature of iron, but the granular nature of resin – surely out of fear that they would take to the air with the parched fragrance of chamomile, which flowed over the ditch from a faintly lavish field of herbs. A sea of flowers was mad with pollination and with bees that invisibly composed an accompaniment to the voice of the transformer. The scent of honey was narcotic.

What oath am I swearing with my hand, still perhaps reaching southwest? Ave! I said, yes, Ave, I love you and never anyone else, I will love you from this moment on with all my heart and all my soul, now and forever, amen.

In the sand a shard of glass sparkled across the entire spectrum. A small bell tinkled. The monstrance of the sun descended into a poplar. And out of the poplar white down. It was possible that something would come from the opposite direction, and I was suddenly frightened by the perilous position I was in. And surprised at the way I'd vowed, adjured, incanted. When I finally abandoned the crossing, I had the feeling that I was someone other than I'd been a moment before. I'd fallen in love, and I was surprised at how certainly I knew it. I realized proudly that it was a beautiful state and that I intended to hold it regardless of whether I ever again saw the being who'd brought it on.

But had this one passing being alone brought on this strange state of permanent excitement? Wasn't she part of a picture, and wasn't that picture part of an atmosphere, part of which I too was?

It was a picture. A picture already many many times turned over in my memories, in my consciousness, so that again and again I am convinced of its perfection. I assure you, Olga, that all of its elements are in their right places.

Back then, people didn't travel by car the way they do today. I had to foot it for several hours. The local that had passed through was the last one of the day.

My shoes comically squeaked. I slipped them off and walked barefoot. Above me the golden evening had already taken its seat, and from the west the front of nighttime was approaching. I've always liked to watch the day rotate through each of its periods. You can hear the tones that correspond to each.

Somewhere a bell tolled. Somewhere someone was unrelentingly pounding a hammer against a scythe. A drake landed on a fishpond and shoveled water. A stubble field burst, shooting water out of sprinklers. A rifle went off twice on the other side of a grove of pines. The train's echo wafted through the labyrinthine nightfall, on a wave of air already laden with dew. It is going from somewhere to somewhere, its route unseen. I hear a periodic clatter, and when through the velvet filter of distance the whistle sounds, it pierces my heart.

I am still standing by the wayside cross. Wilt thou permit me to pray here, our Father who art in heaven, but in whom I no longer believe? Before this shrine, I would like to recite a few words whose source lies in the traditions of my childhood. Hail Queen, full of grace, I am with thee, blessed among rivers and the blessed land of thy life.

I arrived at Hrádek after dark. The bright rectory greeted me with open arms. I was looking forward to dinner. As I stepped into the entry hall, there, coming through another door, was Olga. With both hands she was carrying a bowl of apples. She was carrying the bowl pressed softly against soft breasts.

I must confess to you, Olga, that it seemed like I'd expected this, like it had to happen, as if already somewhere someone had premeditated it, and now it had been theatrically arranged. So I didn't feel at all surprised. I would swear that you too were not amazed. But the pyramid of apples wobbled and one of them rolled off.

That's why, once again that day, I had to catch a falling apple. And I did. I placed the apple back into the bowl and put my other hand beneath it, as if telling it not to tremble. Beneath the bowl I felt your hand.

Over the past twenty years I haven't once been forced to reach like that in order to catch something. Not even a pencil that felt like rolling off a table. On many occasions I've walked through a fruit orchard and, with thoughts of you, have observed the perfect architecture of ripening fruit. Whether it's hanging from a branch or already lying in the grass. Not a single apple has felt like breaking off so that I can see it fall. I don't remember ever seeing that happen, and yet it happens all the time. Believe me, I would run and catch it before it hit the ground, even if between me and the tree there was a fence and half a hectare of garden.

When, much later, I told you about this, and in detail, I was ashamed. Isn't it comical? Isn't it preposterous? But you just smiled and said:

"I too could describe in detail the picture of your appearing at the rectory that evening. I could draw it. The refraction of the shadows made by the candlelight on the table. I could draw it for you in detail. How you came up to me and how you caught the apple falling out of the bowl I was carrying. What you said when Štěpán introduced you to me and when he introduced you to Václav. Our double portrait reflected in the mirror. If we were to remove the mirror's glass surface from its frame and plunge it into some imaginary developing solution, it would be possible, even after all these years, to peel from the glass the silver foil on which we were recorded."

Daphne

Before I'd spoken with you that first time, you had already, for several hours, perhaps for the entire millenium, been part of my atmosphere, my landscape, my world. In me you had already performed, on the stage of some random plain that, right on schedule, a train was passing through. So when I spoke with you, and they were ordinary sentences – good evening, I have arrived so late, yes, I'm hungry – already it was unmistakable: I belonged to you. How happy I was to utter those ordinary sentences. For I felt that you knew as well, even more unmistakably: you belonged to me. You promptly conveyed this too, although you simply delivered a few ordinary sentences yourself – sit down and you'd bring me something to eat, but it'll take a while, because I have to heat it up.

While she was preparing my meal, I talked with Štěpán and with Václav, who was introduced to me as your husband. I wasn't surprised at all, nor was my heart broken. I didn't need to have any claim to you, I didn't need to ask for your hand or push you to get a divorce. I hadn't even imagined sleeping with you, can you believe it?

Not even the image of kissing you. Not a single erotic fantasy, although I often daydreamed about women I knew or didn't know, incredibly vivid dreams. I am good at imagining acts, apart from you or performed by us together. But I have never been good at imagining the extraordinary nature of your intimacy. In my imagination I loved you like my native land-scape. I was present in it even when I was not actually passing through it, but sitting before my board, drawing line after line, an infinite number of points.

We talked together long into the night, almost until morning. Štěpán brought some good wine up from the cellar and told us stories about people from the villages along the border. After the war, they forced out fixtures in the villages who happened to be German. I think this was wrong, unwarranted. It was the fascist regime that was overthrown, not German people or the German nation. But we didn't want to understand this and so we drove Germans out of our land. And us? We were driven out of Europe. As if the decisions of several presidents could abolish the thousand-year tradition of a land that had always been bilingual. Instead of reaching an understanding between the languages, they chose to clear them out. But I won't get worked up over it.

Each of the people who left due to the common crime of war and the common guilt that accompanies it, brought with him an individual story and destiny, and they themselves did not necessarily have to be burdened by guilt. These people never returned, of course, but their stories remain.

Does no one know the no-man's-land right in the middle of Europe? The singular, unforgettable experience of dead, depopulated villages and hamlets. Abandoned cottages, wide-open churches, at the tavern no one sitting with a glass. But soon new people are getting a hold of the glasses, the cottages, the churches. Patriots and zealots, desperate people and farmers who at the beginning of the war had been driven out themselves, swindlers and displaced persons from faraway lands who found within them the seed of Czech descent, and perhaps the stories too. So they planted the seeds, one with faith in God's star, another with faith in the red star and the bolshevik hammer and sickle, and the seeds came up. They came up abundantly. Today no one's much interested in any sort of faith, but rather in the shared yields of cooperative fields, which keep on getting larger. It's all an historical narrative now.

Václav bred horses. He told us about his little farm and described his horses' temperaments, the way one would talk about one's classmates. I was very surprised to learn that Olga was studying painting at the Prague academy. Of course, I assumed that she was devoted not only to Václav but also to those most well bred of quadrupeds. Didn't she, on fragile, restless ankles, walk as stately and with as great a stride as the aristocratic horse? And her hair? Did Václav not love the horse's mane expressly because he'd known Olga since childhood? They grew up together in a village, and their childhood love was so open and matter-of-fact that very soon it was no longer childish, and later it managed easily, without embarrassment, to bridge the yawning difference between their talents. Václav knew how to talk to horses, and it was said that he and Olga understood each other, as well. Olga knew how to paint and draw, and it was said that she asked for a pencil and a brush when she was very small. But I think that if they hadn't given her paint or lead, she would have scratched her pictures onto rock.

I was moved by several stories of their childhood love when Olga told them to me much later on. For example, their wedding. Secretly, so that no would know, they lit candles in a chapel and they were married by a priest, the then young acolyte Štěpán, Václav's classmate in their two-room school-house.

Mea culpa, mea culpa, the little acolyte should have responded at mass, but because back then Latin hadn't yet wanted to settle in his head, he would say: Meanery scenery.

"Meanery scenery," said little Štěpán, dressed in an acolyte's gown, and with string made of jute he bound the two children's hands.

I was well able to imagine the scene and the scenery. As a boy I too liked to play at grown-up things. My most beloved game was to play with my little brother Béda in a dappled corner, a chosen corner of the world, where we would build ourselves a building.

Before leaving for Paris I will visit Béda and we will encamp in a dappled corner of his asylum. We will sit together beneath an elderberry that has lost its flowers and leaves, for it is autumn, nearly winter of the year one thousand nine hundred and sixty-seven. Then, as always when I leave him, Béda will tell me to stay with him at the asylum, that I belong there too. Or, Mikuláš, if you know of another dappled corner, I will go there with you.

All I know of is a single woman, dear brother.

Next, the little newlyweds went to a fair at a neighboring village. In the midst of swings, shooting galleries, and merry-go-rounds an itinerant photographer was setting up a colorful booth. Nowadays they don't itinerate like that anymore. Václav and Olga had their picture taken together. In the background was an intensely lit, primitively painted panorama of Prague, with Charles Bridge, the Castle Hill, and the Church of St. Mikuláš.

They couldn't talk enough about how their life would be together by the river, in the ferryman's cottage. A place I visited with Olga. The ferry doesn't run anymore. There's a concrete bridge across the river now, but the ferryman's cottage still stands there on the riverbank. That is ... is it still a cottage? Knocked-out windows, pulled-up floors, wounds where doors once were, and there, in a dappled corner stenciled blue, a damp straw mattress where someone else most likely slept, and probably not alone. But yes, clearly, it is still a house. Four lines making a square, two lines meeting in a point – the roof – and we can begin again, Olga, beneath it, even with the plaster coming off the wall carved with the emblem of your sex. In the grass we found a rusted, coiled cable, which once had guided the ferryboat.

A big wedding and they became adults right away, as if Olga had passed her end-of-*gymnasium* exams. Štěpán performed the ceremony, the first the Church entrusted to him, but of course afterwards the newlyweds recorded their marriage as a civil one. To take pictures, however, the newlyweds did not leave the church. They considered this conventional. Štěpán took their picture in the rectory garden. Lit by an uninhibited sun, the picture's background is a fruit orchard in the bloom of a conventional spring.

Then, when we had our first dinner, I didn't know about those photographs, but I had the feeling that I had known Olga for a very long time, although for the first several hours before this I had only caught a glimpse of her, and that on the platform of a passing train. When later they showed me one of the photos, and not without childish self-love, I still did not suspect that it would be in that orchard that we would bury Václav and that to see you today, under the panorama of the Castle Hill, I would cross Charles Bridge and that, witnessed by St. Mikuláš', I would say what I was about to say. Plain and simple words. I've prepared them well.

Olga moved into her studio in the old cottage in Prague's Vrtbovský Garden. Sometimes I would get together with her in Prague. We would go to art exhibits and walk together through the gardens and lanes of Malá Strana. We had the thorough, unmistakable feeling that we loved each other, but neither of us needed to give this voice other than in the footsteps we took on our walks together. It was an abstract love and it accompanied us like one's accent as we experienced the cultural miracles of Prague and the Czech landscape. It was beautiful to hear music and then know that somewhere there was a being, some sort of angel, who had the nature of a gilded baroque statue and in whom you are present like an enduring picture, not at all like an appealing thought. That we belonged to each other, and we knew it, did not at all mean that we had to be together. It was enough for us that we did not think of each other in terms of commitment and that we could spend hours just talking. So how are you? You can see for yourself: well enough. And you? Yes, so so, too, basically. Are you painting? Yes, I'm painting. And you? I'm drawing tiny dwellings. And in the blue spectrum of night colors we said goodbye without the kisses our youth had a right to expect.

Olga spent most of her time with Václav in Hrádek, where once again I came to visit Štěpán. In Hrádek, Václav had obtained permanent possession of a small farm left behind by Germans. He started a horse farm there. A letter written by the Minister of Agriculture was evidence that his possession of the farm applied to him and to his children. A few years later, the forcibly collectivized village deliberated on the minister's letter, but Václav did not live off the land, he lived off the horses.

In the fields, they were plowing the balks. Some of the settlers still resisted, but then the cooperative made them all sign a document. Whoever didn't sign, whoever resisted socialization, would be forcibly moved to another region, would be discoursed to death, worn down, signed out, shut in, put in his place, condemned, and then released so that he could wear, sign, and shut *himself* down, out, and in, always pointlessly. Today everyone farms in concord, as if nothing had ever happened. And for the last decade, little has, not even a snowstorm. When I was small, we used to go sledding on St.

Mikuláš' Day. Now there's just a picture of snow glittering all silvery on the television and everyone is on the whole quite satisfied. After all, what's the point? We very decently eat our fill and drink our fill and get a good night's rest, and children study to be engineers. It's the way of the world. As certain as the changing seasons.

Occasionally, Olga, I feel like crying over the way everything in time diffuses into common contours. Do you feel that it would be more masculine were I only to ponder it?

Then, Václav was in an exceptional situation. During the revolutionary period, one of his friends became a deputy minister. A person with such an office and with boundless power in his sphere of influence could on certain important occasions make changes even to the party line, especially when both he and one of his colleagues loved horses and, smoking on and on through endless meetings, longed to air their lungs out in the saddle. They went to Hrádek to hunt.

No one knew quite where Václav belonged. Events were careful to bypass him. All anyone really knew is that important people rode his horses. So it came to pass that in the period when many of the Hrádek cottages were at the mercy of mice, Václav was able to make costly renovations to his farm. Whether it was actually his, no one could accurately determine. I drew plans for the renovations. A beautiful country residence came into existence. Olga made a large studio out of the old granary. She painted diligently and what happened around her was not her concern.

Václav had drainage pipes placed in the hayfield, so that acidic grasses wouldn't grow there. This diversion was happily carried out by the cooperative after an instrumental intercession to raise construction expenditures for the uncommonly enormous pigsty. Back then, they called the pigsty "the Colossus." Václav had only to speak with influential functionaries and suddenly there were millions, not to mention construction machinery.

They envied him. Václav had guns. He was allowed to shoot both rifles and shotguns on the grounds of the manor, as the fearful used to call the cooperative's common property. They had had to surrender their guns, but many preferred casting into a fishpond or digging in the garden, as they had under the Germans.

Soon came a wave of political trials. The leading political figures were personal friends of each other, as well as of the leading political figures being convicted of treason. Today we are permitted to know that they were not treasonous at all. They have been rehabilitated, many of them posthumously. After the wave of trials of the mighty came another wave: trials of the small. According to the theory of the escalation of the class struggle, treason and sabotage should be found everywhere. During this period I had already resigned myself to my ideas and my projects, and I patiently drew housing units and prefabs. When all is said and done, people have to live somewhere and I have to make a living.

I read classic novels and took walks in forests. I dwelt in an oasis of my own, an internal world, not a joyful one. It was a cheerless time. I buried my papa, I buried my mama, and I even buried my high-minded plans, aesthetics, and architectural style. But I grew accustomed to the fact that it is possible to live even without a style. I took my brother off to an asylum. Unlike him, next to the life of a citizen I developed a parallel existence of my own. It allowed me to keep reason close at hand.

Olga, didn't you live in a similar oasis? I irrigated mine with the passivity of my ideas. You painted. It's great luck that a painter's employment is her dreams.

Even Hrádek wasn't spared. First they arrested Václav's friend, the deputy minister in Prague. He was convicted of high treason, but because he confessed to what he did not commit, he didn't get the noose, only fifteen years in prison. Later he was judicially rehabilitated, and later still politically. Now he is once again working in the ministry and looking forward to retirement. They say he will write his memoirs. And your Václav, Olga, for a long time he has been lying in the ground and we are preparing to go to Paris. I have decided.

Štěpán was never able to give many sermons. He performed mass in Hrádek only once a week, and then later only every other week. Church ceremonies were replaced by civil ceremonies. The only time prayers were said was at burials; almost no one requested last rites.

Václav fell off a horse, it was whispered through the village, and soon it turned out that, because the cooperative had invested in it, the hayfield was truly the property of everyone. But because no one mowed it, it became overgrown with weeds. Bewildered, the horses stepped gingerly through the high grass. The fences were split for firewood. The horse farm was declared unviable and the breeding of horses suspicious. Václav had to surrender his guns. A truck came and took the horses away. No one knew where, but the word around the tavern was, an abattoir.

In order to at least hold on to his nice house, Václav became a fattener of pigs for the Colossus. But this did not rescue him. On the farm he had renovated, the cooperative established a nursery school. Olga's studio was where the children napped after lunch, on little daybeds. Václav wanted to follow Olga to Prague. He wanted to be near horses and found a job at the race track stables, but the Colossus would not allow him to sever his working relationship with it. So he moved into the cottage of a farmer who had declined to joined the cooperative and had then been forcibly evicted. Václav painted the cottage white, fixed it up, and brought into its stable a single horse. It was no celebrated thorough-bred, but rather a dray horse that didn't trot and didn't gallop, but Václav was once again in the saddle. When Olga came from Prague, he harnessed the horse to an old wicker gig, all upholstered in leather, and rushed to meet Olga at the station.

Then the Colossus was struck with the plague. Animals perished by the dozen. Finally they had to be shot, and even Václav's horse had to be put down by a hired hand. A plague commission judged that there was sabotage, and sent Václav a criminal complaint. Right before they came to arrest him, Václav attempted to flee abroad. Someone informed on him. At the border station, they dragged Václav out of his hiding place in a train car piled high with a cargo of planks. Olga learned that evening that the escape had not succeeded. She was on the verge of going to Berlin, where she planned to take the subway to the West. Back then, Berlin had not yet been bisected by a wall.

They sentenced Václav to twenty years in prison. They took into account not only the pigs, but also the horse he had ridden around persuading people to join his sabotage, and the conspiracy he had no reason to confess to, but to which his friends had confessed in order to save their necks. Václav's attempt to escape across the border made matters even worse. He was put to work in a uranium mine. After a few months in the forced labor camp, he escaped. He was shot and wounded.

Olga and I were visiting Štěpán at the rectory. Exhausted, feverish, with a severe case of pneumonia, Václav appeared in the entry hall. I scrutinized him just the way he must have scrutinized me when for the first time I entered the rectory and caught the apple that had fallen from the bowl Olga was carrying to the table.

Now Olga caught a piece of dried mud that Václav had brought with him in his sleeve. It was a cold spring. We put Václav to bed. I went for a doctor we could trust, but it was too late to help. He signed the death certificate.

Do you remember? Early in the afternoon a snowstorm comes out of nowhere and in a few minutes the green fields are covered in snow. On a baroque prie-dieu stands a pewter chalice. In the chalice a flowering daphne twig. On the bed lies Václav, and Olga, so much resembling a gothic madonna, covers him with a comforter all the way up to his chin. Then she looks at us, at me and Štěpán, as if to ask whether she was right to cover him only to his chin. We said nothing. We wished that Václav were only sleeping or at least that his death were only a momentary feigning of sleep.

These are my three principal sins, actually the only ones; I don't know of any others. I'm no good at feeling any way other than Christian, or if you'd prefer, Štěpán, theologically. My first sin is that I put up with tedious, servile work without a word of protest. The second sin has to do with Jarmila. I was not frank, not a genuine husband to her. The third sin is fixed in my consciousness, in my memories, like a painting.

The sun is shining from under clouds of snow. Honey-golden light is falling on the white tiles of the stove, and I wish that it would not only look so warm, but warm us too. It is cold as Václav's visage. I touch his temple and look at Olga. As if I have suggested she shoot him in the head, Olga covers his face with the comforter. But this seems inappropriate, and she smooths the comforter back down to Václav's chin and covers the entire body with a red velvet bedspread, still adorned in lace with the embroidered symbol of the chalice, the host, and the initials IHS, Jesus, Christ, Savior.

And that is my third sin, and I will not make confession of any of them, although I would like to apologize for them, all at once to everybody, including Jarmila and now Olga. Who would understand this? There is the sin of living without freedom, the sin of secret love, and the sin of looking at everything with the pride of aesthetic enjoyment.

At the foot of the bed a priest's shadow. The tiled stove glows coolly. Dust swirls through the golden rays of the sun, and why not out into space? Didn't my idea of universal architecture come from the fact that each space, even the sitting room of a country rectory, is part of cosmic space, and that only with the reverence of this viewpoint should a builder have the right to wall it in?

Olga has just smoothed the bedspread, and now she places her hand on her chest. Her tall figure collapses into a gothic arch. A black velvet ribbon weighs on her hair and even on the pale blue of her dress and the dark blue of her eyes, in which I catch a glimpse of the blue spectrum of night colors, although the day still hangs in a shallow light. Beauty, indifferent to the human condition, incites me, and independent of personal fortune and hope I feel perfectly joyful and free of restraint, like a dreaming man who floats above his native landscape.

Olga catches me looking at her. She smiles and reaches out her hand as if warding something off or as if feeling she has an obligation to catch a flying apple before it hits the ground, and then suddenly she turns toward the window. She rests her head against the window frame. Beyond her lie snow-covered hills already preparing for the thaw. For the first time, Olga begins to cry. Her narrow shoulders tremble. Štěpán comes over to me, places his hand on my shoulder, and says:

"Don't cry, Olga. We will be with you, always."

When it grew dark, Štěpán brought two candles and placed them on the prie-dieu next to the pewter chalice that held the daphne. He lit the candles and we went out. We felt that Olga wanted to sit alone with Václav. We stayed up all night in the hallway. We spoke very little. During the night Olga came out twice for new candles. Each time we went upstairs with her, lit the candles, and placed them next to the bed.

None of us dared think aloud how we were going to bury Václav. No one could know about it. They would take Václav from us, and take us in as well.

I remember the dialogue we had just before dawn. I had fallen asleep with my head on the table. I remember the smell of the wooden table top. For two or three centuries bread had been placed on it, and books bound in leather.

"What's that clattering?"

"Snow on the branches. It's melting and then freezing again."

"I would like to know who is the guilty one."

"When you ask about guilt, Mikuláš, you still seem to be asking in a religious sense. Is this the way you meant to ask your question?"

"How should I ask it?"

"For a long time we have not lived in a world circumscribed by doing justice and doing wrong. Now we have different poles than this: chaos and power. We cannot know who is to blame, we can only know who is sacrificed and who is condemned. Go to sleep!"

"I'll stay up with you. It's light out now. If it were summer, the birds would be chirping. Štěpán, can you believe it yet?"

"Look at this!" Štěpán pointed to his crucifix. "It is a crucified man. He is dying. And what were his last words?"

"I know. He is a forsaken man. As we all are, on the threshold of death."

"He is also redeemed."

"But to what other, new sort of world does he go?"

"To the story that has been written, and it is gospel. And the Church. And the liturgy. And tradition, morality, fellowship, art. The spiritual world that we constructed on a single cross and a single crown of thorns."

"There is not just one single cross. You are avoiding the answer."

"I don't believe you really want to know," said Štěpán. "But I will act as if I do."

"Are you in love with Olga?"

"Yes, but I act as if I weren't."

"Out of principle?"

"No. My holy forefathers sinned more than I."

"So what form does such a love take?"

"The form of a priest. I, Mikuláš, am a priest. What form of love do you know?"

"I know of one form, one form exactly. A building. Four walls, a roof, two people inside, man and woman."

"Because you are a plain man, a humane man, Mikuláš, and an architect."

"I am only a plain man, Štěpán, no longer an architect. A single rational building, which I built over time, or actually adapted from a barn and stable, it was theirs and they took it away. I do not build, I patch together abstract cells, and sometimes I have the feeling that concrete people never live in them. Sometimes I lose my own concreteness, as if I were no longer a plain man but only ... the plainness between chaos and power."

I could still smell the aroma of bread and leather-bound book in the grooved atmosphere of old wood, and like wood I slept.

When Štěpán woke me, a very plain man was standing in the hallway, but it was clear to me that his plain clothes were a cover for police work. The first perception upon waking is as powerful as the perceptions of a child. The face of this man was imprinted in my memory like my first childhood recollection, when my father turned me upside down to the landscape.

Other equally plain men were inspecting the church, mortuary, barn, granary and all the nicely formed objects, large and small, that no longer served any purpose. They had only their still flawless, baroque form and their memories, but perhaps there is a sort of sense and even purpose to them. My plainclothesman finished inspecting the hallway and went up with us to the guest room.

Václav's corpse is lying there, on the antique bed, tidily covered by comforter and bedspread. On the headboard of the dark walnut bed is a fine inlaid carving made of cherrywood. On a cloud an angel with outspread wings inclines its head, as if asleep, against a long mouthpiece lying in one of its hands; he is trumpeting. In the other hand, reaching up into the heavens, are stars. The headboard's carving is echoed, like a mirror, at the foot. Only this other angel's hand does not reach up, but rather with a quick movement tries to catch a star that is in the midst of falling into the angel's feathers.

We could hear footsteps above us. Olga woke. She sat up in her armchair and looked at us with big, still unfocused eyes. On the prie-dieu imaginary candles with imaginary flames melted ever faster. The real ones had already gone out. On the candlesticks hung rings of stiffened wax. When morning came, the daphne flower had noticeably unfurled.

With the tips of his fingers, with curiosity and feeling and expertise, the plainclothesman stroked the carving on the headboard, and he marveled at the fact that nowhere, not even the tiniest bit, was the baroque veneer flaking off. He breathed in the air of the room, beautifully scented by the cabinetmaker's work. Had there been such a favorable climate for three hundred years? Do you know what glue does after a mere hundred-and-fifty years? Yet from all those years the veneer is scarcely pared at all. The air, favorably dry as well as damp, acts on the wood like a press.

"Beautiful, graceful work," said the plainclothesman. "If it were not so apparent that the bed belonged to the state, I would try to get you to sell it to me."

"It does not belong to the state," said Štěpán, "it belongs to the Church."

"This is not something we will discuss," said the plain-clothesman. "It is an angel of death."

"Why not an angel of blessed sleep?" said Štěpán.

"I understand wood. I am a cabinetmaker."

"But then why," said Štěpán, "why are you working for Bezpečnost?"

"You mean … Fízl, right?"

"I meant only to ask."

"So, did you mean Fízl, or not?"

"Yes, meant, it seems, but you see, I didn't say it."

"Why?"

"I didn't want to offend you," said Štěpán.

"Thank you," said the plainclothesman.

"You mustn't thank me. I do my best. Each of us in his own position," said Štěpán.

"And my position forces me to ask you to remove the bedding. It would suffice to pull the bedspread down off the face," said the plainclothesman.

Olga rose from her armchair. We stood motionless around the bed. Then Štěpán pulled down the covers. The pale, smooth face of the corpse appeared, and the plainclothesman gave it a long look. Then he said:

"He was shaved after he died. By whom?"

"By me," said Štěpán.

Olga started to collapse. I held her up. The two men stayed by the bed, on separate sides, looking into each other's eyes. Nearby floated for one an angel of death, for the other an angel of sleep. On the floor above us we could hear them slamming the lid of a trunk. Then the plain man, the humane man, whose name remained unspoken, replaced the covers, carefully arranged the comforter under the corpse's chin, or rather over his shoulders, and then covered his face with the bedspread. As if with compassion, he smoothed the folds in the bedspread, crossed to the window, and said, meant only for himself:

"Damn it! I feel no duty whatsoever."

"I am at your disposal," said Štěpán.

On the other side of the road in front of the rectory stood a police van with all four of its doors wide open, to air it out. Yesterday's snow had already melted under the morning's sunlight. The driver was leaning on the van, getting himself a tan. Above the hill next to the cemetery a nimble, flimsy cloud was swirling around. An endless parcel of land on the hillside was being dragged by six tractors at once. There was no smoke coming from the houses in the village, only from the nursery school.

The loudspeakers started up. Merrily and vigorously they took the march out of the village, out over the fields, all the way out to the forest, and along with it came the voice of the cooperative's president. Before lunch, Zeithamplová and her group to the manure! Líbal, Vinkule, Říhová, Horvát, fourteen hundred, industrial economics meeting. A short musical passage. And a bus excursion to a castle near the Vltava River, registration tonight, no later. In conclusion, a sad waltz: "The Scarlet Petticoat," truly my favorite...

"You will be at his disposal," said the plainclothesman. "He does not ask much of us."

"I will do what is necessary," said Štěpán.

"Soon. Or possibly right away."

"Yes."

"We don't have a single witness here. Can I be assured of that?" said the plainclothesman.

Štěpán looked at us. I tenderly embraced Olga. She put her head on my shoulder. This is the only time during that period that I held you, Olga.

"Yes, you can rely on it," said Štěpán.

"Absolutely?" asked the former cabinetmaker.

"Absolutely," said I.

That night we dug a grave. But we did not know how to take Václav out into the fruit orchard. To simply carry his body went against our grain. Sit him in a chair? He fell out of the chair. Olga went out to the garden and took a walk among the trees.

"Why not place him on a table?" I said.

"Which one? None of them would go through any of the doors unless we turned it sideways."

"You don't have any sort of plank or board?"

"Come help me look."

Olga stood over the grave. We found white planks and a black plank, but they were all too narrow. We broke a ladder in half. We carried Václav out and buried him on a ladder.

Since it was a dark night, we couldn't see each other's faces very well. The only witnesses were the trees, some just about to blossom, others just having blossomed, and the elongated square of the rectory's walls, which gave a bright outline to the shadowy garden.

When we threw dirt onto the body, which was denied even a casket, I was so sad that I felt no emotion at all, only the darkness around us, which seemed to have disposed of space. The darkness was intersected only by our shovels' phosphorescent wooden handles, which had been fingered smooth.

Štěpán performed a ceremony. In corduroy trousers and wool sweater he sang the liturgy. He did not make a long speech. He consecrated the grave, we filled it in, and in baskets we carried the excess dirt over to some nettles by a wall. We placed the turf back where it had been before.

Olga simply watched us. An even more silent group of saints held in their invisible hands tall candles similar to the slender, lime-bleached stones of the fruit orchard. Through the garden went the soft footsteps of Jesus, who did what we had apparently neglected to do, but in fact could not, would not do. In the morning the turf on the grave had been carefully tread flat.

I did not dare look at the place I presumed she had placed her forehead, to see if the daphne lay there, nor thereby determine whether it was only lying there, or growing.

Snowman

"I need to be on my own," Olga said to me, and I respected her wish.

Sometimes I stopped by the Vrtbovský Garden to see whether a light was on in her studio, and whether I could see any shadow but hers. I waited until I heard from her, as promised, but I didn't hear from her, as if she had forgotten me. And Štěpán wrote me that she had not shown up in Hrádek for a long time, although they had been regularly corresponding. I envied him. What could they have so regularly corresponded about?

I decided that I too would write Olga. However, it seemed absurd to mail her a letter from a Prague post office, especially when I had so much time and lived so near. In the meantime, we didn't even run into each other by chance. Or wasn't this a matter of chance?

I threw the letter into the box with Olga's name on it, in the entryway of an old building. I stayed a while in the courtyard, looking at the sculpture atop the garden gate. It was a baroque Atlas carrying the world on his shoulders. If I were a sculptor, I would like to treat this theme in a modern way: Atlas carrying the world inside him. But I realized right away that it would not be graphic enough for a sculpture. It might be possible to paint what Atlas carried around inside him. But Olga would be angry with me: it is a literary conception, and literary conceptions do not belong in paintings.

When I saw Olga coming, I quickly hid behind an old cabinet that was standing there, certainly not by chance. It was just perfect for hiding behind. In the midst of his eternal exertion, Atlas was looking at me from beneath his globe. The cabinet was redolent with spices. The scents seem to have broken up and spread in the form of individual ribbons. But marjoram was missing.

In the meantime Olga had opened her mailbox with a shiny little key, read the letter, and passed right by me. From an unbelievable distance right to the city's historical core, via an acoustics system from somewhere out on the periphery, flew the whistling of a train, and it pierced my heart. And in my heart I felt grateful for it. I caught myself thinking something that made me ashamed: inside me, I tended you like a picture. I wanted to make sure that it was still vivid. I just wanted to see, and nothing more.

Then, with the good feeling that I had saved the postal service some work, I took a long walk along the Vltava River. Under Charles Bridge I sat down in a small boat and had a smoke. I found some flat stones and threw them at frogs. Things can't be so terrible in my city when on the riverbank there are flat stones to be found. From the tramway, with a worsening feeling, I followed the plain that extended all the way to the wall of the game preserve. I liked the game preserve and its long avenue that led to the emperor's summer palace, which was built in the shape of a star. It crowned the plain known as White Mountain, and it stood there back in 1620, when we were defeated in a single battle at the start of the Thirty Years' War, and we lost our kingdom forever. Czech history is the history of defeat. Olga, should I count for you how many times? How many splendid bridges, how many splendid castles, how many ideas, feeble at first, that ended up kindling Europe, how many courageous princes, beloved kings, and especially one broad-minded Holy Roman Emperor; how many wars. It always began with a well-meaning insurrection, but why get worked up over it. Unfinished as we are, we do have the cross.

It was with something like disgust, with the feeling in my soul that I was reprehensible, that I would avert my eyes from a construction site. I began to build one of the first high-rise developments in Prague, for which I, to indict someone, with my own pencil strokes drew an endless line of points of tedium. Instead of barrack-like blocks, I imagined a park with a white house in each of its dappled corners.

I would meet Růženka for a drink at the Czech Crown, across from the gates of Hvězda Park, but I would meet Iveta there as well. I got to know Iveta at a library I frequented. I've never set any store in having my own books. I have no interest in being surrounded by literature. I have only a few books that are dear to me, and these fit in a suitcase beneath two shirts, two undershirts, one extra pair of briefs, and a sweater. Olga, this is all I'll be bringing with me to Paris.

Iveta and I liked to talk about the minor-key loves of Anton Pavlovich Chekhov and the major-key loves of Lev Nikolayevich Tolstoy. We used to go to concerts together, and when we came home from them, we played alone, each our own chamber experiences, in both major and minor keys.

Because it is a memory fixed in the period when I threw the letter into Olga's mailbox, and it is connected with the scent of spices in the old cabinet, I can determine precisely that it was at the Czech Crown that I would meet Růženka. She drew up designs with me, and for her too it had been a long time, even if it was more bearable for her than it was for me. She would smile, she would sing, and from morning till night she would eat apples, and let me take bites, and she would keep writing things in her colored notebooks. I was afraid they were love poems. She was plain, freckly, with glasses set on a fleshy nose. But when you watch someone

eating fruit all day, she gains a fruity sort of charm, and then
you rejoice when you realize that she is not creating poems
out of her wild imaginings, but rather writing down and even
thinking up riddles.

> It has a head, it has two eyes,
> and it has lots of plans.
> It has no feet, it has no horns,
> and yet it stands.
> What is it?

We solved riddles together and that was enough. By
daylight with pencil in hand, in darkness by sense of touch,
we made beautiful guesses: what is a table and what is a chair,
how bread tastes and how salt tastes. Who is lying how and
on what, lying on a bed, and over the bed a building. We
were cheerful and we were curious, and again and again I
would catch myself thinking, and I was not ashamed: Would
I see yoú, Olga, would I see you this time again, you in the
freckled rows of her forehead, you in the fence of her
eyelashes, you in the fishpond of her delight?

I liked Růženka. All she ever asked me was – what is it?
Never did she ask me what I was thinking. I was grateful to
her for this. I did not have to be frank, and therefore cruel.
Nor did I ever ask her what she was thinking. After all, what
is frank, what is true and genuine, about displaying the pictures in your head? Isn't it actually the most artificial things
for which we were chosen, to which we are condemned? And
if so, then what's required isn't being genuine, but rather art.

When Olga called me at my office and said that she
would like me to come visit her, and I did visit her, I would
bring along my girlfriends. That's how Olga came to know
Jarmila. I felt that what Olga wanted, that what she actually
needed, was for me not to be forsaken.

"You can bring someone along with you," she told me several times, so that I could have no doubts that her being single made no demands on me at all.

Whenever I came with someone, always with prior warning and according to her wishes, all her paintings would be propped, paint in, against the wall, except for a few, as if they were public and official. There would be at most one easel with a canvas, and it would be blank. There were also studies from her student days, which reminded me of French painters.

Whenever I came alone, and that could be whenever, the paintings were all paint out. Olga sometimes even worked when I was there. We told each other about our experiences, and Olga liked it when I told her about a new book or shared a new anecdote, and like a child she proudly laughed when she solved a funny riddle.

In the studio she wore a burlap dress girded with string made of jute. The dresses were always smeared with all sorts of colors, and this suited her.

"Why don't you work in a smock?" I asked.

"Because they have buttons."

"All I do is sit and stare; I feel like having some herring. I'll take out the bones."

"What's left after a fish has been eaten is beautiful, haven't you noticed?" said Olga. "Unlike the bones of livestock."

Spots of color on the thin warp of her burlap form provoked me into imagining new pictures, and how astonished was I when what I'd imagined appeared, painted on canvas. Of course, sometimes we have the impression that we have already lived through a particular occurrence. I have this feeling in parts of the countryside I know I haven't visited. This field immoderate with meadow-saffron, I've already walked it once before. That clump of trees, it grew inside me long ago.

You always say, Olga, that painting is the greatest pleasure in the world. I've never told you how much pleasure it has given me to share with you your painting. Was I just a spectator? And when I walked the countryside, was I just a pedestrian? Wasn't I part of the landscape, like the shy deer that so often crossed my path? Even my breath, observable in the frosty air, was part of the observed landscape.

Again the daphne blossomed. Olga, do you remember? Again the linden trees released their whirling propellers into the air. Again the larch suddenly went rusty. And the first snow fell, and before it fell on us and on the earth, it melted.

We were always good at finding ourselves a sizeable piece of empty countryside, but we didn't feel overly free in it. As if on our walks we had been condemned for an undefined crime. We also drank our wine with an incomprehensible feeling of culpability. But it never occurred to us to just have water or to just stay in Prague.

"He's having a helluva time! He's running himself ragged!" Olga said, laughing at a young rabbit.

"Do you envy him?" I asked.

"It's hard to say. He can't paint."

When the soft, swampy turf wobbled under our feet, we looked around us with alarm. It was no longer possible to make out the two hills in the distance, one just a little bit lower than the other, which now blurred together under the influence of twilight, and suddenly we weren't quite sure whether there actually were two of them at all. We didn't dare look into the eyes of the stray souls floating above the swamp, but instead looked down the firm, wide path, which was leading us to a clear strip of sky. Do you know the constellations? I'll point them out to you. Cygnus, the Swan; Sagitta, the Arrow; Delphinus, the Dolphin. And there is the Corona Borealis, the Northern Crown. And where is the

Koruna česká, the Czech crown? In St. Vitus' Cathedral on Castle Hill, locked deep within the vault. Already nothing but an historical treasure.

Is it still said that love is born in the eye and descends to the heart? Yes. Certainly. But during the secret mourning she harbored then, I did not manage to get her heart to yield any sort of word, let alone a more private stirring.

I continued to grind the cold pigment of this strange abstraction, so that I could investigate, so that I could comprehend, where it is born and where it descends. But each time I would just end up returning to myself. I empathized and I was moved more than is appropriate, more than a man's nature allows, but at the same time I keenly examined the spectrum of my own feelings, of the tow of events, and of the colors of the regime which, as I recall, changed like the time of day or the time of year.

I am a parallel person. I stand outside events, but I breathe their atmosphere. Does it seem to you, Olga, that love is too indifferent? If so, you would have to avert your eyes from the landscape and its trees, whose beauty makes no other claim than to be perceived.

We were still walking abreast on the long path, which we luckily knew did not suddenly end. On our left, kilometers of pine forest; on our right, meadows and short oaks, whose leaves rustled beneath our feet or were finally preparing to fall. In the distance, a naif painter of late winter was suggesting to us notions about the reality of the central Czech hill country, whose elongated forms were divided from the earth by a dream threshold of mist. In the foreground to the diagram of our walk, and always associated with it, the courageous outline of Točník, the crumbled royal castle, with its memories that even this earth once had firm rulers.

We tread upon a carpet of anemones. White, pink, and blue flowers, it made me sad, but we couldn't fly over them, and Olga, you said:

"But why be sad? Like God's body, grass doesn't care if it loses parts of itself."

Then we came to a colder valley. Even there, not a single vestige was left of the snowfall, except for a snowman someone had built on the path, up ahead. Olga broke into laughter and then broke into a trot, as if she wanted to throw herself into the snowman's arms, but the cold, snowy figure did not let her fulfill her wish. It was too reserved, it dwelt in a granular immobility. Olga's tall, narrow shoulders collapsed and trembled. Fortunately, I was nowhere near her. When I came to where she was standing, she was smiling once again. Even the snowman was smiling.

Once it was one snowball on top of the other. The steep angle of the late winter sun had been slowly reducing the snow, and this was certainly not by chance, but according to the clearly defined laws of thermodynamics, which can be calculated, and the sun had also been thinning the snowman's body to a minimum. It was surprising that the large head had survived on its pediment of snow, which recalled the shaft of a hatchet or heavy mallet. In the hollowed-out body, stumps of icy limbs, pierced by twigs, still survived. And on the twigs, silken pussy-willows. I would like to know whether they were inserted before the reduction, or only later, and was the insertion done when the twigs were still bare and bony, the way one imagines a snowman's hands?

"It's a marvelous feat of pride to imagine, in spite of summer, that I will never melt," said Olga.

The earth is round, Olga, that's something your Atlas must know something about. On it are bands of eternal, primeval forest and eternal snow. Our slab of Bohemia is so small that one cannot even make out its curvature, and the seasons take turns, coming round and round, sometimes fiercely, sometimes so that you don't even know. Name them, Mikuláš, in order! Yes, teacher, sir! Spring, summer, autumn, winter. Do you recognize the colorful pictures hanging on the blackboard? They never completely tally with what we prefer to watch from the school's windows. Where we are, flowers grow underneath the snow, and snow falls on flowers, as well. There's always something that outlasts each season. But these are details, and I won't get worked up over them.

Olga got married. The wedding was in Warsaw, the honeymoon in Paris, the exhibition of her paintings in Rome. I sent telegrams and thumbed through the atlas of my feelings. It was a nice folio edition. Orographic maps and hydrographic maps, maps of the incidence of rare, protected flowers, maps of forests, fishponds, and wayside crosses, where snails crawl and where heather sparkles. And of course a political map, as well. How, without a battle, Šumava was given over to the Nazis, and Czech officers, again and again, gave the command: don't shoot! How across Charles Bridge all the way to the Prague Castle the communist militia marches, and how due to some sort of baroque magic the saints' statues, on both sides of it, smile in pious embarrassment. I became especially fixated on the place where the Battle of Lipany was fought. The Czech commander directed the hopeless battle from atop a knoll. The nobles' cavalry came at him from the rear. The aforementioned hamlet trembled under an exhausted sky. Watercolors laid waste the field. A second line of poplars moved off toward Kouřim like receding charioteers. With the gothic taunting of a swallow you look into the level distance to the Church of St. Barbara in Kutná Hora, and between your fingers you rub wild roses, which burst forth out of the memory of boulders. There is no one anywhere around, and therefore you are bold enough to be ceremonious. You approach the gravemound, wishing to touch your forehead to its black form. Abstemiously, from here in all directions, you wish to manage your mourning with painstaking vigilance, so that sentimentality doesn't come at you from the rear, and quite anonymously you wish to pay your respects to the fallen, who have long been anonymous themselves. But if those who have long been grown-up were, like boys on pear trees, to suddenly frighten a watchman with sticks, you would be less surprised and less disgusted. You do not touch the gravemound, and you quickly leave behind the golden sign a patriot once engraved:

To the memory of a battle lost

Idly, I continued to thumb through the pages. Whenever I tried to designate Olga's portrait as my horizon, I instead sank through another stratum of landscape. Her picture remained unchanging. Nor did I change when I married Jarmila. It was just an occasion to commit against her the sin of frankness. This makes me sad. If I had known in advance, I would not have been so frank with her, or I would not have started at all.

Sometimes Olga would make an appearance in Prague. And sometimes she would write me. She would describe for me one European city or another, and enclose the catalogue of an exhibition. She was successful. It's what I wished for her.

When I responded, I would expatiate with relish on what was new in the forest at Beroun. All sorts of things were happening there. This year the blue irises were growing in circular clumps. The pasque flowers have passed away, the rocks weren't very well disposed toward them, and it's driven the pheasant's eye completely out of its mind. I never mentioned daphnes. And imagine, they've gone and white-washed the St. John tavern, and the hens are no longer allowed in. What else am I doing? Oh, you can imagine for yourself. Nothing special.

And nothing special is how I drew my housing cells, according to and in anticipation of set standards, arrranging them like legos, also according to and in anticipation of set standards. Designing cubes that were a little unusual gave me a great deal of pleasure. At the prefab factory I sometimes parted with my drawing board. There weren't any experiments, only momentary attempts to do something else, something more interesting and more liberating, but the results were not much to speak of. I always returned to my little cubes. Our population likes to move into them. The flats are clean and bright, hot and cold running water, children always merry. When all is said and done, just about everyone wears store-bought clothes as well; if I chose to inspire in them some sort of discontent, it would probably be a mistake. What should I tell them? That we live without style and that beauty has turned into a Cinderella? Does anyone care?

The windows of the high-rise development sparkle. It's a nice late afternoon. People are coming home. Somewhere music is playing, somewhere else the aroma of goulash. In front of one of the buildings, someone is turning the earth in the garden and planting possibly perennials, possibly annuals. Nothing special. Why get worked up over it.

I married Jarmila, and six years later, without any sort of fanfare, I got divorced. I was frank. It was completely my fault. Letters from Olga stopped arriving. Then I learned from Štěpán that Olga had been here for a long time now. Now she too was divorced.

Did it pierce my heart to learn this? I think it did. When I read Štěpán's letter, I thought that in the distance a train was whistling.

Of course, she came because of me! I smiled at the arrogance of my imaginary love. But I did not look her up. If she'd wanted to see me, she would have let me know, long ago, that she was back in Prague.

That year too, one autumn day, I was walking through the Malá Strana gardens and parks to see the colors of the leaves, to see them starting to fall. On the Kampa my plane tree had visibly aged. I found it troubling – won't it survive me? The chestnut trees at Lobkovicz's were more golden than they were last year, but perhaps it only seemed that way to me. I preferred not to visit the Vrtbovský Garden. That fall I was very depressed. I wouldn't have liked Olga to catch me in such a melancholy mood.

I caught a rather ordinary flu at the end of the summer. It took me a week to rid myself of it. But despite my thermometer being back to normal, a strange fever stayed with me. I felt panicky. I couldn't sleep. I would catch myself looking at a book, but not reading it. The needle spun around record labels for a long time, and I didn't even know that the music had played. When I shaved, I didn't look at my face; I shaved as if by memory, on automatic.

Where was I looking? Was I thinking about something? Was I recalling ideas or memories? I don't know. It was as if I were looking into a void. I hadn't experienced this before. My eyes always drew pleasure from focusing on something, fixing on something. A landscape. But where is the horizon and where are the trees? A book. But where are the letters and where are the lines? Olga, where are your paintings?

It was as if I were living unconsciously. I stimulated myself with coffee, but the strangely empty space in which I was suddenly and unexpectedly stuck was only accentuated by the more powerful pounding of my heart. I ran and refreshed my face with cold water. Was it cold? I suffered from dizziness, like what I experienced when I entered *gymnasium*, when I went to the podium and knew I didn't know what to say.

At least I could work, plenty and hard. Work. I drew what more or less had been prescribed. But there was the certitude of white paper and black lines. What I would have liked most was to sit at the drawing board twenty-four hours a day. I arrived an hour early and I left when I wasn't able to hold the pen between my fingers anymore. At this stage, my eye, independent of any sort of feeling, keenly followed the puppet theater of black on white: endless string of points after endless string of points and you have a straight line. My friends, after all those lines I never saw anything strange. I drew more or less without any concern, except for the vacuum I filled with the regular, ordinary work to which I was inured. I needed it like the daily quota of sleep, which I could no longer fill.

When Dr. Rychta, from Komplexprojekt, came to me and told me that they might begin doing something with my old project, it made my hands tremble with excitement. This had never before happened to me. Something about me wasn't right, or more precisely: something about me was wrong.

I turned to Kormund for advice. Kormund recommended that, without any hesitation, I grab the opportunity.

"You see! Your time has finally come."

"My time? Of course not. But perhaps things will now go a little better for me," I said. "I'll be glad. And above all, my old project will be glad."

"I'll buy a case of champagne!" said Kormund.

"I'd prefer to wait a little while," I said.

"If Rychta himself has tread a path to you, it's a done deal. I don't recall him ever coming to anyone about anything.

There are big changes in the wind. They're discussing fundamental issues. Rychta needs you. I think you have a chance,
you and your old project. I hope you won't let that chance
slip through your fingers."

This happened this very year, nineteen sixty-seven. I had
carried on my fundamental dialogue and dispute with Dr.
Rychta fifteen years before. Rychta was now director of
Komplexprojekt, and in our field he had the final word. That
he had come to me proved that I'd been right, but it was
even more gratifying that my old project had preserved its
value. Even Rychta was now proved right.

During this period, Olga, we ran into each other again,
and of course it was not by chance. Of course it could most
likely be calculated using an appropriate formula from the
calculus of probability. Inevitably, it pierced my heart, as if –
as you came through the intersection in front of the National
Theater – a train coming from the south were whistling, but
it's possible that somewhere something actually was making
that sound: a tugboat on the Vltava, a factory siren in
Smíchov or in Holešovice, the pitiful klaxon of a city bus
lyricizing our memories.

Suddenly my life was good again, as it had been long ago
during my student days. I pored over the documents
concerning my project. They were kept at Komplexprojekt,
and since Rychta personally oversaw them, the archivist gave
me everything I needed. At home, in a trunk I had inherited
from my marriage, I found yellowed sketches and memos. I
was gradually re-assembling the contours of my old ideas.

Olga, we were gradually re-assembling the contours of our
even older love, which until then had never been put into
words. But we did not, in any form, employ the word love, or
similar words, or any of their more vague relations. We
thought these words, but they were not inflected in our

mouths. Something had changed between us. We needed to talk it out together, but we related to each other in the form of memories. And we expressed ourselves in images, so that, because we had in many cases a shared past, or at least parallel ones, the images of our dialogue took on the appearance of memories.

We kept surpassing ourselves in the increasingly fine and precise drawing of details of what we could never forget. It was the fractional shifting of a mirror suspended above a landscape, a spreading out of the symbolism of things and of the stroke of colors from the temporal spectrum of nature; the taste of sausage eaten in front of a country tavern, the dying sound of a pebble thrown onto thin ice.

I told Olga about my project, why it hadn't been implemented and how finally people were starting to show interest in it. I confided to her my hopes, but also my doubts. Should I be more involved in it? After nearly twenty years, change my entire way of living? With all the troubles I expected, was it really worth it? With every project, it is necessary to defend and to battle to victory. This is a very definite and for me decisive moral problem. And finally there is the question whether I am still an architect at all. I no longer feel like an architect.

"What do you feel like?" asked Olga.

"Like a man who feels on good terms with you," I said.

Playing with the past had to stop at once. Whenever I thought about Olga, I was actually thinking about the past. Even the first, most present moments when I saw Olga, seconds embellished by the whistling of a train and the carved frame of a mirror, had the character of an imprint of the past: I must have already known you; I had already heard the whistling of that train, I think some time in my childhood; I had already been exposed to that mirror.

We had discovered a new stratum of time, and it was the present, and it had a personal character. We had discovered a time that was like a person. This personal time was measured out in dialogues. Even the future was included in our dialogues. It was plain and simple. It could not be other than shared.

Love is born in the eye and descends to the heart.

I must shift this proverb around a bit. I want to express myself. But I'm afraid of invalidating it.

Love lies in the heart and rises to the tongue, I thought, and without regard for the fact that I was ashamed of conventional words and, like a dying man, under the influence of a picture of my entire past flying through my thoughts, I said:

"Olga, I'm in love with you. You can't just go away without me."

"I came here only because of you," said Olga.

"So we will stay here together," I said.

"We will go abroad together. Things will go better out there," said Olga.

"We're home here."

"What do you mean by 'home'?" said Olga.

"Being together," I said.

"Then it doesn't matter if it's here or there," said Olga.

"Turn that picture upside down. There or here," I said.

"Make up your mind!"

"About what?"

"About yourself," said Olga.

"That's certainly a big responsibility you're placing on me."

"So is freedom," said Olga. "Do you want to experience it?"

"That's easy for you to say: you made a clever marriage and got yourself dual citizenship. For you there is no problem. You can go here and there, as you wish."

"What do you mean by 'clever'? I think it was rather unfortunate. And I'm no longer young. I no longer want to go here and there," said Olga.

"I have been in love with you from the first moment I saw you," I said.

"Why didn't you ever say it?"

"Was it necessary?" I asked.

"It wasn't even possible," said Olga.

"You were my aesthetic conscience. You were the silent word with which I addressed the landscape," I said.

"How long can someone live through such a little word?" asked Olga.

"Very long, Olga, for a long, long time. Which is more, thinking about love or experiencing it? Plato's myth of the cave, with its fire and shadows, appeals to me a great deal, but that is not my problem. My question goes something like this: the parallel existence of two worlds. That is my freedom. Am I boring you."

"No! No! Keep going!" said Olga.

"After thinking so much about my project, do you really believe that I don't want to see it come to fruition?"

"What do you really want, Mikuláš?"

"Nothing. I learned to live on just a bit of fantasy, and I wanted you to be with me in that freedom."

"Be a bit more reasonable. We cannot go through our entire lives just together like that, living on atmosphere, on ideas."

"And you, Olga, you don't paint reality, no, you paint only your ideas."

"But I paint, and it is work," said Olga.

"I found another sphere in which to live, parallel, personal."

"What place do I have in that sphere of yours? Is it personal or parallel?" asked Olga.

"You want me to change."

"Yes. Love is change. Come with me!" said Olga. "If you actually love me. Do you really know at all?"

"It's the only thing I have no doubts about, but it's complicated," I said.

"It's difficult," said Olga.

"You're right, it's more than pleasure," I said.

"And you can see that I'm not afraid of it, I even yearn for it," said Olga. "It's been nearly forty years, between us. We've aged a little. So make up your mind. Out there there's more freedom not only for my painting, but for your barebones life as well."

"Give me a week, Olga, and let's hope that we still have forty years ahead of us. I'm more at home here, as I've said. Making up my mind is something I'd like to fiddle around with."

"Mikuláš, you even want to experience making up your mind. So experience it, experience it with all the fantasies you can muster. Your aestheticism is ruthless, do you realize that? But I understand it. I understand it because I'm a painter."

I had more than my barebones life, as Olga called it; I still had my old project. And Rychta was seriously interested in it now. But it's only a project. Olga, you can take your work with you. I made up my mind in a moment, but it took me a week to come and tell you my decision. Those seven days and seven nights I wanted to have the forty years that were past and, let's hope, the forty years in the future to devote to weighing the arguments. Did I think it through seriously? Responsibly? I shouldn't have agreed to export my barebones, idea-embellished life; I should have given my consent so that you could export your picture-embellished destiny. I could also have talked you into staying with me in Bohemia. I might actually have done it. I might have showed you that my landscape is not just an undercover burial ground.

I think I made the correct decision. Olga very much wants to live abroad. Opposing that, all I have are the atmospheric arguments of personal feelings. So I am bidding farewell to my landscape and crossing Charles Bridge, with what sort of feeling we shall see.

I crossed Charles Bridge with a good, downright festive feeling. I hadn't felt like this for a long time. I gave myself up to the feeling. The bell of St. Vitus', in the Prague Castle, was just beginning to strike. I believe I was smiling blissfully. Several people looked at me, possibly even statues.

The Čertovka Canal, flowers from St. Mary's Under the Chain, and now I'm here, Olga. I will go with you and here I am telling you:

"We will go together, Olga, abroad. I've only been to Paris once. It was right after the war, I was seventeen. Yet I already thought I'd been put on earth to design buildings. An architect on the verge of aging has the feeling that he is here to experience something important. And possibly that's why he still designs buildings. But we will go away, visit a place that's old and good. We will drop in on Štěpán. What will Štěpán have to say?"

"I spoke with him earlier this week. He said that he was sorry to hear it, but that he understands completely. He said that if he were in your shoes, he too would go."

"But how could you have known that I'd be going? What if I had decided differently?"

Olga smiled and kissed my cheek. That's the way she kissed Václav when they were little, I thought. She had had a child's naïvely beautiful face. Even her smile was precisely reproduced in the marriage photos of their childhood. I remember it well. Olga said:

"I knew."

I kissed the tips of Olga's fingers. My lips touched your dear skin covering those tiny bones so good at guiding brushes, those until then only abstractly loved hands so good at placing into the reality of a picture dream images in ground pigment mixed with oil. I felt I was at a crucial turning point in my life, I was experiencing a change, and her big black eye with its purple sheen was looking out from the shadows of its lashes. I looked out the window. In the stroke of the colors of the breaking night, the Church of St. Mikuláš stood above us like a solemn baroque witness.

"How could you have known with such certainty?" I asked.

But I didn't need to ask. I knew precisely what Olga had meant. When I crossed Charles Bridge on the way to Olga's, with that downright festive feeling, I had already played out her words. They were the same words long ago articulated in the music of the whistling of the train as it passed through the sunny landscape. It didn't pierce my heart.

I wished that I would once again hear the words. I wished that I would hear those particular words coming from her mouth, and I hoped and believed and persuaded myself that Olga read my eye like a primer. My words had already, long ago, descended to my heart.

A short pause. In a second, in the fraction of a second, like a dying man, once again I see the history of my life quickly unreel. It's not actually a history, just a number of pictures. Several portraits of people dear to me, landscapes of my land, my project. And between the taking in and the letting out of oxygen, between the one and the other beats of the muscle in my chest, the emptiness in my head fizzles and in its foam I once again see just a picture. Olga goes and lies down beside my words at the bottom of my heart. She lies taut as a string before it creates a note, taut as the freedom of a white canvas. As a word lies, or a body. They want to be joined. They want to be more. They want to turn into each other, just as my father once turned me upside down to the landscape. And me? I had already heard what Olga would say, and not until she said it would I once again have that special, good, downright festive feeling that I had heard it once before. Olga will say: It's plain and simple, Mikuláš, because you love me.

"It's plain and simple, Mikuláš," said Olga, "because you don't have anything to forsake."

If at that moment the towers of St. Mikuláš' had silently or with a rumble turned upside down and collapsed into a pile of building materials on the rotting parchment of its builders' drawings or even on the spirit that conceived them, I would have been less surprised.

I felt like a clean-cut tree suddenly standing in a dead calm, an estranged stump still preserving its center of gravity. For a few moments, I had to hold this impossible position. It was very difficult. Everything started falling, toppling, as soon as Olga said what she had said. I couldn't say that now I won't go, that it won't happen, that I've had second thoughts about it.

I didn't have second thoughts at all. It will happen. Change is functioning. It dazzles me like a sudden natural phenomenon, a thunderstorm that is immediately followed by a striking climatic change. Everything is blanketed by an airtight stratum of ash. It's not enough for you to go to sleep in a dignified manner. You become fixed in an unfinished gesture. Suddenly in the middle of summer it is snowing. You fall asleep on an aristocratic couch and wake up under a guillotine. At the wheel of your car, you light a cigarette and never finish smoking it; you see the oil slick on the road ahead, and already you know that things are out of control, that already you are forever past the point.

So, Olga, you think that I don't have anything to forsake. You think that I should be checked through with you like an empty trunk.

Swiftly and deftly I held a screening for just myself of what I needed to do. I had the same feeling as when I drew the housing blocks of the Prague-East and Prague-West high-rise developments. Impossible to just knock off, but possible to professionally execute without personal commitment. What's the use. There is no relinquishing of the will to shape a style, no relinquishing of personal hopes. All that's required is to understand the necessity of the plan and then arrange within it the cells of a life. It makes me sad.

Above all, I didn't know how to make it clear that some sort of love took place, that something changed. She couldn't have noticed anything yet. I turned the fixed gesture into movement, a small roll of pictures running again without interruption: the arm is now animated. The tongue, may it stir! Let there be the word!

I imagine the space as a puppet theater. It is necessary to see the half-played scene to the end, in the form of a dextrous dialogue. One or two more monologues on top of that, and then for the envoi a short depiction of the future. We will settle in the Latin Quarter. We will found a small gallery. You will paint, and I'll do my best. To live we'll sell paintings, make social contacts. Interesting. I will publish some essays on the theory of architecture: democracy and space; style in an overpopulated world; cubicle dwellings in the metropolis and the personal feelings of today's man.

"Or would you prefer to pursue your projects?" said Olga.

"I will be left with my style," I said. "And I prefer to imagine projects. For me it's the ideal situation."

I imagined how to get out of this situation at least until this evening. Plain and simply, I wrenched and wormed myself free from everything, but how to get out of her real, actual space? Which way to escape? Tea, an open bottle of wine, and a clock on the wall ticking terribly slow.

I smiled. Olga smiled too. We talked about our visits to the countryside here at home, and about our visits to the countryside out there in the big world. My little puppet sat for exams in geography and Czech history. My shadow, fastened to the wall, was exhausted to death. I wanted to sleep and my heart was pierced, as if a train were permanently whistling.

In those long nighttime hours you realize, with all the melancholy you can muster, that hell is the free and easy pouring forth of dialogue in whose content you no longer have any interest. Your disgust is so great that it blankets everything, even the memory of a pleasant book, even words that are sincerely believed and that were once beautifully and unforgettably expressed. You understand the suicide's yearning: to shut oneself up!

Even the compressed wisdom of the proverb suddenly appeared to you as rambling as a walk in the mountains. By morning the rain will have turned to snow. It seemed to you that your tongue was entering the realm of freedom, which is not bounded by necessity, but rather circumscribed by love. And meanwhile you drag your feet through the conventional.

Already, it isn't raining anymore. A viscous flow of snow falls in heavy pieces, yet not even a damp dawn comes. You began with words, soon you will reach the body. Awaiting you are the conventions of living matter.

Until the day breaks, until I go back across Charles Bridge, I will once again think up variations on the proverb. Such is my nature: Until I went back across Charles Bridge I had the feeling that I myself, once a long time ago, must have played out a third variation on the proverb ... and then suddenly I thought of it: Love is born in the eye and dies on the tongue.

Finally dawn rises beneath the mist. In the outgoing night, visibly and audibly, but limited to a meager spectrum of colors, the snow thaws. I observe the shades of gray strewn within the white and black lines. Our naked bodies softly outlined in charcoal. Euphoric, Olga weeps and says:

"Once again! Please say it once again!"

"I love you, I'm in love with you, in love, in love!" I say, and I don't feel any of it at all, neither in my heart nor on my tongue.

I have only one thought in my head: To be on my own again, an individual procession, carrying a picture of a banner. The collar of my plainclothes overcoat turned up! And my hands in my pockets! Slowly across Charles Bridge. On my lips a single yearning: a cigarette!

My eyes roam and scrutinize objects and, according to their density, calculate how long I must lie next to Olga before nothing strikes her as having changed.

Finally Olga falls asleep. I place the blanket over her naked shoulders, so that later she isn't cold. She gives a grateful smile. So that she doesn't have a shadow of suspicion that I am indifferent to her, I kiss her eyelashes before I go. What I will do tomorrow I do not know. Olga smiles and says:

"I'll make you some coffee."

"Just sleep," I say. "I'll have breakfast at my drawing board."

"Let it go! At least today," says Olga.

"Can't. Someone would have to do it for me."

Boulder

On Charles Bridge the streetlights were still shining. A pedestrian was coming toward me. A single pedestrian, it might even be me, the alter ego of my mood. At least now I know what I will do. I pull up my collar, light up a cigarette, and like a soliloquist I say to myself a sentence I've heard somewhere before: Love is born in the eye and dies on the tongue.

He speaks to himself a bit more: I don't have anything, you don't have anything, to lose. If you don't have anything to lose, must you gain something? Broad-minded, you retain your freedom until taking the decisive step, but it is presumed that you cannot do otherwise. What you loved to look at suddenly you hate. As if something inside you has changed course. You have a sickening, downright nauseous feeling. Your beloved's eye does not look at you with love, but with scrutiny; it finds you guilty. It does not, however, discover in you your feelings, intricately structured with the history of this love, but coldly, eternally it judges what is inside you.

For twenty years you preserved your personal, internal freedom and independence, and it wasn't easy. What was all that preservation for, when with utter certainty a beloved woman could tell you that you don't have anything to forsake?

I wanted to be pure, and I remained empty. I have only myself, my barebones life, and you, you can pat yourself on the back, for someone still cares about you and wants to travel with you somewhere. Did I feel offended? More caught unawares, surprised by that one sentence, that one gesture, which cast away, cut loose, condemned me to myself.

After the blow, I could not enjoy my cigarette. It made me nauseous. I leaned over the stone railing and looked down into the river. On the Malá Strana side of the river, stonemasons were already working among the sandstone ashlars and boulders. They were jointing and hewing new blocks of stone so that they could be precisely substituted for old bits of the bridge's gothic material, which faithfully, but to no avail, guards against the disintegration of our false saint Jan Nepomuk. The sandstone's disintegration in Prague's climatic zone, with its considerable variability, has certainly reached its point of completion, so that the renovation of the bridge, dear father of our country after whom it was named, is essential.

I smiled. Although I'd decided I wouldn't get myself all worked up, I thought of a political association. Our climatic zone is exceptionally variable, you can practically watch things disintegrate, everyone talks about renovation. We used to call Charles IV, the Holy Roman Emperor, the father of our country. Our current president, Novotný, has been given the people's nickname, Pop.

The impact on me of the baroque-embellished gothic statues surrounded by tubular scaffolding was both comic and pathetic. As was the view toward the Knights of the Cross and over the weir toward the National Theater. So what sort of true beloved, Bedřich Smetana?

In your head you hear the aria, "Beloved, oh so true, until her dying day is due," but you are not watching a scene from *The Bartered Bride*. You are remembering the year 1948, you see the people's militia marching across the bridge. Untouched, virgin rifle straps shine on workers' overcoats. The Communists are taking power. In their step you feel self-confidence; they bear the collective thought and pathos of their class. I watched closely and registered the double impact of the historical moment, the impact of both the impression and the conception.

The impression was magnificent. The revolutionary picture carried me away. The conception was sober and severe. I stood there, watching. It was the beginning of a new epoch and the end of the old democracy. With the intensity of a still very young man I could feel inside me how they intersected and how they clashed.

Twenty years elapsed, and once again I am standing here looking into the water. What elapsed? My personal time – and nothing happened. I just aged. I'll be forty.

With a completely commonplace feeling, with a feeling of coldness, and with twinges of conscience that I wouldn't be able to concretely explain, I walked slowly toward the other side of the river. I looked at my watch: I still had some time. Even today I would not be late for work.

I sensed to the left, on Letná Hill, against a dim, misty sky, a dark, gigantic catafalque with an outline similar to the terrace-like pedestal of the Stalin memorial that no longer stood guard over Prague. You didn't believe that the people who built the memorial would pull it down so soon. Too bad, now it would be an historical relic, a tourist curiosity, certainly the only one of its kind in Central Europe.

Can you still recall it? Twenty meters high, a stone generalissimo wearing his official overcoat like an enormous filing cabinet, and pressed against his back a group of figures, types, the people. At so large a height and bulk, his only warrant to the beauty of nature was that of the quarry, and to the monumentality of art that of the primeval sphinx. And yet for one very short era it was a gigantic caricature of sculpture, remarkable, more than interesting. It was an unforgettable phenomenon, with its own peculiar aesthetic.

Sticking up into the sky above the city were clumps of stone and concrete that had lost their human contours. They had blasted the statue, but it hadn't broken into particles, as was planned. The impaired body had remained standing, embellished with twisted and prolapsed pieces of steel and iron rods. Resembling a romantic look-out tower that wars had blasted and bolts of lightning had smashed into a sur-realistic anatomy, only now had the sculpture become a sculpture, as if an abstract genius of formative death had given it a touch of micro-blasting.

But what was this sculptor's name? I don't remember. The names of most sculptors are even more forgotten than the names of those whose statues they make. It's a sad tale.

When the ministers who decided that they would put a statue of Generalissimo Stalin up above Prague then went on to demand that Stalin's eye be as high as the cornice of Prague Castle, every sculptor laughed. It was utterly impossible to hoist such a stone colossus onto the banks of the Vltava. The cost would exceed the budget of the largest of dams. They would have to reinforce the river bank. They would have to shoot concrete into the river bottom. The foundation would have to be more solid than that of a skyscraper. Even the transport of materials looked to be problematic. The bridges cracked at the mere thought of being burdened by such unusually large boulders. With such heaps of money and labor, they could have built places for thousands of families to live.

Every sculptor could easily imagine the giant ogre down to its smallest details, for example, his boots hewn from stone. It might be interesting to have the boots stand all by themselves on the hilltop, surrounded by blazing torches. Or the generalissimo could be barefoot. Only there is a difference between a sphinx's claw and the big toe of the Chairman of the Council of Ministers. The sphinx, which is possibly divine, can go barefoot, but the barefooted never decide to go down in history as politicians.

Wouldn't it have been more realistic for the government to have authorized not the building of a statue, but rather the building of a sphinx? And wasn't it shrewd to calculate how big a wad of cash an unrealizable proposal would quite surely bring?

And so one man depicted it as a gag, told it as a jokey, unreal yarn, so certain was he that the project would never become a reality. When later he saw the statue, which after many years of construction loomed like a stray boulder above the river and the city, he shot himself. It is said that in his story there is something bitterly personal, something desperately romantic. Who has documented this?

In the meantime, Stalin died. The statue in Prague was unveiled like a posthumous child. In attendance was Nikita Khruschev, who later unveiled the generalissimo as a despot.

It was a damp evening, the anniversary of the GRSR, the unpronounceable abbreviation it is our habit to use on this occasion. One more anniversary of the Great Russian Socialist Revolution, celebrated in Prague with a parade of the masses and a demonstration in Old Town Square. Then, it seemed to me that one of the sculptor's eyes had survived his own death, and even the sculpture's death, and had levitated up next to my shoulder to watch the show with me.

Spread along the river a silent city. I stand beside the sculpture's ruins. I study a church tower; St. Týn's and St. Jakub's; city hall; St. Mary of the Snows; the rippled rooftops in a dim, watercolor light all the way to Vítkov Mountain, where the Hussite warrior Jan Žižka is sitting on a horse that looks like a mammoth, such a nonsensical monument from our patriotic, bourgeois era. From a distance you can even see his mace, and that's certainly something. The smaller the nation, the larger the statues, but I won't get worked up over it.

Along the embankment at the base of Letná Hill, stretching to the left and to the right, are processions of Praguers holding banners, slogans, and pictures of politicians. The dearest of generalissimos is already missing among the portraits. At the bridge, the crowd fuses together into a powerful current, and the living matter streams toward Old Town Square. Brass bands play for the marchers. I hear music from the heights and from all directions, the marches break overhead and interlace into an outlandish rhythm, which now recalls a broken-winded waltz, now a bustling polka. As the now single procession jostles its way across the bridge, the music starts dying down, and as if on command the armies of laborers turn their heads. The crowd of people shuffling its way from the government's Malá Strana face to the left. The throng of people marching its way from the laborer's Holešovice, as if given instructions, right face! During that brief moment the music stops. All you can hear are footsteps. The collective vision of the mass of taciturn people marching past is fascinated by the statue, which just the day before had been a symbol of unshakability. Today it is a geyser of bursting fantasies flashing into the sky. Tattered rags, a ferrous fossil of the stormy cloud of a revolution that has blown over. Already given an autopsy with dynamite and jackhammers, the torso is scrawled all over with the black lines and curves of steel reinforcement rods.

In the short moment of embarrassed silence, a passive, people's satisfaction is felt, but there is a marionette feeling to it, as if with the common pull of useless shame this view of something supra-individual is quickly adjusted by individual concerns. Suddenly the heads all face forward once again. It is not advisable to look, more than in passing, at something freshly blasted. A pause, a deviation from the ranks, could to the fellow-marching leader of one's party cell be interpreted as censuring the regime, which has remained, which has endured.

So, Olga, you say that I don't have anything to forsake. I shivered with cold and accelerated my pace. The indefinite twinges of conscience I bore within me, she gave them more definite contours. They began to weigh on me like boulders. Olga, you forced me to do some balancing, and I'm no good at rejecting one thing in favor of another.

I was still looking at the spot where once the monument had stood. Nothing was standing there anymore. On this empty spot I could sense history, and it is my history, too, Olga. And you want to ask what of it remains inside me? I don't know. I only know about several synoptic nutshell versions, and I bear within me a record of several pictures, each with its own intense atmosphere.

So I crossed Charles Bridge and along the old king's way I walked at a good pace to Old Town Square. At that hour the streets were empty. Olga, can you understand how lonely I felt on those empty streets, and that it was more than mere homesickness?

I have produced nothing and I have experienced nothing special. I would say, if you'd like, as part of my balancing, that all I've done is live, and that I've lived and still live in a specific place. Why should I apologize for that?

Trunk

In a corner of the square, across from Týn Church, is a partially open window. Out this partially open window flutters gray cigarette smoke shaken by the rattling of a typewriter. Jarmila is frantically smoking and frantically working, as always. She is still up translating some classic, and it's morning already.

Temptation is a powerful thing. I will go up, I will knock, and I will ask if I can stay. I'm exhausted. I'll call work and tell them that I'm sick. I'd like to sleep a thousand years. In my stupor, I hear disjointed sentences from our past together. I can't forget.

"Till you find yourself a new apartment or if you're ever truly in need, yes, you can come by. Consider it your natural, domiciliary right," Jarmila had said.

Never had I taken advantage of what was for me an unnatural domiciliary right, and I didn't want to do it now, either. At first sight of Jarmila, I could tell it wasn't a good thing.

"You're always in the midst of a crisis, and it's so exhausting," said Jarmila.

"What do you mean by crisis?"

"Always dismayed, disgusted. You look like you've just thrown up. And it all comes from your not doing anything," said Jarmila.

"Every day I go to my board and draw," I argued in my defense.

"If it doesn't interest you, then why don't you give it up?"

"What would I do?"

"You have to answer that question yourself. Is every architect in Bohemia being eaten up by tedium?"

"Did primitive man have architecture? Those men who still slept on the ground?" I asked.

"That abstract talk of yours drives me crazy," said Jarmila.

"Of course they had architecture," I said to vindicate myself. "The architecture of the sky above us, the architecture of clouds and trees, of steppes and cliffs."

"Why do you talk and why don't you build?" said Jarmila.

"That was the original space," I said to defend myself, "a space with nothing built yet, circumscribed by no sort of dogma. I would like to return to such a space."

"In the second half of the twentieth century, you want to lie in a cave? I prefer to lie around a pool," said Jarmila.

"A dwelling is an artificial space. House is a technical term for an ancient, spiritual feeling of home. Although the architect expresses himself technically, the point is to not forget one's human calling. Every space that I design, I should conceive as a part of nature and as a part of cosmic, universal space. Back when it was a cave. Even a baroque church. But barracks, no."

"You always talk about the primitive and the original. But what have you achieved?" she said reproachfully.

"I have written a few essays on the topic."

"That's not any sort of production."

Jarmila thought that when she married an architect, she was also marrying buildings. But what could I possibly build? Only something to think about.

Jarmila had aspirations, even for me. I never succeeded in convincing her that this was her mistake, not mine. It's astonishing how much our world is in motion, in transformation. Doesn't it seem to you that this is the epoch of the nomad? What difference does it make that one Mikuláš Svoboda doesn't build a thing? At least he happily thinks his thoughts. Am I less human because I don't produce anything? Because all I do is ponder?

"I know the word for you," said Jarmila. "You're a loafer."

I didn't feel the least bit offended. I just smiled and calmly took exception. No one has ever offered me so much as a free slice of bread, and I would not have accepted it. I've given this a great deal of thought. I turn over to our society the relevant taxes. A straight line is an infinite number of points. I've never been late for work.

"You grind, it's true," said Jarmila, "but empty-handed. Don't hide behind your workday! It doesn't take much these days to earn a living, at least in our zone of Central Europe. No problem at all."

No problem, it's true, but for me things were slightly different. Jarmila sensed this, and right from the start was envious of my peculiar, secret discontent. She searched for its origins. Although in the end she resigned herself to it, she hated my acceptance of my work as bare necessity. She was even willing to talk with me, at the table and on walks, about my pipedreams. For example, I would elaborate upon my ideas about how Prague should develop. I would whole-heartedly reject the building of high-rise developments on the city's periphery. On the contrary, a green ring of trees should spring up out there. The socialist state has the means to do anything; it could rationally plan into the future, near and far, and meanwhile all that's necessary is to regulate the headlong expansion of the metropolis into nature and the nonsensical concentration of its inhabitants.

And Jarmila was grateful for all the free time I had. Never did I hurry. I enjoyed cooking. Around the time I married her, Jarmila stopped living on nothing but yogurt.

She ate with relish, she ate passionately, and she was good at appraising my culinary performances. I truly liked serving meals. I would have felt completely happy as a waiter, but I became an architect instead. Not something to get worked up over.

"You're a damn magician, the way you pull things off," Jarmila marveled, but all I'd said is what I thought, that preparing good, original meals counts as an art:

"Experience is in books, feeling in the heart, pipedreams on the tongue."

"Each time, you say something different."

"Because each time, I cook a different dish," I said.

When I didn't feel like reading and I couldn't listen to music because Jarmila was translating, I would roam around the Old Town. On especially damp evenings, I would sit in my chair and draw little pencil sketches or study tourist maps. I would picture myself walking through familiar landscapes, and I would imagine what I might do with them. After a century's time, this valley could be embellished with tree-lined lanes. And there a string of fishponds would not be too difficult to revive. That chateau, long, long dilapidated, its English park gone to wilderness ... but never mind.

Often I just sat and looked into the void and imagined what it would have been like if we hadn't kept losing every war, if a king had been more aggressive, if in the year 1938 President Beneš had given the command to oppose the Germans with armed force ... I leafed through reference books in order to refresh my memory of certain dates. I felt like a pensioner, except that regularly I went to work.

Jarmila was translating an interesting array of stories into our mother tongue. I see her looking at the dictionary. I get up and help her find a word. She is grateful to me. We hug. That is what I was grateful for.

The atmosphere of the picture of our apartment was that of a cloister. Jarmila's diminutive, renaissance profile stood out against the lamplight. With her slender fingers and short nails, battered from her eternally clattering those keys, she held fast to her practically eternal cigarette. The spiraling of her smoke flirted with light and shadow. On the floor a rug cowered like a Persian, and among thousands I found the one word she needed. What more could I ask? Already Jarmila is spinning the word into a sentence and I am going to take a bath. Things are alright. Everything is normal, nothing's going on. You are sated, and around you lie things that your father would have considered unattainable luxuries: a gold ring, cologne, a bottle of red wine that, obligingly looking forward to being opened, has partaken of the room's temperature.

I rest my forehead against the bathroom tiles and register my thoughts. Are they thoughts? I don't know. More the feeling of the words as I say them: I am not myself, I am not myself, I am not myself.

I look around me. The soap has a sweet scent – another luxury. I'm ashamed of it. Why? In their red-and-gold cup a pair of toothbrushes bear witness. A pair of laughably tiny panties hangs from a thread. In the gas water heater attached to the chimney one can hear the drafts of air. Outside, the wind is whistling deliriously. When the wind wails like that, they say someone has hung himself. Statistically this is just about certain. And what is it that's syllabilizing itself in your head? What's being syllabilized is – now, now, brown cow, ready, set, go, go and don't come back!

Be reasonable, you say to yourself. You think you can do anything, anything can come into your mind, your head is an undefended no-man's-land. What you will do is momentous, decisive. What will you do? You will smile and run a bath. After all, I do love Jarmila. That's why I married her, in order to be with her, in order to forsake her. Before going to bed, she likes to stretch out in the bathtub. And before we go to bed together, Jarmila says:

"If you don't feel well, go see a doctor!"

"If all the people in the stories you translate were so frightfully material, would you have bothered to translate them at all?" I said.

"The body has fevers, as does the soul. The soul's fever is tedium," said Jarmila.

"It's deeper, Jarmila, irrational."

Jarmila is angry with me. She reproaches me for my reflections on modern architecture, and for being an old, romantic man. For not wanting to talk about my feelings and for not wanting to hear about them either. She is curious about sensations, they are concrete and she wants to discuss them, even when we're making love. And she is beginning to suspect that I have another woman on my mind.

I still don't have the courage to be entirely frank, I'm still afraid to tell Jarmila, out of consideration, so she isn't hurt, that I constantly return to that one predestined moment. As if an abstract world had a claim on the way I look at things and the way I express myself in images. Especially in a marriage, this is something I have to come to terms with.

Again and again I looked beyond the wall. In the blue spectrum of night colors I was still attracted by a perfect mirror of love hanging above an oval landscape.

I should have been frank right from the start. Taking so long to tell the truth greatly complicated my life with Jarmila. By the time I finally did tell her about the strange, abstract feelings I had for Olga, it was already too late.

Right at the start, I should have broken with Jarmila, but should I reproach myself as well for being overcome by longing for a vivid woman and for refined, aesthetic situations?

I smiled. What might Štěpán have said? Štěpán might have said: Mikuláš, for you even a crucifix is an aesthetic situation.

Even now, when I am once again living in my memories and when memories even include what I not long ago lived through with Olga and what put me into this new situation, I perceive the situation as an aesthetic one. It's the only way I am able to experience it.

So I stood there in a corner of Old Town Square and slowly made up my mind to command my feet to remove me from this spot and take me to my office. There, I will shave, make some coffee, and get to my drawing. Actually, I am rather looking forward to my pencil.

But I was still standing there in the archway before the Týn Church. Day is breaking, swiftly, materially. I look up at Jarmila's window. From the silent square below, you can hear the rhythmical ticking of her typewriter. Occasionally there's a chime. It's like Cinderella diligently shelling peas.

Cinderella, so delicate, so tiny. And so very, very beautiful that even a man who didn't love her found her tempting, even an overarchitecting soul like mine. Making love, that is the perfect music, she used to say. Music is vibration. Vibration is a physical quantity. It is possible to know it, so that we can master and exploit it. Don't be afraid to cross the borders of shame. The senses work for us. You say a straight line is an infinite number of points? Love is an infinite number of sensations.

She read ancient Indian and Persian books on the art of making love, and she read modern pornography as well. And this inclination led her to use her philological talents, where you gave as good as you got, dear Jarmila. When faced with divorce, some women crack up, weep, or complain to their girlfriends. Jarmila started learning Chinese. It's quite possible she's already translating from it.

But I know, Jarmila, that I'd be oversimplifying and maliciously caricaturing you if I were to presume you just wanted everything to be rationally explained. You had your own secret, and as far as I'm concerned it remains one.

Once I came home without making a single sound. Not a click out of the key in the lock, not a clack from the door. I slipped off my shoes. I had a present in a bag. There wasn't an occasion, I just wanted to surprise you, delight you.

I didn't make a sound as I crossed the threshold. I looked for you among the engravings on the wall, my view wandered from the writing table – piled with paper and books – from the writing table, wide as a marital bed, to the bed, wide as a writing table. Rows of reference books on the shelves, colorful emblems in the Persian rugs, a baroque openwork baldachin, and finally I saw you in a mirror that reflected you out of your room. In your room the air is clean. Special. Incredible. You're up, you're not asleep, but you're neither smoking nor working. Jarmila sucked on her cigarette even when she was naked.

You are sitting on the rug in front of the trunk, and on a piece of oak inlaid with bright stars are scattered strands of your even brighter hair. They merge with the star beams and sparkle together in the halflight.

Jarmila looks nowhere in particular and smiles. I am touched by the paired emblem, one leaning against the other: a closed trunk and a smiling woman.

As if you were flipping through the pictures in a picture book or reading a chronicle that never ends, you were visualizing objects that had at some time been placed in the trunk but at some point disappeared. Bolts of cloth, books, pewter bowls and glass goblets, gloves, tablecloths, and maps, certainly some sort of weapon, someone's letter, purple ribbon, in a secret drawer a gold ducat. In one era grains of

wheat, in another era just the void of interwoven woodworms. That's how good you are at visualizing. But you, you don't know, you don't know at all, how to visualize what lies behind the smile of a woman for whom you are bringing a gift.

You know those smiles that are parts of speech, speech that's not dominated by a verbal treasure, but expresses itself best in a smile. You also know those smiles that are parts of speech that prefer to summarize their express treasures in an unexpressed gesture of the lips and facial muscles, and you remember them. These smiles are meant for you, they confide.

But you also know smiles that guard against confidences, that are only ostensibly emblematic of the delicate movements of the soul. Here you pick out the somnambulists, there the lonely walkers in the countryside. You observe the music listeners in the twilight and you recall the many portraits of gifted painters. You are not the one being addressed. You observe in silence the occurrence of sublime enjoyment, which once, in antiquity, found itself a sculptor.

You are surprised, touched, silent. You obey an order not to shoot at an angel flying past. At least you ask for permission to look at a work of art. But while you might be allowed to stand with impunity in front of paintings and sculptures, because your intimacy is cloaked in art, Jarmila's nakedness and her smile, half-open like a butterfly, suddenly ordered me out past the threshold, like an obedient stranger who by chance enters someone else's bedroom.

Jarmila turns her head. Her eyes are fixed on the mirror. I am still looking into the mirror, as well. Where was she looking? Was she looking through the mirror? Did she see her own face there? She could see it there, but she didn't have to. She could see my face, too. I wasn't sure about the angles of incidence and reflection, so I couldn't make any calculations.

When I was home by myself, I would sometimes make a study of this enigmatic angle in order to figure out whether she could or couldn't see, had or hadn't seen me in the mirror. I would like to figure out what sort of experience she was traveling through. There was only one thing I knew with absolute certainty, that I was not part of that experience.

Like Jarmila, I too used to sit before the trunk and look into the mirror. Before it I am before a threshold, at the spot where I stood back then, and I set up a clothes rack topped with a hat so that I can most perfectly lay out the situation and judge whether we'd recorded each other's presence. Neither of us ever brought it up.

Yes, it was only an instant. How much time does a smile take? Suddenly I retreated into the corridor and very loudly, as if in alarm, I made the key click in the lock and I slammed the door and I cried out, Nazdar! Hello! I've got a present for you! And two fresh sausages! I'm steeped in smoke from an absolutely impossible meeting, and I'm going to take a shower. Can you hear me?

Jarmila was already at her typewriter again. And in her mouth she had a cigarette, on her forehead a little vertical crease. It suited her. It reminded me of the way orientals decorate their foreheads.

I dozed a bit. The clatter of the typewriter lulled me into a pleasant sleep. I had a short but vivid dream. In the trunk, piled one on top of the other like bolts of cloth, are two two-dimensional women, one big and tall, the other tiny. I shut the lid, consigning them to darkness and dreams. I feel I'm asleep, but in my dream my memory of the dream is unbelievably vivid. By touch I can distinguish the warp and woof of diverse fabrics. They are warm and delicate, their softness is vivid. In the winding of skeins I can finally feel three dimensions. A pinky without a nail.

After twenty minutes I woke up. In dictionaries I once again found a number of words with the right distinctive meanings, dictated them to Jarmila, and then went and polished my shoes. I polished my shoes long and carefully. My performance even embraced Jarmila's shoes. I became absorbed in my work for an entire hour; it was just the sort of little extra-employment pleasure that ought to be fairly remunerated.

I flipped through photographs of and documents concerning Chateau Pustověty. Old records and maps, a little history, a chronicle of the estate. The chateau was – over the next ten or fifteen years, more or less – to be renovated. Kormund was my intermediary. I was supposed to draft a preliminary overview. It was an absolute delight.

After which I brought in a pitcher of beer and we dined on the fresh sausages. Do you taste the garlic? It has a carnal aroma. We made up tall tales about its source. Jarmila was happy. Or just content? She had once again completed a good and thorough piece of work. For that matter, so had I. Why, during such a nice meal, did I not feel myself? How did Jarmila put it? Let's calculate in ourselves what is uncalculating! Sensations! How many do you have? A lot, plenty, and they're nice. No one would believe that there's something eating my insides out. And I don't impart it to anyone. Only once did I tell Jarmila, and I've always reproached myself for doing it.

There's a pause in the typewriter's clatter. Jarmila opens the window wide. She has discharged a task and has surely, once again, met a deadline. I know exactly what she will do now. She will bend over, breathe a sigh of relief, and raise her arms as if readily surrendering to her long-awaiting enemies, who have finally arrived and are ready to disarm her: weariness and fresh air. The cigarette smoke around her flutters like imitation lace curtains. She looks across Old Town Square towards the Castle. I like that view, as well. Then she watches a pedestrian coming toward me through the square. He asks me for a light. I attend to it. The light of the tiny matchstick illuminates my face. Suddenly, at the same time, day breaks. A dark cloud passes, the sky is torn open. Jarmila must recognize me, she must see me. Do we wave to one another? Without a single gesture, I remove myself around the corner onto Celetná. I don't want to look back. But my imagination is occupied by Jarmila's naked body. Why? Who gave the command? I should already be seated at my board, drawing.

I sit at my board. This is my indifferent certitude. I suddenly feel dizzy and my heart is pierced, although I don't hear the whistling of a train.

I am sipping my coffee. My teeth feel an infinite number of pieces of finely ground, caffeinated powder. A straight line is an infinite number of points. The telephone. Project Documentation. Svoboda. Which one? Mikuláš. Block A/Sixteen will be at our disposal on Monday? Of course. You can rely on it.

I work quickly, deftly, practically just by touch, like a blind child making a wreath. And I put together a balance sheet. I put together a balance sheet as if I were about to die. In any event, for one particular woman I do have to die. To offend someone, to forsake someone, to let someone cry on her blanket is not any sort of art at all. I must devise a viable way of becoming indifferent toward Olga. I need to find a sentence of my own that would manage to turn Olga upside down, to reverse, expunge, revoke. I am not good at hurting,

I am not good at actively defending myself, I have to find myself another form of resistance.

I marvel at this. What do I really want? And which cold, insensitive constellation of burned-out, faraway stars determines the fate of someone who wants to be indifferent, who wants to be unloved?

From an infinite number of points, comprising a life, I seek to draw a line, to depict some sort of story, but I see neither a beginning nor an end. All I see is a number of points equally distant from a single center. A story, what sort of story? There is only a spot of color which in man, who is used to looking at pictures, evokes concrete ideas and associations. I see small animals, human figures, the undulating horizon of the landscape.

Project

I visited Štěpán at the Hrádek rectory in order to ask his advice. Midsummer's Eve was balmy and long. It was as if I were once again making confession to him. The eye of the Crucified was watching us from a sweet-smelling brier bush.

Soon after I completed my architecture studies, I obtained a good position at a design institute, thanks to Kormund. I was given a very interesting project: to propose an overall solution for a worker's residential development near the Beroun ironworks and lime kiln. I proposed terraced buildings in a wooded terrain about fifteen kilometers from the industrial properties, beyond a series of rolling fields, outside the radius of descent of industrial emissions. Simple forms: wood, stone, glass, concrete. Grass and trees, even a sky with drifting clouds, were obviously part of the buildings. I wanted to connect the development to the industrial properties by means of an electric railway.

I worked very quickly and very hard. My project thrilled me. I had an idea for a modern town that would remain in harmony with a part of the landscape I had a personal connection to. In a village not far away, my Uncle Boleslav had a small farmstead, where with my brother Béda I spent the holidays of my childhood. There Béda and I played in a dappled corner. Out of stones and planks we built ourselves a wall that separated us from the garden and which, in our fantasies, roofed by sky and plum trees, were at the same time the rafters of an imaginary house. How carefully we placed stone after stone around a little basin, on which we sailed spiders around in paper boats. My game was now continuing into the dimension of adulthood, and perhaps I didn't appreciate that it is truly a professional's greatest joy to realize his childhood notions and still be paid for it.

The director of the institute rejected my ideas. But he told me that he respected my conception and that I mustn't doubt this. The approach is progressive, informed by the best traditions of modern architecture. He mentioned the Russian revolutionary avant garde, Scandinavian architects, and the major figures of postwar building design. He opened a cabinet, offered me a cognac, and then also took from the cabinet several foreign publications, which we flipped through with great pleasure. What he particularly valued about my project was my understanding of the needs of workers and their families. Yes, of course, this is how we should envision socialist architecture. But unfortunately, in Czechoslovakia today, no one would authorize such a project.

"Who do you mean by 'no one'?" I asked.

"You ask? You ask – who? Absolutely no one!" said Dr. Rychta. "And that includes committees, representatives, delegates, commissions, presidia, authorities. Speaking more generally – the state, the patron. We live in a world of precise societal connections and political contingencies. Don't you see it, feel it, experience it?"

"Let's submit the project to the workers' consideration," I proposed.

"We can't deal directly with workers concerning fundamental questions. We can deal with them only through the mediation of their functionaries," said Dr. Rychta.

"Are they actually their, that is, the workers' functionaries?" I asked.

"They are functionaries," Dr. Rychta stated.

"You yourself, sir, you have a significant, I think, a very significant position. Get our proposal authorized!"

"In the first place – it's your proposal. Second – as a matter of principle, in front of co-workers, you refer to me as Comrade! Third – now is not the time for me to try to get anything authorized. The exigencies and tendencies are clear. Build quickly, build cheaply, near factories and according to a single model. I don't need to tell you which model. Build tactfully, inconspicuously!"

"Today we should build our workers' housing worse than a capitalist would have eighty years ago?" I objected. "On the road across from smokestacks that spit out ashes? And in the future the highway will head west."

"First a highway will be built heading east, and that will last at least twenty years. Only then will Prague allow this area to have a highway to the west. Then we'll let everything fall into ruin. It's really a question of whether after twenty or thirty years the aging factories will still be producing anything. But now there is one clear, relevant exigency: two thousand apartment units for each of four to five five-year plans. We must fulfill this exigency according to given, clearly defined notions. Consider this a provisional situation and do not try to bring together aesthetic aspirations and sociological issues. Fulfill your tasks. This doesn't mean you can't preserve the continuity of your thought processes. Keep it up. The future will show that you were right."

"I object to sentencing a generation to ugliness," I said in opposition to Dr. Rychta. "Children will grow up in barrack-like courtyards. We will decorate wretched, deplorable blocks with turrets, pseudo-renaissance concrete columns, and slogans with folky ornamentation. A worker comes home from the factory, looks out the window, and there's the factory again. Children will swallow ashes, sunshine will always be on the other side of a smoky curtain, and no one will get a thoroughly good night's sleep. In this socialist realism there is nothing either socialist or real."

"No architect anywhere in the world can build outside the era in which he lives," said Dr. Rychta.

"What sort of era is it that forces me to build like this?" was what I asked.

"You cannot stand outside the era all on your own. Do you want to try?"

"Does the era want to stand outside of me?" I declared somewhat pathetically. Every pathetic declaration has its own atmosphere. I clearly remember that atmosphere, and I'm ashamed of it. But I don't think, even now, after nearly twenty years, when all sorts of things have changed, that the declaration has lost either its personal urgency or its civic legitimacy.

Dr. Rychta gave me a mournful smile and said:

"Whom do you want to convince? And by what means? You walk, you sit, you draw, whatever is asked of you. You're still young enough to go against yourself a bit. In ten or fifteen years you'll build differently and we'll look back at this painfully embarrassing episode as we look back on an illness."

"May I be frank with you?" I said.

"Please. It will remain between us, between our four ears alone," said Dr. Rychta.

"Sir, how will you yourself, in ten or fifteen years, look back on your paper 'Czech Architecture in Light of Stalin's Writings on Linguistics'? Will we really survive this illness? I mean, morally?"

"You want to be frank, then be frank. What do you think of my paper?"

"You are good to talk with me like this. Thank you," I said.

"I too was once young," said Dr. Rychta.

"This is excellent cognac," I said.

"As beleaguered as we are, what's left? Several drops of frankness and a few decent human beings."

"Do those decent human beings also have a gram of courage?" I said. "Who will help us through?"

"Europe is divided, the whole world is divided. And the line down the middle of the Elbe is definitive. I'm relying on developments in Russia," said Dr. Rychta. "After ten or fifteen years, we will be building your development. Stalin will die and the revolution will return to its original conception."

"That seems reasonable," I said, "but right now what can an architect like me do? Wait for a head of state to die?"

"I already told you," Dr. Rychta said.

"When you wrote your paper – please, we said we'd be frank – weren't you ashamed? I know your earlier work. You went against yourself."

"They are only tedious words, my friend," said Dr. Rychta, "a small tax paid at a high rate, and it allowed me to save the institute, to keep quality people, to reinforce our position. Things will be better. If you don't believe me, join us when we get together and laugh at papers like that."

"You laugh at yourselves?"

"A little self-irony doesn't hurt. And your ability to experiment, that isn't something to take for granted. Be reasonable: no society on earth will see with your unrestricted vantage point. It will always turn against you."

"I can also turn against it," I said.

"Then try! Who else will talk with you the way I'm doing now? I'm talking with you as a man, as your friend, as your older colleague, but don't forget that I am the director of this institute. Do you want to shout your truth? And then? All you'll do is brand yourself, and nothing will come of it, nothing at all."

"I'm not talking about truth. I'm proposing a project," I said.

Dr. Rychta was exhausted. He took off his glasses, rubbed his eyes, and then looked at me. It's odd to see eyes one has always looked at through lenses. The eyes were flaccid, defenseless. As if they were suddenly not themselves, not like other sharply observing eyes, but only parts of a body, like fishponds in a landscape. I looked at the director's eyes, and I wanted to ask him to arm himself with glasses once again.

In the countryside I never felt that I was being watched, although I was certain the countryside is also looking, has its own eyes, is defenseless. Its passivity always moved me. When chilled through, I would often huddle beside a tree or sit in a woodcutter's cabin, while I and the landscape shook from the wind. Often the landscape would build me not only its own relief, but also an eye with which to see into its heart; its strata of time are not only geological. In the strata I read words and followed gestures and made out signs filtering under the surface along with the water of human destiny.

Sometimes there were eyes fixed on me, they weren't looking, but they communicated in the manner of human eyes. The director had not yet put his glasses back on. Through a spot in his eye I sank into the stratum of his thoughts.

What is truth if not a project? How can we convince ourselves about the truth except by implementing designs? A line in and of itself is not true, it contains no truth, is only an infinite number of points; we can comprehend it as incidentally resembling the straight lines of a mass of stars that have been spread out on a board. A line stands in opposition to truth only when we give it finite form. Truth is directly dependent on our will. We do not have truth if we accord with reality; accord is just fragmentary and we will never know what reality actually is, but we can always know precisely what it is we want. Truth is something we have when we build projects according to our proposals. Truth is construction, and each thing we build is a creation.

Dr. Rychta gave another mournful smile and said, "Call to mind the way a peasant moves his hand. From his palm he lets seeds fly into the soil. The motion is a projection of ears and bread. The peasant controls his motions, directs his project. Of course, his lord directs his project as well when he indicates that here a row of trees be planted and there a chapel be built. Factories and cities grow as they wish, and communication binds the earth not the way we wish, but the way that is most expedient. The era when the architect stood at the source of the process is long past. We simply marvel, friend, and to respond to what we see, we begin to look for new intellectual and technical devices to help us account for and understand the rampant growth. People wish to live, and this requires places to live."

"I certainly don't want to pack them into prefab housing units," I said. "I hate the concepts behind their rampant growth."

"So let's talk business," said Dr. Rychta. "Move from the development group to the project department and you will work on the documentation of a high-rise development in accordance with established directives. I did not make the directives, so don't aim your reproaches at me!"

"I thought that at least you'd allow there to be a competition."

"It is not permissible to have an alternative design. It would be considered a luxury and a violation of the directives."

"Why did I work on this? Just for my own amusement?"

"Did you enjoy it?"

"Yes, greatly. I must say that the work gave me a great deal of pleasure."

"So like it and stop grumbling! At least you relish your work."

"I'll pack up the proposal for my project and go. I won't draw unsightly things. Excuse me, but I won't decorate prefabs with little garlands."

"Your proposal belongs to the institute. You did it as work for hire. You can pack up your jacket, but I can't release you. I need every able pencil," said Dr. Rychta.

"You don't have the right to hold me against my will!"

"I have the right and I have the means to enforce it," said Dr. Rychta. "And if I were to release you, where would you go? No alternative exists. This is it. Where do you want to retreat to? You'll find, let's say, something slightly more interesting, more interesting of course only in a relative sense, but you are a principled man, you project your principles into every situation and into every engagement. You are an individualist. You want to implement yourself. For you architecture is only a means for you to project yourself personally into space. But if you want to work in real space, you must surrender your notions."

"Why don't you give this real space a name then. I don't trust this sort of abstract defining. You speak of an era and a world and their tendencies as if you were speaking about mathematical formulae. Yes, why not, but please have the courage to substitute concrete names," I said.

"If you introduce concrete names, concrete data, and the concrete decisions and decrees of concrete organs of power, what names will you give them?" said Dr. Rychta. "Names are permutable, easily replaceable. Power is transferable, perhaps not so easily, but without fail. Names can only paint over or indicate events. The question is much deeper: what directs us?

One name – Stalin? One slogan – socialism? I have no name to give you, but I know that it gets its way. It is something collective, enormous, anonymous. It is more than elemental. If you wish, it is talent, but not individual talent, and it certainly has neither aesthetic aspirations nor moral conceit. It looks out for itself and it is definitely outside the liberal tradition."

I asked Dr. Rychta to give me a few days to think about it, and he gave me his consent. My project was locked up in the storage room, and he recommended that I take a vacation and then sit down at my board like all the others. But I still imagined that I had a choice, and I went off to see Štěpán. I wanted to ask his advice. Dr. Rychta was right when he said that things wouldn't be better at other institutes or design departments. But I still had one possibility and I wanted to talk it over with Štěpán.

When it comes to scents, one memory relates closely to another. Out of the rectory cellar, right in our direction, came the pungent aroma of apples that ripened early. We bit into some good black bread sprinkled with salt, to accompany the red wine. And back then, I was doing so well that even a difficult problem could not upset me; instead, I found the situation more interesting than shattering.

"This is my body, and this is my blood," I said.

"Mikuláš, yes, all that's left to us are ceremonies, private ceremonies, ceremonies in intimacy," said Štěpán.

"Beautiful," I said.

"Empty," said Štěpán, "but perhaps I do not give beauty its due."

A star flew so low in the heavens it seemed to sizzle. We walked around the outside of the rectory, its stucco had been roughened by the primeval rains. The sundial, now a moon-dial, preached from its blue luminosity about transience, a subject we wanted to laugh at. Dew sparkled on the burdocks. In the nettles were shiny colored balls a careful farmer had once thrust onto sticks above currant, gooseberry, and raspberry bushes, now long gone wild.

"The end of architecture does not quite mean the end of man. So I will not propose any more projects, I will just live, exist, but I will remain myself alone," I said.

"Beware of big words," said Štěpán. "I know what an architect is. I do not know what a man is. I do not wish to remain just myself alone. Remain something, that is the only way you will be someone." Štěpán pointed out the shadow of the cast-iron Christ in a brier bush and said, "Look! It is only a symbol of him now. I wanted to bring tidings of his resurrection, but I do not believe. Why not at least be of service. Peace be with you! I exchanged the mission of a priest for the role of an actor, and I am not ashamed. I would be ashamed if I were to act or bear myself poorly. I enter into the spirit of the role before the altar and in the cemetery, and I feel disappointment whenever I take off my chasuble. I prefer the reality of liturgical gestures to the reality of so-called ordinary life."

"Disappointment, disappointment," I said. "In Prague these days a new term is making the rounds: the 'disappointed communist,' the communist who's become disillusioned, lost his faith. They hang their own general party secretary and put out a placard: Comrades, Trust the Party!"

"Always this twisted principle," said Štěpán. "Sacrificing your own man and believing that there is some sort of purpose that is higher, suprapersonal, historical. Founding a church. Founding a nation. Miserere! Me, I do not know any purpose other than the personal!"

The rectory orchard, so often traversed by former generations with their humble prayers and modest meditations, now began to shake all over, as if rising up in protest against us. We looked at it with alarm. Dawn was spreading in the form of shadows, and granular sunshine was dusting the curtains of dew that audibly fell on the leaves of the bushes and trees. Right up to the dark fishpond in the distance it shone like a divine eye. Floating over the ground was a gentle spirit.

"It's a lion's den and a fiery furnace," I said.

"And no one will get us out of it," said Štěpán.

"But the countryside is beautiful," I pointed out, and I told Štěpán how, even now, although I've been a disbeliever for so long, I pray beside a cross in a field, and how sometimes, when by chance I stop by a church during mass, I kneel before the altar and take the sacrament.

"Such a heathen," Štěpán said with a smile, "to appropriate sanctity like that, out of an aesthetic and spiritual overflow. In the name of the Father, the Son, and the Holy Ghost I marry and christen and perform last rites out of duty."

"If my calling required a God, I would fabricate him," I said. "I would design him. But all I require is a rational patron, and that's something I cannot fabricate. My mind refuses, but it wants to engage my capacity for nonsense. Yet I refuse. So I will not design projects. At first I was frightened by these notions, I felt as if I were rejected, forsaken, but then I said to myself: you have acquired more freedom. Isn't it a point of departure, a way out? Somehow I will earn a living. You yourself said that you know no purpose other than the personal. And I, Štěpán, am a personal architect. I wouldn't be good for any other sort of work."

"First we renounced our God, Mikuláš, and now we are starting to renounce our callings. What is left to us?"

"I feel myself being seduced by a singular temptation – to live, to be, to exist and nothing more," is what I said.

"And what about your education, your dreams, your reflections on a universal architecture, your conception of the Czech landscape? You are retreating into yourself. But what does it mean to retreat into oneself? Hasn't someone already tried this, in this era of ours, which countenances everything but contemplation? I am a priest, probably a poor priest, at least a problematic one, but I am, I exist by means of this office. What is it you see yourself doing with your freedom, Mikuláš?"

Štěpán gave me a slight, mournful smile, and the sun, which had just risen and which, with just one of its rays, had found its way to us through the dense, low-hanging branches of a broadleafed tree, illuminated a single point of Štěpán's face. It seemed to me that the retreating night's colors were passing a blue spectrum through his eye.

"Come out into the full light," I said. "It makes me feel nauseous. A sign!"

"Mikuláš, beware!" said Štěpán. "I am that I am, God in his power defined himself. Do you, in your anxiety, wish to define yourself in a similar way? When you left the Church, you made confession to me. For us it was already just a game. I haven't forgotten your gentle smile, which I observed through the grille of the confessional. My friend, Your Reverence, you said, I have nothing to confess, may you and even your God forgive me."

"Yes, I have nothing," I said, taken aback, and once again with all my heart.

I said this the second time in the rectory garden. We could still walk through the garden without any misgivings, without having to steer clear of any grave. I was still deciding what I would do, and I had not yet felt the weight in my hand of Jarmila's tiny body. Today I would confess to three things. That I gave precedence to beauty over compassion, that for nearly twenty years I did work for hire, and that I wear my heart on my tongue.

The first time, Štěpán continued his reflections: "Theologically speaking, you abominate sin. But from a layperson's point of view, you do not wish to sympathize. Work through in your mind the extremities of your position, take your absolute standards to their logical conclusion, and when you have done this, you will know that being a saint amounts to being a martyr and that dissent from the provisions of a dictator means revolution. When you've worked it through. And if you do not choose to work through such dangerous ideas, then don't start playing with them as if they were pure existence, pure conscience."

I was still very young. I was angry and I was afraid. I said: "Then what is your advice?"

"I have no advice for you at all. I am just analyzing your situation."

The conversation exhausted me. Štěpán noticed this and sent me to bed. But before I went, we picked some juicy, spicy radishes. Sprinkled with salt, they were unforgettable. It was at this same spot that we later buried Václav.

Week by week I sat at my board and drew. I've been drawing at my board right up to the present day. Let it be said that I have also done some designing, but it was something I contemplated more than did. What happened to make Dr. Rychta suddenly interested in my old, personal project?

I went out to buy a couple of rolls. And the couple of rolls I ate. They were delicious, flaky, and flavored by the caraway seeds they bore. I am thankful that someone bakes good rolls, I would like to congratulate him and wish him the best of luck.

As an architect I too would like to bake such good rolls, just as tasty, personal rolls. But as an architect I'm in a more difficult, no, an impossible position. I imagine everything other than as it is. Dear Štěpán, three five-year plans later, I have to admit that you were right. The alternatives are clear and simple: tedium or revolution. I merely played with these ideas, I worked them through to their logical conclusions, I have a big enough imagination for that and a straight line is an infinite number of points.

My personal scruples once again took on a more concrete shape. I worked them through, long ago I worked them through, and I did nothing.

I chose a beautiful calling. I know of no calling more beautiful than architecture. Right from the start I knew that to be an architect also meant being conflicted. Why did I retreat, and where did I retreat to? Those with power are more potent, I tell myself. But now to each of my yeses I will add – but.

And if it were possible, I would like to apologize to everyone I did not firmly stand up to, did not defy.

Vineyard

When in Russia in fifty-three, Generalissimo Stalin finally died, there was a great deal of discussion among the Czechs about whether his name and his monuments would die as well. Surprisingly, Nikita Khruschev brought the discussion to a close in just one session at the Kremlin. Stalingrad was renamed Volgograd and they blasted the monument on Letná Hill.

The news of Stalin's death reached me in a small town on the Elbe. We were delivering to our patrons several prefabs, each with two to three hundred housing units. Building by building, they were indistinguishable, and the street was still swampy and not yet lit. Over the entryways we set ceramic symbols – a rooster, a swallow, a sunflower, a fish, and a hammer and sickle. The architect, who knew something about modern, purposeful construction, was ashamed. But if he were to see the happiness and good fortune of the families that were moving into the new buildings, he would have to reconsider. Would you want to spoil the happiness of these lucky people with a remark about moving into barracks, about moving into a space that fell far short of the concept of home? Would they feel this way at all? And how would you explain to them that it was you yourself who sketched out this discordance?

Even in this small town they held obsequies for the departed generalissimo. I joined the gathering of mourners. Flags flew at half-mast. The citizenry came dressed in black, as if a collective relative had died. Torches burned. And then came a funeral procession of troops, whose leaders wore across their chests black sashes with silk tassels. A young poet recited a funeral ode.

The music was agonizing. Weeping women held broken flowers. I did not doubt the sincerity of their tears any more than I did the sincerity of their broken flowers. I think I entered into the spirit of the throng, whom fate had set to music, a common, melancholically resonating being in a frame of mind thoroughly, unbelievably controlled from a distance of a thousand kilometers, from the Kremlin's mausoleum all the way here, to the street of a small town on the Elbe. I saw people who were genuinely in despair. But there were also people who'd gathered only out of fear of their neighbors or only out of curiosity; they were affected by something grandiose and attracted to the irrational gloom of the jointly felt solemnity of terror. Like a fan, the soul of the nation spread open in a spectrum of feelings ranging from resigned self-enfolding to the self-assurance of grief.

Dead was the prodigy of power, who made decisions even about you, whether or not you liked it, whether or not you knew, whether or not you agreed. Directly or indirectly, but in any event substantially, he affected your life as well as the life of your project, and no one could avoid him from the Pacific Ocean to the banks of the Elbe. And this was no god, but just a man.

We were fit into a gigantic pyramid. There at the bottom, on criminals' cots, lay the political prisoners. At the pinnacle, propped up by believers and by functionaries who toed the mark, stood he. The ceremony of mourning, which had been joined by such a multitude of people, like never before in history, turned the pyramid upside down, but each of them already knew that no power could stand on the grave of the dead leader. What would follow?

For us architects, the release we felt was like a day breaking. We could have a look around the world, profess sound reason, and here and there buildings would rise that were downright interesting and original. Again I tried to unchain myself from my drawing board, but I had neither the luck nor the drive to make any headway. Again and again I would return to my board. All in all, there was more room for imagination, and we tried hard to provide the apartment blocks and prefabs with reasonably more humane views and somewhat more individual layouts.

In this more liberal atmosphere I published a few essays on the theory and history of architecture. It was more viable for me to think about these things than to fight for them with committees and commissions. I was not permitted to publish certain of these essays. The censor returned them. The editors apologized. They agreed with me, but they couldn't help; I got myself all worked up, but to no avail. At least I could have interesting discussions with these smart, learned, power-less intellectuals. It was during one of these conversations that I met Jarmila. She was translating some things for an editor. I had come to pick up a rejected essay.

I had already crossed through, thought through, and thoroughly experienced our countryside, back and forth, to and fro, and so I became her champion. She has been violated. Run down. She is dying. She has been exploited vulgarly, ruthlessly. In the dismal outskirts of the industrial cities, the obsession with production is transforming her. The country-side is endangered, and since the countryside is endangered, so are the people who live in it. The Czechs are a small nation in the middle of Europe and they have nowhere to retreat to in order to begin anew. If we do not fundamentally transform our way of life, our nation will lose its character. To ruin the countryside means disposing of bread and water and air. And they can't be imported. From where and in exchange for what?

It would be unjust to indict a government that didn't care about anything. But it cares about itself so much, and so little about our countryside. We have by and large capably unfurled a net to conserve our nature and our cultural relics. I however want to point out a fundamental misunderstanding. From its one and only body of nature, can such a small country make provision here and there for a tree, conserve now and then a forest? Isn't it necessary for us to put this question in its inverse form? Shouldn't the entire countryside breathe freely and shouldn't our laws, if we are truly a civilized people, specify, define, and make provisions concerning all that will destroy the countryside?

During this conversation, Jarmila was sitting on a table. I offered her my chair. She declined, with a smile.

"I can't sit on that sort of chair," she said. "No one knows how to make a good chair anymore."

"Someone should first make a good drawing of such a chair, dear lady," I said.

"You say that with such self-assurance, as if you could do it, as if you were ready to build such a chair yourself, dear sir," said Jarmila.

"What sort of wood would you like?" I asked.

"Something ordinary. Spruce, larch, or fir."

"You will have such a chair," I said. "For Christmas. But you must give me your address."

"How do you know that I don't already have a good chair? Or that I could find room for one?"

"You'll see. You will sit in judgment on it. You shall decide. If the chair does not appeal to you, I'll chop it into firewood and before your eyes I'll burn it in the fireplace."

"Who has a fireplace in Prague anymore?" said Jarmila.

"I will even build a fireplace," I said, "if there's a free chimney where you live."

"Aren't you promising too many good things all at once?"

"It'll be a struggle," I said. "Art is one thing, but those patrons. Those patrons."

"You too are complaining? You too?" said Jarmila. "I get the feeling that I'm living in a vale of lamentation. Do you get the same feeling?"

"I absolutely never complain, I just make statements," I said. "May I ask you to dinner?"

"When and where?"

"Now."

"At four in the afternoon?"

"By the time we find the right table for us, it'll be six," I said.

"What a waste of time," said Jarmila.

"What would you be missing?"

"Heaps of words."

"We'll come across a few," I said.

"Are you so sure?"

"Certainly. The air is filled with vagabond words."

We wandered through Malá Strana and went across Charles Bridge, there and back again. The historic backdrop of the city provided the occasion for conversation about history. Does it seem to you that Czech history is a history of defeats? Why not a history of new ideas, even a stimulus to Europe? Why in Bohemia are the ideas never brought to fruition? They're implemented elsewhere, but to our nation they don't return. So, do you see how ideas can be defeated?

Of course, the air of our city was congested with vagabond words, which hooked onto us and which we dragged behind us, rustling on and on like kites with tails of autumn leaves. It was autumn again. And it was getting dark. Again that undying person was walking along, dressed in beige, wearing a hood, and with a bamboo pole he was pulling at the rings of gas streetlamps so that they would light our way.

The symbols in the baroque ornamentation of the buildings signified our passage: a cloud, a wheel, a scale, a snake, a heart, a key. The key was gold. From the square in front of the Castle we looked out over the city, at the hermaphroditic Church of St. Mikuláš, the roundness of its dome and the slimness of its tower. And when we went down the old Castle steps, our eyes solemnly roaming across the outspread organism of antique roofs, we experienced a doubly native sensation, a sensation of the bygone history of the city as well as of the just beginning history of our love, which was going step by step down into the colorful mist of the tortuous lanes of love, and I had once again the special consciousness of movement counter to reality. Weren't we also going up the stairs, all the way to the point where one begins to feel the tow of the blue spectrum of night colors?

In the mode of the era, the pubs were smoky, the restaurants overflowing, the wine bars filled to capacity, the managers sullen. We looked in vain for a cheerful temporary home for our dialogue. Feeling like refugees brought us closer. In Jungmann Square we ate standing up at a grilled kielbasa stand, and in front of Old Town Hall, right where once upon a time they executed our noblemen, we tossed the coin we got as change. Heads, we go to Jarmila's; tails, we go to my place. Tails was the tail of a lion, and home we went to my place.

"You can sit down on your chair-to-be," I said.

"You have imaginary tendencies," said Jarmila. "I prefer sitting on more concrete chairs."

Then, in quietly flowing conversation, caught unawares by incalculable sympathies, the two people introduce each other to the worlds of their childhoods, the worlds of their notions. They relate stories about what has long ago been demarcated as their adulthood, and when the words grow weary, they try to assess the demarcations of their bodies. They're still young, and they think that this is beauty, they don't want to give it a name independent of themselves. So they give it their own names. I was glad, Jarmila, that you liked my name. Perhaps you still like it, independent of what has happened between us. You liked to call me by my Christian name and I liked to hear it.

When I would leave Prague, we would say goodbye as if I were going off to the Turkish War, although I was only going to spend a few months in Moravia. We shared many moments of blissful intimacy. Blissful? For you, Jarmila, certainly. I already had my doubts, even if my love for you was sincere. Didn't my sincerity include even the sudden and unexpected encounters with loneliness and, even in the most blissful moments we shared, the surprising view somewhere beyond the blue spectrum of night colors? Don't cry, I'll be back in just a few weeks.

A tiny woman is lying in bed and her name is Jarmila. I speak her name with love. She is naked. I am kneeling beside her, as if I were praying. While the miniature body is reaching out to me, I still have a moment to think.

"What are you thinking?" asks Jarmila.

Which of the loving and which of the loved can ever truthfully answer this question?

"I wasn't thinking about anything, I was just looking at you, because you're so pretty," I said, but I know that I was fondly deceiving her. I didn't have the courage to be more frank.

It's true that I was looking at her beautiful little body, but mainly I was formulating how, in just a moment, I was going to make love to her. I was projecting the shape of love-making onto the creamy form before me, and then I would implement it, as when I draw. From the first, soft contact of pencil tip on taut sheet of paper, to the final, rapid stroke and the bit of shading with which I complete the drawing.

I want to make love to you, Jarmila, beautifully, and that's what I was anticipating in my thoughts. Are you insulted? You were very pleased until I spoke up.

In the overall blueprint drafted with delicate, refined precision, there was one non-material element, and it was a lie. Do you love me? Without hesitation I answered yes.

In Moravia I eagerly threw myself into my new work, my new project. The field of archaeological studies needed an architect. I had to draw up plans for work relating to the development of the countryside, with the prospect of constructing a museum, a place to do research, and a tourist hotel, as well as renovating a nearby castle, with its surrounding buildings and an ancient hamlet. This interested me. My architectonic reflections could spring not only from nature and history, but also from prehistory. I could test out my conceptions on a small plot of land in a completely concrete task. I easily surmounted the distance, and I welcomed parting from Jarmila as an opportunity to make decisions. I contemplated marrying her.

After several months' work the funding came to an end. The drawing and the digging remained half finished. The digging and archaeology groups ended their camaraderie and went their own ways home.

We set a farewell bonfire among the graves of the old warriors, in whose debt we still remained. Again we felt self-reproachful. We were standing in the middle of what was once a cathedral, which we would like to resurrect, at least its floor plan. At this crossroads there once stood a city larger than Paris.

"Here everything passes before it comes to pass," one of us said.

And this sad, pliable song, baroque as a matter of fact, appealed to us, had an impact on us, or perhaps only on me, the way its melody validated the moment. And didn't I have the temptation to presume that those moments together before we went our ways – those furtive smiles that didn't want to confess to any feelings, those glances that saw an ancient sword crumble as it was being unearthed – that everything for us was in that condemned moment more important and more precious than if we were making a champagne toast in celebration of the completion of our discoveries and projects? Some day someone will do it. We had experienced the insubstantial beauty of the first attempt.

We still had several weeks of cleaning up, and when we'd finished, I accepted an invitation to a vineyard. Southern Moravia was in the midst of summer, with its wasteful padding of flowers and weeds. I stayed there until the grapes ripened. I helped them attend to the vineyard, and there, for the first time, I truly understood that before a person drinks, he must sweat. It was a blessing. The songs in the cellars, even those based on wild Hungarian rhythms, struck me as sad, almost Czech, as if bidding farewell.

What was I parting from? From what is known as youth, perhaps?

I was exhausted before I began. Shamefully I looked for reassurance in the silent wisdom and good humor of the vintners. Each of them cared for his own piece of the vineyard and from its grapes he pressed his own wine and drank it. All I could look forward to now was the infinite number of points that constitute a line.

I invited Jarmila to come taste the new vintage. She was pale but cheerful. She had managed to complete a translation just before her departure. She handed it to the editor just before the deadline. I admired her for it. Her time was hers.

And she was enthusiastic when I took her to a mountain hut with a view of the countryside. It once housed a watchman, but the vineyard didn't have to watch for anyone anymore. Downstairs a fireplace was at our service, and a crude wooden table. Upstairs were two straw mattresses with rough blankets, and on three of the walls glassless windows with wooden shutters painted green. By which of the windows the sunlight came and fell on us in stripes, we could judge how long we'd slept, whether we'd woken early or not until evening.

Evenings we would sit in the vineyard and look at the empty landscape as if into our future. It was broad, it was plain, it was fruitful. We drank down a nice crop of grapes and promised each other all sorts of nice things. And we got what we promised. We didn't promise each other love, we were very much in love already.

Am I sorry? No, I'm not. But sometimes I remember as if it were happening now. I think of you, Jarmila! I remember when we went back down to the vineyard. At the chateau, music was still playing. We were good and drunk, and we wanted to keep drinking by ourselves. So back up we went. At the first terrace you stopped and said:

"My footsies won't get me up that. Call a sedan chair for two, lined in velvet, a chair right out of the Renaissance! Or do you know of any donkeys? Or a horse? Or at the very least an elephant!"

I picked you up and carried you through the vineyard to the clearest strip of sky, right in front of the darkness where our hut stood. You were lighter than a small basket of sodden grapes. Your head was resting on my shoulder. You laughed a quiet little laugh. Without touching a toe to the ground, you straddled me like a randy dancer, and then with a long, rocking motion I held you aloft with more than a loving hand.

We were a single two-legged creature ascending through the vines, whose leaves demurely rustled. Something alluring rustled in us as well. Reaching the top terrace, we stepped into the moonlight. On a white wall fell the four-legged, armless shadow of a tall figure with two of its legs swinging against its hips.

In the light and shade, a one-horned creature approaches the wall. It embraces the wall. The shadow play and the actor fuse. The tiny woman leans her back against the wall. The wall bears her weight, the wall that looks like the frontal view of a man, with the man's head sticking up above it.

Beyond the wall the blue spectrum of night colors. A streak of mist. The sheen of water. A hill with a chapel and an ancient cross, which sparkles like the spikes on a new instrument of torture.

The woman shouts in a sing-song voice, and it's clear from the shout that the woman is young. Along with her contralto, waves of her hair are tossed about between the living and lifeless walls. The man is plucked out of the ground and remains suspended on the stone wall. He presses his knees against the wall and bears the woman as the wall bears him. For an instant they both become walls, they turn to stone under the pressure and stress, like a boulder forever set in its place, and then they fall. The wall remains there, standing over them. The stone is sorry that it's not human. At least it can still feel the warmth of the sun.

The wine is cool, it shimmers. We poured each other glasses and for a long time we didn't speak. Then Jarmila said:

"If only the wine knew how much we're enjoying it. That's something I would wish for."

We sliced the bread and broke the slices. This is a memory of love. I remember one certain woman and one certain period I experienced with her, I experienced with you, Jarmila.

Once again I can hear your lovely contralto. Once again I look beyond the wall and see the blue spectrum of night colors.

And I don't know whether I should apologize for loving and, at the same time, looking.

But the spurs of life are every bit as eternal as its women. The autumn mists came and I was once again seated at my good old board, my dear pencil points perfectly sharpened. The points on my lines are also sharp, and infinite.

Dappled Corner

Our wedding was in no way ostentatious. Ultimately, even our divorce was quite civil and peaceful. We didn't have any guests at our wedding. We had already buried our parents. There was just my brother, Béda, whom we borrowed from the asylum for half a day. And as my witness, Kormund. When I asked Jarmila whom she wanted to invite as her witness, she didn't know. She had a lot of acquaintances, but not a single friend. She thought of Olga. This surprised me, but I welcomed her choice and considered it a good sign. I think that Olga too took her role emblematically. Dr. Rychta passed on to us a fine gift, a post-White Mountain engraving of Charles Bridge. Štěpán came from Hrádek, a basket of apples in hand.

Jarmila was disconcerted by Béda's crazy smile. She was glad when we put him back behind the walls of his institution. But he was completely inconspicuous. He went with us for a stroll. He just kept looking all around. Not for a moment did I leave him by himself.

"I understand," said Béda. "You're afraid for me, but don't be! I won't carry out any subversive activities today."

We took him to see our flat. He stood by our bed of conjugal proportions and picked up a little yellow pillow.

"As if nothing had happened, as if nothing had happened," said Béda. "How ordinarily yellow it looks. I could almost believe that there is peace."

When Béda came home from prison, he tried several times to commit suicide, until he forced the doctors to place him in lifelong commitment. My brother had been sentenced to six years in jail and after only two years he'd come home.

Béda would always dig holes in the ground, looking for buried treasure.

"What are you scraping around like that for?" This time I couldn't figure it out.

"I've got an eye on my heel and it's looking," said Béda.

"Through your sock?" I was doubtful.

"And through the ground," said Béda, and he actually found some treasures: a nail, a red bead, the tip of a plow blade, a wooden sphere big as a tennis ball. Then he dug up a genuine treasure, a little pot filled with pieces of quartz. When we picked through the stones in our dappled corner, we found a coin mixed in. We would have liked it to be gold. Uncle Boleslav too, when we took the coin out to the field to show him. Back then, Uncle Boleslav still did his plowing by hand. The plow was pulled by a cow.

I was allowed to hold on to the handle and walk by myself behind the plow and see the earth turn and the blade glisten. You never forget the scent of freshly opened earth. Today nothing comes close to that scent, the world wants to be chemical and mechanical, but why get worked up over it.

Just as Béda dug in the earth, I too had my own obsession: I liked to look out at the countryside from up above. I would go sit up in a tree for a long time, and from a cliff known as Crow's I would scan the brushstrokes of the fall colors of the forest, from Točník all the way to Křivoklát, while my brother studied his pebbles.

Uncle Boleslav was a factory worker who farmed, and he made some money on the side acting as a sexton. In those days, they still rang the church bell regularly in our village. Now they don't ring bells anymore, or only occasionally and at places that don't want to give up their character, that is, they're rung ornamentally.

"He fell asleep," said my aunt. "Take the key and go ring the Angelus! But don't keep it up till midnight."

Uncle Boleslav was asleep with his head on the table. Béda was lying in the garden, delving into a geology book. It was the first postwar summer vacation. When I showed Béda the key, he just shook his head and pointed downward; he didn't have the time. He was earnestly studying earth's treasures. I was getting ready to start my architecture program.

Inside the tower you couldn't see a thing. I climbed by touch and by memory, first the stairway, then the ladder. Somewhere in space the works of a clock were gently clicking. I opened the belfry gate and looked out at the landscape in all directions, feeling that it belonged to me. And wasn't it mine? I certainly belonged to it.

To the north and northwest an endless forest, to the southwest a line of blue hills crowned by the setting sun. To the east limeworks and ironworks smoldering. In the name of the Father and the Son and the Holy Ghost I blessed all four directions with the thousand-year, true and universal priesthood of a seventeen-year-old boy. This inspired sensations in me, and I was fervently possessed by a congruity with the church tower in which I stood and through which I grew conscious of my being. Thank you, God, that there is peace again.

I pulled the rope. The metal clapper beat against the big bell, whose multilayered, harmonious voice filled me with the vivid knowledge of a happy moment. I myself was the bell's clapper, and the bell, and its voice. I was no longer tormented by any past regrets, nor enthralled by any future longings. I was supremely free, on good terms with heaven and earth, kindred to angels, saints, and even God, in whom I still believed in my fashion, but no longer with prayers. In a brotherly way I was at one with Béda, whose little body, deep in study, lay in the garden under the canopy of a hickory, at one as well with the folks on town greens and out in the fields, and even with the toiling pickup truck stopped at the crossing, for in the distance the smoking local was shuffling along the tracks. Into the roaring in my ear, the bell of a railroad crossing tinkled like a wayward acolyte. In the peace and quiet I was even at one with the naked Russians, based on the other side of the village, who were blissfully paddling around in a fishpond; there were no longer any bullets to place them in jeopardy, and their sentimental accordion, with my baroque angelus interrupting it, gave the impression of a quiet organ responsory. I even came to an understanding with the dead at the foot of the church, among whom lay one of my ancestors and a Russian captain of the guards.

We were fine at imagining. We expanded the dappled corner we had built in Uncle Boleslav's garden. Bohemia is a small land, one of the smallest in Central Europe, and we get along like brothers. Béda was a communist, I advocated a multiparty system. Now we don't quarrel anymore.

Almost within sight of my tower, just beyond the landscape's divide, which took the form of the protracted comb of Brdy forests, Béda was conducting research into iron ore, but in this area ore had, since the beginning of the world, set its heart on being scant, insufficient. Carefully studied and analyzed specimens of rock and soil did not choose to yield to my brother's enthusiasm, and they were equally indifferent to the requirements and standards of the central office, which to reinforce the workers' initiative offered a large goal-oriented bonus and sent into the field an experienced ideological worker, whose propaganda stirred up the young geologists as well as the ancient strata of earth.

In the meantime, they were building a smelter, whose imported apparatus looked forward to the first delivery of high-quality ore. They also built quarters for the working class, which in this backward agricultural area had sprung into existence in conjunction with the new factory, fortifying the socialist consciousness of waverers, peasantarians, and mine-farmers.

The committee of functionaries and representatives of the central office, who had traveled to see the results of the research and construction, were satisfied with the attractively thought-out notice boards and the cozy red corner in the newly built plant, but they were not satisfied with the final report. They took the unfortunate Béda back to Prague for instruction. This is the sentence that decided Béda's life:

"Comrade, you must work things out honorably with that ore of yours!"

And going down in the elevator, there was that kindly, eye-to-eye pat on the back:

"So, keep your head high! What else are we here for? But you realize that we can't include your numbers in the plan. Think those numbers through again! We must get started!"

"It'll be over as soon as it starts," said Béda.

"Leave that to us! If there are raw materials, there are raw materials. If there aren't, they'll be imported. But above all, don't go hiding anything from us. There are other authorities who will have to deal with your numbers. With political authorities you are always agreeable. Security doesn't discuss, it interrogates."

And then there were a couple of passing remarks made as they parted:

"Again, we would like to fill the position of deputy in the ministry with a competent man who's been put to the test. So you have a chance, you have a green light."

"In the elevator," Béda told me, "I felt sick. I don't know if it was how much I had smoked at the meeting or the way the elevator was swinging back and forth. A queasy stomach. Or a collapse. You can cling to the walls, but you're aware that inside that car is the only place you can hang on. You're closed in and you're being pulled down somewhere."

"Let it go!" I said. "You can't extract iron from paper."

"It's a lot more complicated than that," said Béda. "I can't even step into an elevator anymore."

When Béda, as a competent fieldworker who'd been put to the test, became a deputy in the ministry, he went up to his office on foot. Were he to enter an elevator, he might have to weather changeable times in his job. Walking the stairs made him eccentric and therefore suspicious: this man does not have faith in anything at all.

"It's an attempt on your mind," I said. "Why don't you defend yourself?"

"And you?" Béda reproached me.

"It has nothing to do with me," I said. "I draw and don't get worked up over it. When all is said and done, people have to live somewhere. I build poorly, but I build. I'm resigned to do without aesthetics, I'm resigned to do without style. Smelters can't be resigned to do without ore."

"Once it is decided to mine, they mine," said the unfortunate Béda. "Freight cars full of slag and iron granules. And the plant is already up and ready to run. What can you say to people who want to work? Admit you made a mistake?"

Of course, eventually someone must take responsibility for a mistake like this. They expelled Béda from the party, dismissed him, and locked him up. Perhaps it was demonstrated that his report on the ore deposit did not correspond to reality and that he must have known this.

134

After two years Béda was released from prison. They dropped the serious charge of sabotage, and he was rehabilitated as a specialist, the victim of an agitator. However, he was not politically rehabilitated; as a party member, he should not have done what he did.

Then things once again changed and Béda was vindicated in the political sense, because he evidenced party discipline. However, he was criticized as a specialist, for it had been confirmed that at the critical moment he proved incompetent.

"You wouldn't happen to know of a dappled corner anywhere, would you?" Béda said to me not long before his first suicide attempt.

What sort of dappled corner could I have offered him? It is only in our memories that we can return to the world of our childhood. No one can provide us with any true shelter. I turn to myself alone. My brother not only turns to himself, but turns on himself as well. I found my sanctuary in the open countryside and in the past confined within baroque stone. My brother found his sanctuary behind a white wall, where now he's raking up the autumn leaves. Our sanctuaries also provide us with political asylum; we don't need to cross borders to get it. However, we did cross borders in ourselves.

Where did I end up? For nearly twenty years now I have not lived a normal life.

"They don't want to know the truth about what's under their ground," said Béda. "So why dig at all? We made a poor decision, brother, but then I've been looking for buried treasure ever since I was small."

I can't remember the moment when I decided to be an architect. The image of a building, of a roof, has been with me so very long. If you say the words world or life or love or sleep, I see a building. It's my earliest memory.

In Uncle Boleslav's attic there is a large bed. I am lying on the bed, and I am not at all afraid, even though it's getting dark. Through the open window I can feel the draft of the blue spectrum of night colors. There is sheet lightning in the boundless distance.

A thunderstorm awakens me. Ropes of rain come through the window and reverberate far beneath the roof, making empty bowls clang. I can't manage to close the window, the lightning disconcerts me so. I run downstairs to the living room, to get my uncle to help me. I call Uncle Boleslav what they call him here: Hey! Hey, do I need help! It's raining on my comforter! The thunderstorm x-rays the naked body of a man on his bed, ready to join vigorously with another body.

"Hey, what are you up to?" I asked.

Uncle Boleslav jumped off the bed and showed me:

"I'm letting the storm know it better not strike the house!"

He quickly covered his third leg with an open almanac, as if he were erecting a building between his legs, and his thumb stuck up from the spine of the book's roof. I took hold of the thumb. When the lightning struck, I could see underneath the striped featherbed, curved like the world, my aunt giving me a smile.

I want to tell you that to live in a dwelling means to make love, and that without love one cannot design a dwelling. But why get worked up over it.

Once I went on a trip with Jarmila, and when I saw on the map that we weren't far from Chateau Pustověty, we visited it. The exposed stone wall had in many places fallen to the ground, but at least it symbolically protected the big old park, which we entered by walking down a gentle slope, between two long rows of poplars standing in a brown, plowed field. There was smoke coming from the burning of stalks and leaves somewhere. The picture before us was tinged a bluish gray, and out of it, almost black, rose a small tower with a clock whose chimes came very close together. They tinkled, like at a railroad crossing. According to the schedule, a train was passing; we couldn't see it, but we could hear its whistle. It pierced my heart and startled Jarmila, and I, because I still didn't want to be frank with her, I diverted her attention from the way I'd been moved by bringing up a memory from childhood.

"That's how I would imagine a dappled corner today. With Béda we would keep house in it and we would buy you dictionaries from every language into every language," I said. "And with Béda we would have something to do all our livelong days. With our bare hands we would restore everything good as new, and certainly somewhere we'd come across some treasures."

The groundfloor windows were boarded over. The pond was overgrown with algae. The statues had been covered in velvety moss and had delightedly disguised themselves behind bushes and weeds. On the first floor lived a custodian, who looked after the extensive manuscript collection. On a column supported by beams, so that it wouldn't fall through the basement's ruined vaulted ceiling, was a plate with an inscription about this being a national cultural monument.

When the custodian became aware of our presence, he ran out and asked in a panicky voice:

"Why have you come? Why are you here? Is it beginning already? When does it begin?"

"You can rest easy," I said. "We're not part of any schedule."

"You have the perfect refuge here," said Jarmila.

"For someone who never tires of his own company, it's an absolute paradise," said the custodian. "And this architect would like to deprive me of it. I want things to stay like this until I retire. It's an art, you see, to maintain things just short of dilapidation. Too shabby for anyone to envy you, but not so gone to ruin that it attracts much notice."

I noticed that this bothered Jarmila, but she didn't say anything. When we were alone, she asked:

"Do you find him a likeable man?"

"I understand him," I said.

"I can't abide melancholics with a program," said Jarmila. "I understand that some people are born with sadness in a corner of their eye and without the ability to resist it. That's just the way it is. But I don't understand how, in contemplative idleness embellished with natural ornaments and historical ruins, someone can be looking for a way out."

"He's not looking for a way out, he's looking for an end or, more precisely, for the form of his end," I said.

"Is he dying?" said Jarmila.

"And so we let him," I said, and I put my arm around Jarmila's shoulders and we went off together.

We still weren't traveling by car back then. We walked to a train stop and at the train stop we ate some plums that we'd picked in a field along the way. This is how I imagined happiness: to be able to sit with this tiny woman at a tiny train stop on an autumn evening before it started getting cold. To pull plums from my pockets, to pass the plums around, and to have on my tongue that strong, unmistakable flavor. We threw the pits on the tracks.

"They won't derail the train," said Jarmila.

And me, just short of dilapidation, but still not too gone to ruin, I was on the verge of unhappiness, although there I was at that train stop eating plums with my own, unmistakable woman. Have you ever noticed? A plum tastes the same, whether you feel good or bad. A plum is so indifferent. Is it less beautiful, then?

I am especially sensitive to certain signs, to certain words, and when someone has an aversion to me, I can feel it through a wall. According to a very complex yet precise formula, it would surely be possible to calculate how it happened that I came to be interested in renovations to Chateau Pustověty, why a chateau would be named "Desolate Sentences," how the concord of surroundings and personal motives brought an aging but not yet dying custodian to this place, and why we had to meet him in order for Jarmila to be able to speak, as if just in passing, such words as: sadness, corner, eye, resist. Jarmila did not yet suspect that her words were addressed to me. I, however, knew that we would have to separate.

The chateau of the desolate sentences is still desolate, we still haven't repaired it. I don't know whether a freshened façade would suit it better. Dilapidated, nearly in ruins, it was close to me, homey as a dappled corner that had long ago tumbled down, and I will not apologize to anybody.

So I still hadn't managed to tell Olga that I wouldn't be going away with her. I'd also have to tell her that I didn't love her anymore. This was the truth, but I didn't want to put it into words. I would have to explain that something she said changed the climate inside me, and I wouldn't be able to do that. I am only good at making observations.

Several years have passed since I visited Pustověty with Jarmila. Several days have passed since Olga told me that I had nothing to forsake. I thought it would be worse, but I had learned how to keep shining the light of kind words on the backdrops of minor experiences, even those dilapidated and nearly gone to ruin, and how not to impede any atmosphere that promises beauty.

We would often plan our future over dinner, a future I'd already written off. The future is always something just

imagined, and yet, out of purely personal motives, I had already stripped it of any right to its own image. Let the image appear. We do not have to embark on it. To you it would seem vulgar and cynical to so deliberately set the stage for the moment you come to realize, on your own and without any pain, that I do not belong to your world. That I have a world of my own and that I cannot forsake it. As a painter it's something you'll be able to comprehend. It is only a picture, an image. It is also a project, a design. And isn't every picture also a project, and mustn't every project also be depicted?

I intentionally took Olga to all the places I called home. The dappled corner was here, and there is its tower. From Crow's Cliff you can see my project as if it were in the palm of your hand. That's how it will be, that's how it will look. You see, Olga, what I must forsake.

"That's a desolate-looking forest," said Olga.

"Yes, of course," is what I said. "But it isn't altogether desolate. For twenty years I've beaten paths through it. And now I have a concrete offer to implement my project."

"Why are you talking about the project? Why aren't you talking about yourself?"

"Because I am an architect!"

"But Mikuláš!" said Olga. "What have you built? I am in love with *you*."

In a few days I'll be forty. We returned to Prague through the countryside, which was already thoroughly white. Snow began to fall. Olga put her head on my shoulder. If I were twenty years younger, I would accept these soft words with devotion, the way the undulating countryside was receiving the fresh snow. The countryside was turning into this fresh dusting of snow, which copied its gentle contours, and it was impossible to imagine that between dusting and ground there was yet another stratum. But in these forty years I found that even when someone tells you that she loves you, first she has to reproach you for something, and always it relates to a designated time, a time you've lived through, a time that's past. Will it seem pathetic to you when I say, Woe is me? Woe is you if you are an architect and you can't show what you've built. Just then, we passed the wretched, deplorable high-rise developments with their wretched yards built along the highway to Prague, those flats, those prefabs for which, with my very own strokes, I enlisted an infinite line's-worth of points. I'm ashamed of them. I couldn't show them to Olga, although the kind snowfall had covered the grayness and transformed the sorrow of the desolate prefabs and their yards into an abstract brightness.

For the first time, I felt the need not only to apologize, but also to accuse someone. But the circumstances, the era, the establishment, history – yes, history already – commissions, authorities, committees, decrees, subcommittees, branch and even umbrella organizations, long-term plans (outline, actual, counter-), capacity, output, prefabrication and out of a catalogue, menus, timetables, newspapers, ballots, party and nation, all of it, what has so concretely touched the course of my life, determined even its most intimate details, all of it lacked the concreteness of the snowflake that just melted there on Olga's shoulder. Who would I blame? It would sound like shouting underwater.

But here is Olga, resting her head on my shoulder, telling me that she loves me. How can she say that she loves me and at the same time that I have nothing to forsake? How can she love an architect who has built nothing? Whom does she love? She loves a blank man. Why then does she hold his failure against him?

You know the words of love, but you cannot say them, you beg for a parable. You don't have to know the words of pain. They translate themselves into your tongue, they sound piercing or matter-of-fact, and they have a relentless ability to wound beyond all curing. I had those words on my tongue, and I wanted to say them, but I said nothing. I was very unhappy, I spoke with the voice of the snow that was illuminating the darkness, and I thought of my mother. I can't pull anyone into my pain.

My mother is tired. She is resting her head against the tiled stove. On her lap is a book, but she isn't reading, she's taking a nap. From her dozing she falls into sleep, but then her head will jerk and wake her up. Again and again. She smiles at me and I keep rattling off the same demand: Mama, come to the look-out tower! Mama, come! Come to the look-out tower!

Mama would rather stay in her corner, which now, in my memory, seems dappled, but I've talked her into it and already I'm dragging her up a steep avenue named Sokol. I know that street well.

"What are you smiling about?" asked Olga.

I said, half frankly, that I was thinking about a street I used to walk along and which, before the war, was called Sokol. When the Germans came, they renamed it Segert. After the war, they called it Keller, but not for very long before they once again renamed it, this time Janáček. Now it's called Kmoch. Funny, isn't it. You can't grow old under a single flag, but why get worked up over it.

I was dragging my mother through the park, whose name has also been changed to something that doesn't suit the nobleman who established it. But the hill has remained just as steep.

My mother wanted to catch her breath, but I wouldn't allow her to until we had reached the look-out tower. For the first time, she firmly refused to do what I asked. She wasn't going to climb all the way up to the sky, unless I were going to carry her up there like a backpack.

"I'll carry you, Mommy, on a chair even," I said, and when I saw with what exhaustion she was cleaning off her glasses, I added, "when I'm big."

"Go on your own," my mother said. "Run up like a bar tab."

"Give me your glasses to take with me," I said, and my mother gave me her glasses and I ran up the twisting stairs of the look-out tower and finally, for the very first time, I saw the city from up above.

The city looked completely different from the way I knew it at pavement level. I felt in control of my viewpoint now, and I doubted whether Czech knights or, later, presidents, protectors, and governors have been so sovereignly and gloriously beheld. Of course, I am now interpreting a feeling from my childhood, when I couldn't have put it into words like this. But it shouldn't be overly pondered: it was and that's that; it was a view, and a view is a picture.

A wide, gleaming river meanders; it couldn't do otherwise. I grasped this then, even without grasping the concept. The city sat like a stone nest right up against a hill on the horizon, but the horizon itself was green: meadows, copses, fields. And without any particular motive, I was faithfully in accord with them. Now prefabs have petrified it all.

The Castle with its cathedral, the palace, the houses and the buildings, Charles Bridge – as if the urban hillsides of Vinohrady and the workers' labyrinths of Smíchov and Karlín, from history up till the present, could have been laid out otherwise, yet had freely elected, for my viewing pleasure, once and for always, to be situated just like this, so that, in addition, we could delineate them on a map. Overwhelmed, I marveled at the view.

Rule and unruliness were joined together in this picture, framed by the distant, extinct volcanoes of the central Bohemian hill country.

"Mama, Mama, look and see," I said, and I put her glasses on.

And then I rushed down the look-out stairs to tell my mother the saga.

"You saw so much," my mother said, "while I just looked into my beer."

I wanted to cry, but I didn't. After all, my father said: Freedom sheds no tears!

In the picture whose details came from the ruliness of the natural environment and the unruliness of construction lay one human element. It took me many years to grasp it. Under the table on which my mother's glass of beer was sitting, on a chair, lay one of my mother's feet. It was already aching something terrible. She died from that foot, and before I closed her eyes, I took her glasses off.

We were already driving through the outskirts of Prague and I knew that its historic core was awaiting us, and in it the events of a late evening known as love. More than anything I've done in my nearly forty years, I would have liked to cry and say, Olga, you're right, I haven't built a thing and it's a miracle that you still love me.

That was what caused my breakup with Jarmila. Štěpán, you say that God defines himself like this: I am that I am. About myself, I can only say that I am the way I am.

"So what is it that I still love about you?" said Jarmila. "What way are you, Mikuláš? You're no way at all! It's true that you're a decent person, but what is there about you to lean on? You're an architect, but all you get from your work is suffering. You can't ask for anything, because you're too much in love with your permanent discontent."

Freedom sheds no tears, my father said. I didn't cry even when I told Olga about my project. It's possible that it might be implemented. But soon we'll be going away together and I'm telling you this only so that you know that I do have something to forsake.

"Would you rather stay?" asked Olga.

"It's just a project," I said, "and I know that you love me."

"Talk about yourself, not about the project," said Olga. "About yourself, not about me!"

"Everything's in order," I said. "I'm packed."

"Could it be that I seem old to you?" said Olga. "Mikuláš, you don't love, you just try very hard. Unburden yourself, be frank with me!"

Under the pressure of the gray spectrum of night colors I saw my life and in it there was nothing truly personal. Only in the countryside does something happen: water moves through a river bed, a bird flies past, snow falls. There's lightning again, and the almanac, which tries to regulate time, provides shelter to my uncle's private parts. And then a few more words. Who? Possibly Štěpán, possibly Jarmila, possibly my father. If you can't work, then you must fight. And if you don't want to fight, you must serve. Béda has raked up a pile of autumn leaves. The leaves are smoldering. From the white institution for the insane comes the sound of sane music. I listen and I can't tell if it's a doctor playing or one of the lunatics. And my father says:

"Freedom doesn't whine over a smashed watermelon. Freedom picks out a new one."

Father, mother, brother, I will astonish you, you will get the surprise of your life. I will bring you a watermelon. What does such a melon cost? It doesn't matter. For a crown and fifty hellers I can pick one up at the store before it closes. But I'm too young to have a crown and fifty hellers. I'll make the rounds of the trash cans, courtyards, and dumps; I'll pick up some bottles, rinse them out in the Vltava, and sell them. But most shopkeepers require deposit receipts with a company's stamp on them. I went from grocer's to taproom, and from taproom to co-op, and not until late in the evening was I able to exchange my bottles for cash.

A thought like this goes through your head, it's a thought you too must know. But the child couldn't put it into words: if I don't bring back a watermelon this evening, I'll die. A melon is green and round as the world. And inside, it's red.

You feel very strongly that you want something, and go looking for it, running, trying very hard, until at last you find a stall that hasn't yet been covered over with canvas and next to which sits a melancholy man, who says:

"So, Mikuláš, go and pick out a green head!"

You pay and you're not at all surprised that someone you don't know has called you by name. You remember this for the first time many years later and you imagine that it can somehow be logically explained, but you don't want to get worked up over it, you prefer just to remember and to accept the memory as a picture, and a picture, Olga, is not painted in order to be explained, a picture is painted in order to be a picture. I look.

A little boy is carrying a watermelon. It is big and it is heavy. That's the way every gift should be, big and heavy, so that before you deliver it, you have to take a breather on the landing. You rest the watermelon against the railing. Low in the sky a biplane is whirring along. You can barely see the pilot, but you wave to him. You even believe that the pilot sees you, that the plane decides to make a change in course, to come back around and glide over your courtyard, its wings nodding as if to say hello. You raise both your hands to the sky and forget that round little world, which can no longer be held up by the single black line of railing with its ornamental brass points. There's nothing you'd rather do than leap after the head.

You are standing over the wreckage of your gift. Red spreads from the green roundness, it looks to you like a bloody mess, and I am to blame. Beyond the flat picture of buildings, from whose windows humanity is looking at you in the form of a black, motionless man, quietly, drowned out by gusts of wind, the free plane is whirring.

My father comes, says his saying, and lifts me onto his lap. He wipes my tears with his knuckles, he kisses my head, and I say:

"I'll never cry again. Cross my heart. I swear."

We walk together all the way to Masaryk Station. Today they call it Prague-Central. On its green towers, the clocks still lit up and still paid homage to President Masaryk. Somewhere there is a drawn-out whistling and the heavy sound of a hammer striking a wheel. We cross zillions of rails before coming upon a fruit warehouse. They're still loading and unloading, even though it's a late summer evening. My father talks with someone and that someone talks with my father. They point at me and then toward the back of the warehouse: Our delivery man, our master! Svoboda, go and choose whichever you want, and don't worry about how big it is.

Many times a gate has opened before me, the gate of physical love, which our memories spiritualize, and the gate of spatial imagination, which materialized at each happy moment when I grasped the handle of our front door; there are also the gates to the dappled corner, Béda, and the Porta Bohemica of the lone hiker in the central Bohemian hill country. But I've never passed through as many gates as there were melons on the pyramidal heap of happiness. My father picks out, carefully picks out the biggest watermelon, weighs it in his hands and, when it's finally clear to him that he won't find an even bigger one, delivers the armful to me.

"What are you thinking?" said Olga. "Must you always be thinking about something, even when you have me in your arms?"

"Forgive me, Olga," I said. "I have this project and I would like to get to work on it. I have to stay."

"I will stay here with you," said Olga.

In the blue spectrum of night colors her face was beautiful as a painting. She wanted to put her head on my shoulder, but gently, as tenderly as possible, I laid it down on the pillow.

"No, Olga," I said. "It will be better for you out there."

I was glad she didn't cry. I was grateful to her for it. She didn't ask for an explanation. For this too I was grateful. She propped her head up on her hand and stared at the white wall, where not long ago paintings used to hang. There were still several nails in the wall. A finite number of them. Black points on a white surface, which I connected to form an imaginary line. I was surprised to learn how easy it was.

"So go," said Olga. "It's morning. And don't stay on your own!"

Paternoster

I took it to heart: to not be late for work. When I no longer had any other principles left, I stuck to that one: to take my pencil in hand right on time. When all is said and done, I've been reasonably well paid, and in the twenty years I've endured my job, I have performed a unique, unsurpassed feat. Which of you, colleagues, when you leave to take your pension, will be able to say that you were never late for work?

I was just walking through the lobby when the clock struck seven o'clock in the morning. But the era was more liberal now. Architects didn't have to sign or punch in anymore. It was just a personal matter now.

It was the same thing with the project I had on my table: very personal, my own project. I was delighted that after almost twenty years I had to change almost nothing. Yet I still wrote several notes concerning implementation, and a short theoretical postscript. Then I threw the postscript into the wastebasket. The project speaks for itself. At four in the afternoon I was scheduled to meet with Dr. Rychta.

I will submit the project, and in the evening I will visit Miládka. That too I took to heart: to not stay on my own. I arranged the papers, placed them in a folder, rolled the rustling tracing paper into a little tube, and looked at my watch. It's not even close to four. For the first time I didn't have any work to do on the project. So I neatened up my drawers, fastidiously sharpened my pencils, and when I felt drowsy, I put my head on my desk. My watch ticked me to sleep, and it felt good. But I couldn't be late for my meeting.

Fortunately, I didn't have to be afraid about falling into a deep sleep. In the half-dreaming spectrum of my memories, I was awakened by one picture after another.

We are standing on a hill, me and my wife. We are looking at the river down in the valley, dug with explosives, the debris carted off. On the hillsides felled forests lie. Also within our view is a camp consisting of a variety of long wooden trailers scattered through the valley to form a jerry-built village. Dust cloaks their tar roofs like an artificial mist. Cicadas and pneumatic drills attempt a summer harmony. And as I've done so many times before, I enthusiastically tell Jarmila what I would do with the valley.

It will take four years to build the waterworks. The nomadic nation of day-laborers, blasters, concrete pourers, and engineers live a makeshift life, while their smooth, arched achievement, all developed beforehand according to the designer's precise calculations, asserts a claim to natural permanence. But why get worked up over it.

"Get worked up, get worked up," said Jarmila. "It suits you."

You see those pine trees? Those solitary larches? I'd like to lay out a village there. Now. Right away. Small terraced buildings in harmony with the landscape. And a nice pub, of course. And I'd draw a road along the contour line, and along that road they would bring the construction materials. Whoever wanted to walk would walk right through the forest. How can someone work hard for four years living in a trailer camp? This little nomadic nation would find itself at home. Their children would grow, and when the dam was completed, most of the people would stay here, on the shore of a big reservoir. Aren't there enough jobs in this area? Whoever didn't want to stay, or couldn't, would at least have a home to remember. And they could come here for solace from the noisy city.

"That sounds perfectly reasonable and perfectly fine," said Jarmila. "And if my experience of the word weren't so detestable, I would say that sounds like socialism."

"So I'll give it a try," I said, and I asked Kormund if I couldn't secure a hearing before the ministry. I had the honor of meeting with the deputy minister. He was a perfectly reasonable and perfectly fine man. Before long he called me and invited me to visit the building site, to get the lay of the land, and to present a brief proposal of my ideas.

"It might make a good example for our large building projects," the deputy minister said as he led me to the paternoster elevator. "We always think in terms of cubic meters of poured concrete, and that's a mistake. We just turn on a switch, the lights come on, and we forget that someone must generate the power. And you are right when you say that abstract men live in abstract buildings, but that actual men must live in actual buildings."

I enter an endless field of aaronsbeard. This is a good sign, because its flowers are dear to me. Floating above the aaronsbeard is an oppressive heat; the summer has reached its crescendo. I think of Jarmila. Behind the air's misty, silver-strewn humidity, the sun has lost its corona and a glow radiates from the heights of space, as if a burning blanket had been spread across the heavens, so that when I test it by reaching my long arm out in front of me, it casts no shadow at all. In this sultriness, the skylark has neglected its song to just silently flutter around. Under this blanket of haze, there is absolute silence.

So there I am, heading through the petrified gold of the endless aaronsbeards, not as an architect, but as a sexual somnambulist. Now I am remembering Jarmila unambiguously. I see her tiny, childlike, boyish body and I reproach myself for having forsaken her. But in Bohemia nothing is very far away. The midnight train would restore her to me. Once again, according to the geography but not the season, the midnight train gives out a long, lusty whistle, but, Jarmila, I've ordered my heart not to let itself be pierced; I will not, for life, embrace this distant sound when I can enter into a lifelong embrace with a living body.

"But Mikuláš! Don't say forever." Jarmila smiled. "Forever is a vagabond word. Say always, always or whenever or wherever."

I would like to make love to you right here and now in this flowery paradise, but since you're not here, I can at least see you with that yellow pillow beneath your head and I can pray: Wilderness of aaronsbeards, let me love Jarmila absolutely. And you, who have translated so many sorts of stories from such a profusion of languages, could you not know how to say this single word in Czech? Absolutely, yes? And in my hand I brought together this word and a single yellow flower, like a secret monstrance. In the still only slightly dissolved mist, the sun abandoned reason and from the heights of space it fell on me in a dazzling, blinding diffusion.

When I reached the horizon and walked across the divide in the landscape, beyond where the land crests and troughs, I imagined these waves absorbing the bustle and noise of our factories and could see in the distance a lunar sea of plowed-under machines and the gigantic torso of a pillar. The true silence of the field I'd walked through, which had been validated by the mute skylark, was transmitting torpor, via its silence, all the way to the large, false, shadowy building. Under the sunless sky, in the milky lighting, objects such as houses, shacks, cranes, funiculars, and human figures were shadowless; they were their own shadows. Sometimes you too have such dreams.

In the flow of these incredibly hot work days, other objects, such as excavators, automobiles, girders, planking, loose and solid materials, trailers and human figures, lay in utter silence and immobility, as if the entire human camp were suddenly struck by an epidemic of sleeping sickness, and the machines were unable to emancipate themselves in order to fulfill their respective functions. The only variation is the harmonica of a despairing, confirmed insomniac.

Inside the shacks as outside under the sun all was truly asleep. With my sense of hearing I found the harmonica player sitting in the canteen. He poured me a warm beer.

"So what happened to make everyone stop working?" I asked.

"It happened to the entire building. A little mistake, and half a billion," said the harmonica player, snapping his fingers.

"But that's insane," I said.

"The beer is usually warm. Don't be surprised. Someone will close it up, and then we'll get rid of the building for the same sort of dough. Supposedly they found some lunatic. First they want to build this desperado a marble palace."

When I returned home later that night, Jarmila was still translating some classic. For the first time I understood what it means when you return somewhere and can say: aaronsbeard, it grows so freely, so unrestrained.

Once again I listen to her lovely, free contralto. Musically, she draws the common sign for the wonderful act of physical love. Never have I listened to music with my eyes shut. I look and I listen. I think. A musical instrument is built according to precise rules, according to which a violin maker makes his calculations, or at least discovers them through experience; however, melody is full and free as Jarmila's joy. I share it

with pride and envy. Stroke after stroke of the blue spectrum
of passion's colors draw for me the basics of abstract art,
which far beyond the wall of compassion I observe as if it
were a landscape. My brain, delicately curled up into a
receptive symbol of sensitive matter and drawn down into the
foamy narrows between your legs, there far below your heart,
finds itself in miniature. Inside of you a divine little finger
pushes against me, as if your back concealed a diminutive
man, reproachfully sticking himself out.

For a long time Jarmila carefully observed my dissat-
isfaction. And then she said:

"I'm not the way to enter into any sort of kingdom. I'm
just a wall. Lean on me! Don't be afraid! Close your eyes!"

"Do you want to deprive me of the last dregs of my
shame?" I said.

"Isn't it enough for you to feel it to the end of every
strand of your hair? So talk about it, truthfully, fearlessly!"
said Jarmila.

"As delicate a woman as you are, please allow me just one
little metaphor," I said. "The truthful, unambiguous words I
have at my disposal are vulgar."

"So let our love be vulgar," said Jarmila.

I took her dare. I spoke. I talked about everything life
had taught me, about everything culture had not, what has
so often been said about women, without any packaging, but
not always without feeling. I talked about my memories going
all the way back to childhood, even what I'd inherited from
the ancient, universal consciousness that has outlived the
death of love and the death of people who love each other.
There were increasingly faint vestiges of words and names,
and then just vocalized and guttural signs, which led me to
yet deeper and until then undiscovered memories of grasping,

moving, touching. And you wouldn't believe that this too was a way of looking at things.

"You don't know yet? You don't know yet?" said Jarmila, and then she whispered: "I want you not to know anything yet, anything at all."

Returned to where cells begin and unite with others in the circulation of heat, of course I do not yet know anything at all, like the leaf of a sycamore, a grain of wheat, or the horizon of a field. My passion has abandoned even its self-consciousness, like an angel falling headlong into darkness. And I have even closed my eyes out of obedience, as you wished and as the god of love commands in the form of kisses. But despite this, in spite of this, in the blue spectrum of night colors you see a landscape, which in your mother's tongue is feminine.

"You're always looking beyond the wall," said Jarmila.

"Beyond which wall?" I was alarmed.

"At the vineyard, that time, you must remember," said Jarmila.

"Yes, we were sitting up on a wall together," I said, "and letting our legs hang down, me and your little footsies."

"It's so good that you're so sweet," said Jarmila. "And that you don't know that I know that you have more to say."

"I don't know."

"You've been deprived of your shame regarding sex and you've learned to feel shame regarding the abstract. That's why you aren't saying anything more. And I'm glad."

"What have you learned?"

"Now I understand a bit better what it is you aren't saying. I'll say it for you. We were sitting on the wall of the universe. Beneath us bunches of ripe grapes and above us bunches of stars. Yours is a metaphorical morality and I have learned to respect it."

"It was a stone wall, Jarmila," I said, "and I'll be frank. The wall's stones were warm. And when I looked beyond the wall, all I saw was the countryside. In me there is a likeness between that landscape and a certain woman, but you are right to say that it's abstract. You mustn't be afraid of it."

"So you were in love with a strip of color," said Jarmila. "Can you name it?"

Which name, what sort of name? According to what sort of almanac and with respect to which atlas? From what sort of manual should I read it out, and how should I pronounce it? Who was named first, the region or the woman who passed through it?

Later I introduced Jarmila to Olga. Their names were spoken as if in passing. They got along well together, and why not? But then I told Jarmila about how the old-time train ran along the shining rails, how it whistled and how each time I heard it, it would pierce my heart, but that I had forbidden my heart to do this again. But that I see amethyst leisurely lying across the Prague night, even when my eyes are shut, this I could not forbid. Do you understand?

It was a mistake to be so frank. I told her everything. In my story, which consists primarily of pictures, what does "everything" mean? It must seem very small to you in relation to the hungry, bloody troubles of the world, but why should I characterize my suffering as greater than anyone else's? It's enough that I've told you that in you I love someone else, something else, and that this has made both of us miserable. So, this has been a very brief lesson on the disadvantages of frankness, on the harm frankness can inflict. This has been said before, but it wasn't given a name.

Jarmila shrank into her armchair and looked at me as if at a concept she could not work out even with a dictionary more universal than any she owned. She cried. She looked like a little parcel lamenting her undeliverability. Then she pulled herself together and said:

"Let's go out for goulash!"

But there was no way we could make it to the tavern before closing time. I'll go there with you, Jarmila, still and always. I would like to know whether I will still and always go away with Olga.

When you stopped crying, you combed and rearranged your hair before the mirror. You turned on a little lamp so you could see better what you were doing. The light illuminated your face, a stone in your ring flashed as in an eye, but it only produced a sparkle, not a stroke of color from any spectrum. From the square we could hear the quiet steps and tinkling of Old Town's astronomical clock. Then the Old Town cockerel crowed, and we walked across the Charles Bridge and back again. We talked softly while looking down at the weir, but it was there we began to quarrel, under the great stone heart of God, bulging out so as to exalt the beautiful baroque fleshiness of sandstone muscles. For some time, we still needed not to say another word.

"Why are you looking at me like that?" said Jarmila.

"It suits you," I said.

"Don't give me a hard time!" said Jarmila. "Try the statues, they're pretty, too."

I put my arm around her shoulder. The clock on the embankment tower was lit. It looked nice, as always. The human marionette with the bamboo pole went from one gas lamp to another, but the lamps were already lit. The gas buzzed like a cloud of golden flies. From St. Kliment's came the sound of a mass, from St. Salvator's an organ chord, and from The Golden Tiger the slamming down of beer mugs and the aroma of their foam.

A black carriage, drawn by two brown horses, was circling the Old Town fountain that looks like a pillory. On the coachman's seat a gray bowler, inside two young people, one of whom was playing Mozart on a clarinet. The humorous song reached us despite the sound of the carriage on the damp cobblestones. The metallic clattering reverberated off the pale-rose rococo half-shells and fell back down to us, and for a moment I felt different, ready for a world in which I could walk without self-reproach.

"Don't be angry. Give me a nice smile!" I said.

"And what is it I should be pleased about?" said Jarmila. "Other than the books I'm translating."

She worked hard. Were she to write the books, she could leave a page unfinished, she could just put the story aside. With a translation you always see it through, you have to make the deadline. She stopped frowning and attempted to faithfully translate into our intelligible mother tongue the text we had jointly encoded. I did what I could to help, and every now and then I would pull from my dictionary just the word she needed. I was pleased when it turned out to be a nice one. Unfortunately, it was more often a bitter one, when all it had to be was truthful. Was I often truthful? I was more often frank.

Jarmila didn't give up. She looked for mistakes and wanted to make corrections. From her astounding memory she quoted all our conversations and endeavored to breach the barrier posed by words, as if there were a manuscript where she could read even what had been written in invisible ink or conveyed between the lines. The mistakes she found were always mine, but I didn't try to do anything about them; all I did was apologize. I myself was the mistake. Of course, every mistake is intriguing, it stimulates your curiosity and reveals the true import of sentences, but when it's repeated, it becomes tedious. And so our love too became tedious and lost its sense of intrigue. But for a while at least our love was conscientious and considerate, and by the end of six years together it had developed the kindly features of an old man, which we occasionally varied through petty quarreling.

"I can't stand it when you mop up your plate with a piece of bread," said Jarmila. "And why do you mop up your mouth with bread, as well? What are napkins for?"

"Please be so kind as to not use matches as bookmarks," I said. "At least in books with golden edges."

"I've told you a thousand times: stop whistling in the shower!"

"If you have to read the newspaper on the toilet, at least don't leave it in there!"

"I don't understand how a rational man can sleep with his head underneath the pillow."

"Exercising naked after daybreak is incredibly unerotic!"

"You carry money in your pockets as if the bills were handkerchiefs."

"You left your key in the door again," I said when, appropriately dressed and not quite sober, we were on our way to the courthouse. "Be careful. From now on, the apartment will just be yours."

When I was fixing up my own apartment in an attic on Bridge Street, I made several trips to Jarmila's and brought my things back in suitcases. I didn't need any sort of vehicle. The heavy pieces remained on Old Town Square, assuring me that little was mine, that I was a quite mobile, transferable fellow. In the meantime I spent the nights in Kormund's studio. His wife furnished me with excellent breakfasts, and at sunset she always set up a folding bed between Kormund's drawing tables.

But a few times I had to spend the night in the waiting room at Masaryk Station, which is now called Prague-Central. It wasn't always easy. Besides the travelers with tickets in hand, it was a shelter for Prague's nomadic outcasts, social and intellectual. Alcoholics, gypsies, and bleach blondes without homes, who began to stimulate my curiosity like mistakes in a poorly arranged sentence. The clean, smooth hands of an official and a brightly-colored jacket testified that this one was a talented artist who had not yet made the breakthrough to a studio flat. There is more than enough remunerative work, but little in the way of flats, and so artists spend their nights where they may, until they find something or until enough prefabs are built to house everybody. A line is an infinite number of points and a city is an infinite number of housing units. Once again I was feeling self-reproachful.

"Good evening," I said at the left-luggage desk. "Here's my ticket. I'd like to be asking for my bag, but I'll just be taking out my coat and leaving my bag here."

Accustomed to heavy loads ... what should I call her, a luggagette? ... she handed me my bag with the greatest of ease and then scrutinized me from behind her counter, on which she was writing something down. I took out my coat, a clean handkerchief, a toothbrush and tube of toothpaste ... and rejoiced: in case of great emergency, I had hidden away in my bag a bottle of vodka.

"Please don't be angry about my imposition," I said.

"It's okay," she said. "What train are you waiting for?"

"I'm not traveling anywhere," I said, and I offered her a cigarette.

Together we enjoyed our strong, fragrant Winstons.

"These may not even give us cancer," she said.

"I'm not so sure."

"But I'll tell you," said the luggagette, "I don't buy American cigarettes. I'd feel bad about it."

"I know," I said. "I reproach myself every time I smoke one."

"One of these costs as much as one egg or two rolls."

"Good things are expensive."

"Not always. Some of them are free."

"No!"

"Mushrooms are perfect!"

"That's true, when you can find them."

Every seat in the waiting room was taken, and it was windy out on the platforms. I felt like drinking some vodka, but I didn't want to drink from the bottle out in public. The snack bar was closed. I could drink it in the bathroom, and for a moment I entertained that possibility, but then I rejected it. I walked out in front of the station and stood on the steps.

I looked out at the street, which was now rather quiet. A cabbie hit the brakes and looked to see if I might have any interest. I waved him on. I wondered whether the concept of universal architecture could be conveyed in Czech. When I was young, I was interested in theology. My conceptology was equally lofty and abstract, but why get worked up over it.

When I proposed the founding of a Department of Universal Architecture, Dr. Rychta adopted my suggestion but threw out the title. No one would have authorized it, it sounded too idealistic and it didn't sound Czech. Out of the department came an institute called Komplexprojekt. Now it's called the Institute for Rational Construction and Ecological Landscaping. It's a highly selective and respected workplace, and I wasn't able to make it through the screening process. Somewhere a document exists saying that at a public meeting three five-year plans ago I did not raise my hand in approval of the execution of Dr. Horáková, that I used to go to confession, and that I did not go to elections. Now I go to vote, appropriately dressed and in a state of moderate sobriety, as when I went before the civil court. But why get worked up over it. Before the war, the Communists got approximately ten percent of the vote; early in the days of the People's Democratic Republic, they got forty. From the time that even I started going to the polls, they've had ninety-nine, and the count is very precise. And yet somewhere a document exists saying that my father took a short trip to Spain and returned with his forefinger shot off, and that when they executed Slánský in the fifties show trials, he turned in his party membership card, and that since my mother refused to iron state property, someone hung above her shop a shield inscribed with the words Liberated Household. Whether there is also a document saying that I married a translator who had translated Boris Pasternak, I don't know. I don't know if someone informed on her or not. That translation made things difficult for her.

There is no document saying that I designed a loathsome high-rise development opposite the Beroun ironworks, that I allowed urban planners to copy my prefab designs again and again, all the way to the walls of White Mountain, as well as in Prague-East and Prague-West, that for a certain quantity of prescribed housing cells I sacrificed our entire body of field and forest. But I have no doubt that every authority knew it.

Just as I was deciding to change my post on the train station steps, I noticed the luggagette approaching. Her shift was over. She was nicely done up, wearing a white coat and over her shoulder a leather purse.

A quite beautiful face, a face that in this poor lighting even appeared very beautiful. I was surprised by how small her hands were, since the muscles on her arms had been built up by lifting bags. And what a soft, delicately harmonized neck she had. I deliberated: Is this woman young or old? A silly question. She is a woman I am scrutinizing.

"I have a bottle of vodka in my pocket," I said. "Would you like to drink it with me?"

We set off for the Žižkov section of town. We talked about traveling, not from the point of view of passengers, but from the viewpoint of baggage. It was very interesting.

"And you know what 'stray baggage' is?" she said. "Forgotten bags that have been left with us for over a year. When we have a ticket with an address, it's no problem. But there are always a few forgotten bags that come back to us. We have to get rid of them."

"How do you get rid of them?"

"A bag is sent a long way, and if it isn't 'stray,' at the end of its travels it's opened, some of the contents are burned and the rest is sold at public auction. But stray baggage comes back to you even from a great distance; there's some kind of catch."

"And?"

"And then it's our problem, us at the left-luggage desk; you see, it can't be helped." She smiled. "We have to handle it, and we do it as honorably as possible."

We walked along the narrow, pockmarked streets of Žižkov. Right down the middle of the street. On the sidewalks there was scaffolding to protect pedestrians from falling plaster, but the scaffolding wasn't safe either. No one had their lights on anywhere. Everything was asleep, like in a ghost town. On the sidewalk lay a bathtub enameled in the blue spectrum, from which there still came the warm, pungent scent of ashes. We stopped in front of a wide-open gate.

"There was a time when this gate closed and when there was a handle. It was brass, you see," said the luggagette, and she pointed to a hole in the wood. "In addition to your vodka, I have some excellent slivovitz and mushrooms in vinegar."

"You're kind, and I won't forget that your name is Miládka," I said. "I'm Mikuláš."

"Mikuláš." She laughed. "Like the saint who on his nameday walks with both a devil and an angel."

I squeezed her small, firm hand. With her white coat against the black entryway, her slender calves, her powerful but adroitly curved body, with dark tresses falling right to her collar, she struck me as being like a backpack whose contents have been arranged from corner to corner, all the way to the last pocket, carefully and with extraordinary skill. Everything in it is essential, there's nothing that on a long march could jostle or encumber. Such a burden carries itself, so that a hiker need carry only himself through the mountains. I had a sudden image of gentians in gently fluttering grass, and I longed for some clean air to breathe.

"Excuse me," she said. "I'll go in first. Watch out for the railing. They used to lower copper kettles down from here. And now I'll turn on the light. Come in."

"Perhaps I should take off my shoes," I said when she opened the door and I looked into a large room without a vestibule. The floorboards were perfectly clean. Just inside the door were red tiles.

"If it will make you more comfortable, then yes, take them off," said Miládka, and she herself changed into another pair. "It's not that I'm fastidious about my floor, it's just that I want you to feel comfortable. But you'll have to go barefoot. My shoes won't fit you."

I took off my shoes in the doorway. The tiles chilled my sweaty soles, and instinctively I stepped onto the floorboards and hoped that my enormous footprint would evaporate before Miládka noticed.

"Such feet!" she said, and she smiled.

"I apologize. This is my second day of wearing these shoes."

"If it's alright with you, please follow me," she said, and she led me through the room into a kitchenette with a bathtub. "Sit yourself down on the edge, and I'll make us some sandwiches."

I rolled up the legs of my trousers and put my feet under the faucet. As everywhere in the world, here in this enclosed space the soap smelled peaceful. Dear God, I thank you for allowing me to wash my feet, I said softly. And I recalled Uncle Boleslav's tower. On nylon threads hung sheer stockings and a few other intimate bits of clothing that were familiar to me. I looked around. Miládka handed me a clean towel.

"A clean towel. I don't deserve it," I said.

"Don't worry about it," said Miládka.

I also washed my face. To look in the mirror I had to bend considerably. The stubble on my chin was heavier and my face was thinner than usual. The blue in my eyes looked gray, but why get worked up over it. Indiscreetly and with a feeling of trespass I pulled aside a lace curtain that concealed a large closet. All the way to the ceiling were suitcases and bags of all sizes, colors, and materials.

"What do you have in these suitcases?" I asked.

"Nothing. They're empty. I've worked with luggage since I was small, by which I mean, since I left school. If you'd like, help yourself. It'd make me happy."

"This one?"

"That's a light carry-on piece. It won't be cumbersome."

"Thank you," I said, and when I picked it up, something inside rattled. "There's something in there," I said. "May I look?"

"It would surprise me a great deal," said Miládka. "I'm sure that all the luggage is empty, in fact, I guarantee it and I'd swear to it. But if there's a rattle, there's a rattle. What sort of gremlin do we have in there?"

I sat down on a chair. While Miládka was cutting a cucumber, I set the bag on my lap and made an unsuccessful attempt at opening it. It was made of good leather and it had a chromium lock. Miládka handed me a box full of all sorts of keys. Never had I held so many keys before. The splendid diversity of form and notch, once meant for a particular function, for now long-missing locks, seemed to be living, breeding products of nature that wanted to demonstrate their vitality through differentiation.

"Play around with it," said Miládka, "or if that doesn't amuse you, pick out another bag."

"I don't know whether I have enough patience," I said, but I tried key after key until one fit.

Inside the bag was a black pistol. Miládka was shocked when I picked it up and aimed it at the clock on the wall. It was already well past midnight.

"There's nothing to fear," I said. "It's just a cap gun and it's pretty old. I wonder if it still fires? This was the sort of pistol we played with between the wars. See, all that's in the magazine is a strip of caps, and they look pretty dry to me. May I give it a try?"

"Only if it doesn't make too big a bang," said Miládka.

I pulled the trigger. It was live, but it just made a dry crack.

"It's funny how it frightens you even when you know it's going to go off," said Miládka, and she beckoned me to the table.

"Here's to your luggage," I said.

"And what kind of toast should I make to you?" she asked. "That you may soon find a place to live? Okay?"

"I'll manage, eventually," I said. "Exactly how, I don't know."

"Then what will we drink to?" she asked, and there we were, still raising our glasses.

I was at a loss, as if she had asked, What matters most to you? I couldn't come up with anything. I wanted to say, To your health or To our parents' children or some equivalent sort of nonsense, but Miládka was looking at me with such sincerity and kindly expectation, I couldn't brush her off with something conventional, and I didn't want to. I searched for something that would indicate to her that I had searched for a toast that would truly make her happy and would be perfectly appropriate. But how to find something appropriate to me? To your health, of course, that's important, but what is it compared to this suitcase? To love: love is beautiful, but would it be appropriate to define this touching concept for her, so that it would weigh as much as a piece of luggage handed across a counter from one person to another person, who has given it in safekeeping for a certain amount of time? Long live freedom! Laughable. What sort of freedom, when, where, for whom, at what price paid in lives and guaranteed by whom? And so I said:

"To Miládka! May she find all the mushrooms she hunts for!"

"Yes, I like that. And may you find yours, as well!" she said with enthusiasm. We clinked our glasses together and she added: "All over!" Another sip. The vodka burned our throats and she said: "May you find yours all over the forest!"

On the wall hung a golden helicon. Beneath this quietly shining instrument, on a small shelf, was a photograph in a wooden frame. Years ago, Miládka was resting her head on the shoulder of a man whose plain smile was not out of duty. There are moments when there is simply you and nothing else, and when this sort of moment is caught in a picture, your smile looks a bit bland. This goes without saying. And it also goes without saying that I recognized him from the picture and then in my memory appeared two pictures, as if they stood on opposite, splendidly inlaid sides of the universe: the picture of an old bed and the picture of one of my sins. My memories of beauty will be forever tied to self-reproach. I smiled.

"Why are you smiling? As if from so far away?" said Miládka.

"I'm grateful for this silence," I said. "To hear silence, that's a scarce thing these days. Thank you."

For a few more minutes, or very long perhaps, since I don't know which kind of time was operating, we maintained this scarce silence, and it bound us together without any feelings of suspicion. Only the bottle's pellucid liquid bore witness that something outside of us was diminishing, too.

There wasn't any alarm clock ticking away. On the otherwise blank wall hung the golden helicon. Several flashing points of its shining edge encompassed musical memories. A festive march. A funeral march. A revolutionary monstrance in a May Day procession.

"Your husband was a musician as well as a cabinetmaker?" I asked.

"How did you know that?"

"I didn't know it, I just saw the golden instrument on the wall."

I examined the helicon, its fabulous curves, and I realized that there wasn't anything on it that was squared, just like music, and along with the notion of round brass-band sound came the notion of a square drawing board. Roundness belongs to play, squareness to work. Miládka, forgive me, I am so extravagantly square and cubic. It's been a long, long time since I knew how to play. A cabinetmaker and a musician in a single destiny, isn't that happiness, plain and simple?

He wasn't just a simple cabinetmaker. In addition to his square cabinetry, he could turn a baroque ornament out of a variety of colored veneers and make an old wardrobe or chiffonier as good as new. And he wasn't just an ordinary musician. With an instrument considered to be just part of a musical ensemble, he passed many hours alone, as if he were a soloist.

"You wouldn't believe how fine a helicon sounds without accompaniment," said Miládka. "It's prettiest on summer evenings. I love to remember how it sounded. I don't understand why he joined the Fízl, why he became an agent. They took him from his workbench, they dragged him away from his music, and we weren't right for each other anymore. They trained him and I couldn't understand him anymore. He was always away somewhere, and when he did show up, he'd be frightfully exhausted and disgusted with himself. When he talked, he made me sick with such insipid, brackish words: assignment, duty. Those aren't words we'd ever known before. The last time I'd done an assignment, I was in school and I didn't like it, and when I saw a pistol in his bag, I was afraid."

"Now *I* have a gun too," I said.

"Be glad it's just a toy," said Miládka.

"Yes," I said. "And what about the instrument?"

"Don't worry," said Miládka. "He won't come back. We were divorced a long time ago, and he left the horn behind. Just like this, hanging on the wall. And why shouldn't it hang there?"

And so you cast a quick glance at the golden horn, which seemed to dazzle and swallow you up, I'm sure you recall the feeling: how often we foolishly stared that way at the sun. Out of the revolving helicon as out of an embossed conch shell that has for ages been displayed in an elevated suburb opening like an amphitheater to the oceanically roaring metropolis, it was as if you'd heard or as if you'd only imagined words ... sounds. You didn't know how to talk about them, you didn't know how to imitate them, but occasionally, unexpectedly, a drab echo of the memory returned: the calls of forest animals, the roar of invisible airplanes, the nighttime ringing of pipes and, through the open window, reaching you in your forsaken bed, those moans possibly of passion, possibly of pain; the skin quivers at the slightest contact and, like a hungry flock, the procession of people presses through the organ; you catch a glimpse of a buzzing fly flitting by, and it's as if you were eavesdropping on the narrative of a lonely soul; you've also heard the buzzing of a salvo of artillery, far off and near as well, and the wavering sound of a siren. You hear yourself and you are saying:

"Yes, Miládka, that's how it is."

We drank the last glass. Daybreak. Miládka opened the window overlooking the courtyard. In the distance, above the city roofs, a crescent moon was setting. In front of a brick wall the dahlias had fallen, picked off by the first autumn frost. In the middle of the courtyard a barrel. In the barrel water. On the water several tiny white balls, ping-pong balls perhaps, which children had been playing with. A gentle breeze propelled them along the surface in curves that could be calculated.

"When it's nice out, I sit on the rocking chair and close my eyes," said Miládka.

"I too like to rock myself sometimes," I said.

I watched the small white forms gently traversing the black surface of the water, and the barrel in the courtyard seemed like a night sky self-contained and self-enclosed. Amidst the strokes of the azure spectrum of dawn colors, the city's streetlights went out like the closing of a piano. I wanted to put my arms around Miládka. Wasn't she standing right next to me?

But Miládka closed the window and asked me whether I didn't want a little something to drink, she still had that excellent slivovitz. I thanked her but said no, liquor is a good companion of mine and I wouldn't want to have a falling out with it, but nevertheless we did have a little goodnight swig, even if it was morning.

"These are the little delights that don't cause any problems," I said. "To breathe fresh air. To pick a plum off a tree, with that thin coat of blue down they wear. I could go on and on."

"Yes, you could," said Miládka. "You could tell the one about me coming out of the train station and looking around … and these hands. All day I've used them to hand people baggage, and suddenly, with the greatest of ease, they flutter around in the air freely as a sheet of paper. Or a handful of dried mushrooms."

She sat on the bed, leaned back against the pillow, closed her eyes halfway, and didn't so much lose herself in thought as reach into her imagination. She halfway smiled. She was beautiful. She was more than beautiful, a singular woman at a singular moment before aging began. Will I continue to see you? Will I continue to trace with my finger that deep crease of yours that passes close to your delicate eyebrow like a sinuous string?

"Stretch yourself out in the rocking chair," she said, and she switched off the light.

I softly rocked myself into a shallow sleep as if on a boat at anchor. Through half-closed eyes I saw the instrument on the wall shining out of the darkness, and the wall was bound above to the ceiling and below to the floor; I couldn't see into any adjacent space. I was inside a building. When for a long while my rocking chair had remained completely silent and motionless, as if a boat sitting on the ocean floor, on the bed, facing the helikon, Miládka began to undress. Without making a sound, the painterly whiteness of her body echoed the vigorous yet delicate curves of the instrument, which now only seemed not to be making a sound. You could hear the tugging of damask and the overstuffing of feathers, and the growth of the pine and the stretch of the glue of her bed, but she wasn't lying down to sleep, she was boarding the bed as if it were a train. For a while, deep in thought, I walked along beside bicycles, which cut a furrow through my landscape, then in front of horses, and then like a child in a load of fragrant hay; this too you must know, you whose head has sunk back into the pillow, the green horizon turning upside down, and along the blue or not-blue path that leads through the landscape, above you and below you, rock a lantern and a white, pot-bellied cloud. The udders of a rowan tree caress your face. And you don't know whether finally, for the first time, you are falling out of eternal vigilance and into sleep, or whether, for the first time and possibly the last, you are as vigilant and grownup as Uncle Boleslav.

I was the one who woke up first. The bed wasn't narrow, but neither was it wide; it definitely wasn't meant for two – this could be calculated – and in no way was Miládka economizing on her use of it. Not that she could. Economically slim and slender were her components – small hands, fingers, earlobes, ankles like belt buckles, mouth like a ligature of letters, crab-apple knees. She had a profile out of Matthias Braun. And above it hair spread across the pillow like a black, brimming sheaf, and then hips like ramparts built for war and a massif of barriers lowered beside the bifurcated gates.

I went over and sat down on the bed, cautiously, so that I wouldn't wake her. I leaned back against the headboard and scrutinized her body lying there, resigned, like a white piece of luggage. Just as I sit in the countryside, leaning against a tree and looking at the hills, fields, and forests. Since I was small I've been a sexual person, I look at a landscape the way I look at a woman, and you are the first, Miládka, to whom I need not apologize for this. However, you too do not remind me of anything, you are like the central Bohemian hill country, the rounded hill on which, it is said, our forefather, Čech, stood and took in the land, those extinct volcanoes, Milešovka and Vlhošt', the pair of Bezděz hills and Háznburk, tits of earth with ruins at their summits, the elongated buttocks of the Krkonoše Mountains and the Czech Karst or, as they sometimes call it, Paradise with its Mousehole in the fissured sandstone walls beneath Hrubá Cliff, walls overgrown with coarse moss and the redness of dwarf heather. And the way your instep arches, so too the little sandstone bridge that leads from the Baroque to the Romantic section.

Next to you I am at home. With silent ardor, I belong with you and nowhere else. You're being admired and your sleep knows it. You smile just a bit, you're already beginning to wake. A soft ripple goes through your body, your left breast loses its center of gravity and slowly pours down upon my hip. Is gravity plucking you from your sleep? But all you do is sigh, you like to sigh, you know something about yourself, there's a dream that's deserting you and you're stretching yourself into the bliss of a slumber that, today, will not be alarmed by the diurnal clamor of your alarm clock.

Under your knee a vein is seriously swollen. Through gaps in the lace curtain, rays of sunlight interfere with what would be your lap. Your anthracite lawn absorbs pink and gold and red reflections that at the same time are turning thin, individual strips – refusing here and now to be gray – to silver. On the broad, moist pathway a supple, sinuous, fleshy leaf. You gave me a nice bag. What will I give you?

I leaned over, so that I could look into Miládka's eyes until they opened. She had to wake soon. Half asleep, she interlaced the fingers of one hand into her hair. Her other hand moved in a slow arc to her stomach and slid on, to my groin. The nail of her pinkie came to rest on the most sensitive point of my body. The sensation rippled my brain into the blue spectrum, but I thought of neither Jarmila nor Olga.

She opened her eyes. I saw two enormous black circles, like two universes before creation, and I felt that I was looking out of them at myself. Suddenly, however, the light made them close in upon themselves until they were small disks in brown, illuminated fields, but again and again those black disks opened all the way, as if taking on the rhythm of her heartbeat. She realized where her hand was lying, clasped her hands, smiled, and said:

"Excuse me, but it was done in sleep, and sleep has nothing to be ashamed of."

I wanted to add, Nor does love, but I couldn't get those words out, so I said:

"Nor do we when we're awake."

Once again, we greatly enjoyed our intimacy and we were grateful for our shared bodies and for the shared light of a day that made love along with us, with affection, tenderness, and kindness, with merriment, gravity, and severity, with rough-ness, cruelty, and fury, with desperation, dedication, and exhaustion, and we looked at ourselves sitting face to face and joined our ebb and flow into a single sea that fortunately remains unnamed, and its blue time enveloped us like the sum total of our lives, to the point where we were astonished.

For breakfast, or lunch or dinner, we drank tea. Was it morning, afternoon, or evening? I don't know anymore. All you can recall is the table, and on the table a teapot with a yellow rose.

"Some bread?" asked Miládka.

"A thin slice. Thank you," I said.

"Butter?"

"Just a bit. Just enough to close the holes," I said.

I wanted to tell Miládka about Václav and about the two angels who stood at the head and the foot of his bed, and about my experience with the plainclothesman, who was Miládka's husband. I thought that she would like to hear about it, as would her forsaken helicon. But I would also have had to mention Olga, and this I didn't want to do. And above all, I remembered what was said: There wasn't a single witness. Nor could I testify on his behalf, although I would have liked to. I had a duty to remain silent. It's too bad that I wasn't allowed to talk. He felt no duty and was very human. I often imagine, I often see him looking through the rectory window out into the fields, and this memory has for me much, much more than its plain meaning.

We went down through the narrow streets of Žižkov, headed toward the center of the city. I was carrying the bag, and in the bag the toy pistol, and in the pistol a strip of caps, one of which had gone off. I had my arm around Miládka.

As we approached the heated Prague-Central station, a light snow began fluttering through the air and mingling with the locomotive soot. Locomotives were rolling onto the switching track and Miládka said:

"Look, those are my chickens."

"My two pieces of luggage are still checked with you," I said.

"Not to worry! However long you want. I'll tack your ticket up on the board, so you won't have to pay if I'm not there when you come for them."

As is usual near a railroad, you could hear the whistling of trains. It wasn't just one locomotive whistling, but at least forty thousand locomotives, or however many trains one could count on this continent, and just in the proximity of the stone platform two or three in harmony, in a major key. From afar, through an empty corridor, through the pungent atmosphere, audibly and at random, came whistles for Holešovice, Libeň, Střížkov, Kobylisy, Trója, and Bohnice, but this time no sharp object was being twisted into my heart. I have some amazingly vivid memories. I recall that nothing resonated in my heart, although I did use to register steam pipes and car horns most sentimentally. I didn't realize then that there was silence in my heart as in a forest; I realized this for the first time now, while recalling it.

What did the cardiologist tell me? The best heart is the one you know nothing about. But lately my heart has been regularly pierced, even when I don't hear a train at all. It was high time that I visited my old boss, Dr. Rychta. As always and everywhere, even now I had to arrive on time. In a drawer I found several vials and tubes containing heart medication. I swallowed a pill, washed it down with lukewarm tapwater, and promised myself that right after my conversation with Rychta, I would go to The Golden Tiger for some beer. In my heart a sharp fingernail kept mispronouncing the r's in its painful soliloquy, my hair was tangled down to its roots, and twice, thrice my gallbladder undermined me, as if a match, burned down and not yet cooled off, were being twisted and crushed into my abdomen. I felt faint, and unfolding before my eyes was a blue tablecloth with white polka dots, but I was able to calculate that after fifteen minutes the medication would be working perfectly. With swift strides I headed across Wenceslas Square toward Rychta's institute, and it seemed that if Archduke Waldstein had died of gout lying in his palace, that is, in the midst of the best of architectural designs, that even I could die. Theoretically, or rather figuratively speaking, I shouldn't have minded. On my walks and during sleepless nights didn't I ponder my death and long ago give darkness the same sort of detailed treatment as my loves? But when I imagined myself in a cold mortuary, my sleepless hand finding on my chin an infinite number of black points, whose keratin intends, after the soul has passed away, to extricate itself for at least twenty-four more hours, I shook with dread. I looked around the Ledeburské Gardens and promised myself that when the trees are in bloom, I would come again and spend an afternoon, and that I would stop smoking, but I knew that I wouldn't be able to keep the second promise. I lit up right away.

I still remember how, that time, I wanted to buy Miládka a blue tablecloth with white polka dots, but that the store had closed, and how even that day I wasn't late for work. I didn't go to work at all that day, and I remember that no one noticed, no one made a single remark about it or asked about it, as if I'd been sitting there at my board like all the others, or as if no one had any need of me at all.

Dr. Rychta received me very amicably. For a moment longer than usual he held my hand in his, and he observed that my hand was cold. For warmth he offered me cognac, and when I drank it, my heart medication began to work perfectly; it made me feel great. For the first time I told myself that I might be an alcoholic, and I don't know whether this discovery pleased or disturbed me.

"It's too late, my friend," said Dr. Rychta.

I looked at my watch. It was a few minutes to four. Dr. Rychta took off his glasses and wiped them with a white handkerchief. Then he said:

"As you can see, I'm winding things up." He pointed to the papers that covered all the surfaces of the office and looked well rummaged through. "They shelved us. They didn't want to work with us anymore. They're a young, aggressive generation, and they blame us for having built in the fifties the way we had to build. There's nothing you can say to them."

"And what about my project? Our project? Isn't it an argument worth making to them?"

"You think that I had only your project to deal with? I had many more projects like that. ... I'd been thinking of the future, that is, I'd been thinking of the present day. Didn't I tell you that over time the most rational ideas win out? But we will no longer be involved. They have their own projects. I am old now. You are the one who has to try to reason with them!"

"I won't go begging to anybody," I said. "I'm no longer young myself. It's exhausting to have to keep looking to people with personal influence just to bring a single decent idea to fruition."

"What do you want to do?" asked Dr. Rychta.

"I'm going away. I don't have anything to forsake," I said.

"Nor do I," said Dr. Rychta, "but I don't like to forsake my calling."

"What will you do?"

"Next year – but it's only a few days away, how time flies – I will be named ambassador to Ceylon."

"That's very far away," I said.

"It's not so far. These days no place is far. An Ilyushin or Boeing will set us down there in a matter of hours. ... Don't just disappear. Write me! Come visit! What country entices you? Canada? Sweden?"

"No country entices me, it's a matter of bare necessity to finally detach myself, and I have an opportunity, a personal one," I said.

"And I wish you all the best. I mean that personally."

"Thank you."

"I thank you as well," said Dr. Rychta.

I came out onto Klárov, went across Mánes Bridge, right through the Old Town to Republic Square. If I can still catch Kormund, I'll ask him to go with me to The Golden Tiger for some beer. I have to cross Old Town Square again, past the astronomical clock, and I do not look up at Jarmila's window. I hop into the paternoster elevator, let myself be hauled up to the fifth floor, and from the corridor I have a good view of the Old Town tower. I knock at the door of Kormund's studio.

"Good evening, Věrka," I said. "Where's Kormund? Could you put some water on for coffee, please."

"Mr. Kormund is dead," she said. She had always referred to him as simply Kormund. "He died in the hospital, but he was killed trying to pass a car. He never regained consciousness."

Věrka sharpened a pencil and tapped the black dust into a tin can. His drawing board stood before the window, on it the half-finished drawings of a proposal I envied him for. On a shelf his jacket, as always absolutely white. Coiled beneath a stand, thin leather shoelaces. Poor, dear Kormund. We are truly starting to go. Because his feet were sweaty, in the studio he always changed into sandals.

"I'm awfully sorry," I said. There was nothing else to say.

"Three weeks ago," said Věrka.

"Why didn't I hear about it?"

"I wrote you at home, that is, I sent you the announcement. And Mrs. Kormundová called you, but you weren't home."

"Home. Oh," I said.

"Were you away?"

"Only for a short time."

"West?"

"No."

"East?"

"No as well. Just in Prague."

"Can I make you some coffee?"

"It's a terrible pity. A terrible pity," I said.

"There's still some of Kormund's coffee left," said Věrka, and she picked up a large tin of powdered coffee from Switzerland. "As well as a case of champagne, for you. If you'd be so kind, when you leave. Don't forget!"

She tried to put water on to boil for coffee, but the electricity was off. I looked out the window. On the square streetcars were standing this way and that. Cars were swerving in and out among them, hectically honking their horns, and the traffic lights illuminated the gray, ant-like teeming of pedestrians who, having been deposited by mass transit, were now rushing along their own axes.

I wanted to ask, Was he buried? And where? Or was he cremated? But all I said was:

"The power's out. Let's hope it's back on soon. I'll turn off the burner, so it doesn't boil away all the water if the outage is long and you forget you had it on."

"I'll do it out in the corridor, where there's gas," she said.

"Wait! Stay right where you are! You're not going to do a thing. Please," I said. "What happened to him? It's hard for me to believe that Kormund got caught passing a car, out of bad luck or bad judgment or whatever. He drove too fast, but he had a good car for it."

"Kormund was Kormund," said Věrka, and when she leaned back, her dark hair fell on the light drawing board.

Her mourning hair was parted in the middle. I knew that she'd been in love with Kormund, even though she knew he wouldn't get a divorce for her, just as he wouldn't for the waitress, architect, doctor, chemical engineer, hairdresser, operator, or opera singer, but Věrka was the only one he talked to about the others. When Kormund talked about them over beer, it always derailed me a bit; I didn't understand where he found the time and energy, and I wondered why he'd ever gotten married.

"I like professional women," Kormund would say. "And Věrka is my first and last, dependable fallback. But were I ever to get married again, I would once again marry Květa. You have only one wife."

The one who oversaw the building of the funicular at our dappled corner, do you remember, Béda? Yes, Kormund was Kormund, and I admired the willfulness with which he drew the designs he wanted to. He was a good designer, and he managed to implement all of his projects. With great bravado, he scattered monuments of perfect, undiluted architecture around Bohemia and in South America, Iran, and even as far away as Ceylon. He belonged to a group among whom Dr. Rychta had the decisive word.

We spent nearly all of my forty years together. Kormund was just one five-year plan older than me. This was decisive.

"But what price do you pay, Kormund," I asked him, "when you don't pay the price of compromising your professional principles? By what miracle do you accomplish this?"

"I subscribe to only one sort of morality: the morality of buildings," said Kormund. "Everything else is politics. Find yourself a vacant site and impose yourself on it! Find yourself some of the people who hold the pursestrings. They're not all stupid, they know what they should be supporting. Suddenly, they'll be making references to you. But watch out! What they say will be about facts alone, and our facts are buildings, not paper projects."

I gave the light switch a click, to see if the electricity was back. The light went on, and then off again.

"Do you know any more?" I said.

"Reluctantly," said Věrka. "Unfortunately." She handed me a little leather case, what looked to be a travel case. "He left this to you, also. It wasn't an accident. He also left me a letter. Instructions on how to do the rest of the drawings for his project. And a remark about you, as well. There's the case of champagne, and then this."

I opened the gleaming zipper and then from the leather case I removed a not so gleaming pistol. It was not a toy. Eight bullets in the magazine, one in the barrel. The safety was off. I marveled at it. Whatever passed through Kormund's hands was dependable. I dumped the bullets into my hand and put them in my pocket for safekeeping. Kormund built beautiful, splendid houses for several government ministers. Glass, concrete, iron, stone, wood, and water. The ministers built several beautiful, splendid public buildings on whose foundations Kormund's signature appears.

The sky above us changed. In my pocket, between my index finger and my thumb, I was worrying the acorns. Věrka looked at me with panic in her eyes. And who can document that that era was completely revolting?

"He was afraid," said Věrka.

And then someone knocked.

"Come in!" said Věrka.

On the doorstep stood the plainclothesman. I recognized his features immediately. Now two things had been added to them: exhaustion and age.

"Good evening!" he said.

The light came on.

"May I go home?" asked Věrka.

"That's not up to me," said the plainclothesman.

"Good night, Věrka!" I said. "May I give you a call?"

"Please do!" said Věrka. "Whenever you like, later today would be fine. Goodbye!"

She left the door open. I closed it. The plainclothesman picked up the case of champagne.

"Champagne," I said.

"Mr. Kormund has left you a pistol, Mr. Svoboda!" said the plainclothesman. "May I look for it? Or do you already have it?"

I took out a handful of bullets and placed them in a line on the table.

"I don't understand," I said. "But in any event, it was his."

"It wasn't his," he said plainly.

"For God's sake, how could you know that?" I said with anger, but then I quickly apologized: "I'm sorry. I'm always getting myself all worked up."

"It's okay," said the plainclothesman. "If you have it, and from the bullets I think that you do, look at the serial number. Every pistol has one."

"Alright," I said, and I raised it up toward the light above me and looked at the serial number.

"Q 467 318," he said matter-of-factly.

"So it's yours," I said, and I handed the pistol to the man who used to belong to Miládka, and I did not rule out the possibility that he knew that I knew this.

"It's not mine," he said. "But thank you."

"No problem," I answered. "He was my best friend. I would like to ask you what happened."

"One group relieves another, my dear architect, that's how it is. And someone must be in charge. That too is how it is. But that someone doesn't want to go. That someone cannot simply go. He has to fight back. But how can he fight back when nothing is threatening him? When he is threatened by his own incapabilities? So he asks small services of people who were once obligated to him. If they fail to perform the services, they go down with him. Many extremely powerful and clever people once again need a pretext for terror. A few shots from a gun are enough, sometimes not even that. It's enough to have the weapon found in someone's flat. It's a sad game and it isn't over yet."

"And Kormund?" I said.

"He was mixed up in it," said the plainclothesman.

For a while we were mum as the pencils that were lying all around us. The light went off, and then on again.

"We always dream up our enemies in advance," he said without any emotion. "That is my experience."

"Then where are the real conflicts played out?" I asked.

"Many conflicts are played out," he said, "but whether they're actual or not, I don't know."

What were we talking about? What, what sort, and whose were the words?

If I were to end up walking through the valley of the shadow of death, I would fear no evil, for Thou art with me... And though I have the gift of prophecy and understand all mysteries and knowledge, and though I have all faith, so that I could remove mountains, and have not love, I am nothing... Disregard and contempt for human rights have resulted in barbarous acts which have outraged the conscience of mankind... But what distinguishes the worst of architects from the best of bees is that the architect first builds his cells in his imagination before building them out of wax...

Memories of new and ancient gospels turned upside down before me like the abstract rosettes and webs of a rattling kaleidoscope. There were images of a shepherd, the pietà, a city destroyed, an oversized portrait of Karl Marx being held above the heads of a roaring procession. If we had not been seated and speaking, and if instead I had been playing over and over, on an imaginary viola, one of Bach's fugues, and if he had been carving a baroque ornament out of a piece of alderwood, I would have been less taken aback. This too you must know, you who grasp nothing at all, yet understand everything.

"I'm glad that we met again," I said. "I would like to ask you something. Do you remember that time we stood by the bed of another of my dead friends? It's so long ago now. May I talk with you about it? With someone who was not part of it?"

"Are you considering exhumation? What do you intend to rehabilitate? One burial? Honor our promise. There was not a single witness," said the plainclothesman.

"There wasn't and there won't be," I said. "You may rest assured!"

The plain man walked out. I stayed in Kormund's flat for a while, sitting with my legs stretched out on top of the case of champagne. I leave, you leave, he leaves, I said to myself. I picked up the box and went out into the corridor. The corridor was long and silent as those in hospitals. The lights were once again on. The cleaning woman was swishing her mop like a ferryman his pole.

I shoved the case of champagne onto the paternoster, and just as I noticed I'd put it on a cabin going up, I realized that

I had loaded it badly, but it was too late for me to either get on with the case or to pull it back out; it was already shoulder height. It doesn't matter, I told myself, I'll let it go up to the attic and then back down. I was on the top floor and I looked at the lit-up sign: GET OUT HERE! I waited for the case to appear in the other elevator shaft and remembered Kormund.

"We won't get out!" said Kormund.

"I'm afraid," I said. "What if it flips over with us inside?"

"Nonsense!" said Kormund. "Don't strain your spatial imagination. It doesn't flip, there's just a normal displacement of space."

With Kormund I rode the turnaround for the very first time. He already had a command of geometry. If our era has any tolerance, you can see it in the way it wastes its talents. Only – what is our era? Our era is our regime, and the regime consists of people who have power over us. How can an architect reach an understanding with power? Kormund managed to. Or did he? He reached an understanding with certain people, but as is perfectly normal, things up there got shifted around.

Tenebrores circumdederunt nos, we are enveloped in darkness, but where is our case, dear Kormund? Where is it turning upside down? Where is it going round? Your post-humous gift is suspended somewhere. The ghosts imprisoned in the bottles have popped the corks, they couldn't bear the fizz, and now they're floating somewhere above the Powder Tower, and I am standing here all alone. Goodness wood-ness, I said as a child, from a single wife twins, isn't that wild? Petr and Pavel. We christened them both with cham-pagne.

What sort of line, what sort of limit did they set for you, which you did not consider to be crossed or exceeded? What sort of vacant site, what sort of crack did you find narrow

enough, tight enough a fit? You aren't coming. You're suspended somewhere up above.

GET OUT HERE! The lit-up sign beside the other shaft has
gone out again. Another outage. The cabins too are stopped,
I notice for the first time. I notice that I am stopped as well,
but I would like to flee, to run, to trot, to walk the way
soldiers walk when they're commanded to. Only I would be
incapable of listening. I am an architect. I am also incapable
of giving orders. All I can do is submit project proposals, and
now even that's passé.

GET OUT HERE! It flickers and once again is lit. The
outage was making a feeble attempt to go out. The paternoster rattled, jerked, and then once again froze. As at
Miládka's, as with Miládka, I hadn't a single thought, but I
couldn't put my head down on her stomach, so I leaned it
against a wall. There was a rattle and a jerk in my heart, but
then it froze. Dancing before my eyes was a red spot, and I
said: Paternoster, paternoster, who art in heaven, we do not
know Thy name. Our kingdom expropriated. The will to
power in heaven as it is on earth. Our daily bread without joy
and our trespasses boundless. The trespassers cannot be
identified. For ours is a life without power or glory now and
perhaps forever, amen. Hail, Rowan, full of grace, I am with
Thee, blessed among panicles, blessed fruit of Thy tree. This
too you must know, you riding in a load of hay, upside down,
and above you rowanberries dangling.

Like the Lord God, who knows no duty, but wants to
behave like a human, the paternoster once again sets itself in
motion, and its bulbs go on. The cabin with Kormund's gift
arrives and I get on and go down to the basement, in your
honor, my friend!

"A ride to the top? Not much in the way of kicks," said

Kormund. "Stay on and don't be afraid. A ride to the bottom is one big kick. You'll see!"

Then, he took my hand. I wasn't even ten years old yet. Now, with resignation, I sat on the case and rode down past the ground floor. And then down, further down into the trembling darkness that smelled like machine oil, rumbling and squeaking; I had to cry and at the same time, seated on that case of champagne, I had to laugh. The superficial shifting of the cabin and the profound shifting of the way I felt, feelings I didn't know how to name, although they mattered to me so much, as if they were part of a project. My lips slipped into a photogenic smile, my teary eyelids glistening like spilled magnesium.

What do they call this? What is a man like me supposed to feel? Pain? Regret? Sorrow? Despair? Sadness? Panic? Anxiety? Contrition? Stress? Grief? Depression? Despondency? Hopelessness? Forsakenness? Loneliness? Rejection? Torment? Misery? Futility? I don't know, I don't know, or ... or the melancholia, eternally counter to time, of blooming geraniums that are being carried out in the heedful embrace of a woman, now a widow, of one beautiful dusk in silent rain at a wall overgrown with a purple cross of clematis. They don't fathom naming. My world defies words now, except for one, the name Kormund.

We were on our way back from fishing. I was carrying our catch. Kormund was carrying the rods and the net. On the porch, in a pram, were the twins, Petr and Pavel.

"Look, a goose, a common Czech goose," said Kormund, and he pointed his rod at Květa. "Why is she holding more than she can hold?"

His wife hadn't seen us yet, she was standing, at a loss, at the other end of the garden in front of a wall notable for its purple clematis. She didn't know how to put her armful of

flowering plants down on the ground. I couldn't define how
what you said, Kormund, made me feel. What you said in
reference to your wife was undoubtedly said with love. What
were the contents of my feelings as I looked at the rainy
spectrum of the approaching evening? Humility? Offence?
Shame? Defilement? Contempt? Regret? Disgust? Sadness?
Panic? Or ... or the melancholia of the eternally blooming
geraniums Květa was still holding in her arms, offering them
with a smile despite the rain, in which she, like the flowers,
was willing to remain. To remain until the geraniums, brought
out from inside, were naturally rinsed and watered by the rain.
There was no stand or platform nearby to facilitate her
putting down the potted plants; she continued to hold this
overabundance. She was determined to be the flowers' stand
and platform. And to them she already was. She remained
standing out in the rain. Then she knelt, first with the pots on
one knee, then with the pots on the other. This too you must
know, so too did you pray beside your bed where no one
could see.

The rain fell harder. Květa raised her face to the sky,
shook her head to get her hair off her forehead, and for a
moment offered her face to the heavy rain, and then slowly,
smoothly, softly, moved by concern for the plants, she
inclined herself so that she was leaning on her hip, with her
elbow pressed into the grass. She put the geraniums down on
the ground. She was enthusiastic about her success, and
although the rain was coming down with just as much enthusiasm, she arranged the pots along the wall at regular intervals.

My internal surface remained unnamed. On one stratum
it came close to being a dream. On another an old memory.
On yet another, something future. But I know that the air's
humidity conferred on me its love for plants with blazing red
flowers. Dependably, the paternoster brought me up from the

basement and I got out. The case of champagne had no rope or wire around it, so I had to carry the unwieldy burden alternately in my arms and under one of them. I looked rather conspicuous. From Celetná Street I turned into the entrance to St. Jakub's and sat down in a pew. After the war, I used to come here every Wednesday to hear Professor Wiedermann's organ recitals. In those days, hooded monks used to wander about collecting donations during the concert. Today one has to buy a ticket in advance. It seems as if not only the monks, but their habits too, met with misfortune, but why get worked up over it.

Out of the twilight the long nave of the church, striped with twisted golden pilasters, lifeless statues of saints, men and women, were looking at me as if they were living beings. Above me hovered a cherub, pointing at me with its slender finger. With a wavy, serrated sword that looked much like a saw, its other hand was pointing the way out of the church.

But I wanted to stay there for a while and listen to the silence of the church and the silence inside me. The church's silence was embellished with the colors of the lavishly curved bodies of angels, and above one of the altars the Virgin's ghost was painted in the blue spectrum. The silence passed through me and left behind fragments of buildings I did not find agreeable. I felt the dissonance. And I felt guilty about my talents, about having destroyed them. Or did the era destroy me? No, the era didn't destroy me, it destroyed my resolve.

From beneath the vaulted ceiling, painted with frescoes to give the illusion of clouds, came the murmur of the non-illusory wind, as if, in order to fly, the non-airborne statues of angels were drawing the wind into their wooden, illuminated wings. Someone up in the choir turned on a machine that drove air into the organ. After a while, the organist began to play, as his obligatory prelude, one of Bach's fugues. I followed the perfect counterpoint of voices which, although conforming to precise harmonic laws, sounded free and unrestrained. At the same time I followed the voices inside me. They did not sound free and unrestrained. I looked up from my chaos and distress, up toward the vaulted ceiling of St. Jakub's, a perfect, pellucid example of baroque architecture which I did not design, and its musical likeness was embodied in the shaded tumult of the organ pipes as well as in the focused luminosity of the paintings above the altars.

So I just observed and listened, and my observing and listening comprised a polystratified and polymorphous order. Inside me, however, this order was neither mirrored, copied, deposited, nor accumulated, as in an organ or beneath a vaulted ceiling, inside me there was a confusion of languages, as in Babel, a tangled spindle of thoughts and the non-rhythmical intrusion of self-reproaches all the way into my heart. Both horizons, the graceful design of the vaulted, long-since impersonal music that buttressed the church, both designs, and even my personal horizon scattered into whirling spots, went counter to me, and I felt as if they were intersecting in my clasped, praying hands. Like the old wooden bench, with its book bound in leather, the bench covered with black scars left by the hot wax dripped by candles long ago and over a long time. Their pale white nun's-time now melted onto me, and over the wall of my dappled corner I watched the child Kormund gathering beads of wax off the snowberries and sticking them on the blue-green needles of the dwarf pine trees in Uncle Boleslav's garden.

I recalled prayers I once learned by heart, and into those books of mine, fastened shut with anxiously bitten fingernails, I whispered:

O grief, delirious dream,
Where freedom, law ...

Archduke of poets, Aleksandr Sergeyevich Pushkin, shot down by a snob on the field of muzhik despotism, intercede for us!

For a while more I followed the organ music, which, suspended in the harmony of St. Jakub's, sounded as if it had no end. Until I recognized the final chords, and then there was a short pause and once again silence, just the murmur of the air I am still breathing, Kormund! I am still alive. Will you forgive me? There are still a few things to try, and what is offered I accept, I don't refuse, possibly from the infinite number of scattered points I will make one final finite line. And now you choose a little freedom, the freedom to rise from the pew, to stand on two legs, to lift the case of twelve bottles of champagne, to walk through Old Town Square and across Charles Bridge, and since I'm resolved to do it, I will. It was plain and simple.

As I walked across Charles Bridge, I had no, absolutely no feeling. I gave myself up to the vacuum within me. Like the moment before deciding, when you don't have anything to forsake. The bell of St. Vitus', in the Prague Castle, was just beginning to strike some evening hour. It had long ago grown dark and it was winter.

I walked along the Kampa, in the Vrtbovský Garden I greeted the dampened profiles of the Braun statues, which have aged nicely, and I rang at the door of Olga's studio. I expected to be dazzled by the light, and I was. And the waves of air that crossed the studio's threshold were warm, but they weren't saturated with the smell of turpentine, poppyseed oil, and beeswax. The walls were bare, prepared for the journey to Paris. I couldn't hear water thrumming through the gutters.

So, once again, does love arise.

You are given tea and tea you drink, and what else is there? You are here and you can't do otherwise; this too you must know. For a long time you saw things upside down, until things stabilized, and finally you yourself. You don't have anything to forsake, you have only yourself, and so it is yourself that you will take.

"And what about your project?" Olga eventually asked. "Is there any hope?"

"It's all in order," I said. "Completed. Approved. We begin to implement it after the new year."

If at that moment the towers of St. Mikuláš', which stood just outside the window in the labile tow of the blue spectrum of night colors, had silently or with a rumble turned upside down and collapsed into a pile of building materials, or if at that moment I were to speak human and even angelic languages with the gift of Jarmila's philological talents and the love I didn't have, I would have been less surprised. I came with a mandate in my heart: we will go together, Olga! I came with an announcement: I would like to go with you, Olga. And it is with an entreaty in my heart that I came: Olga, please take me with you!

I felt like a clean-cut tree, a stump still with a center of gravity. Another change in climate. A natural phenomenon, a stratum of ash, an unfinished gesture. But you already know the situation, that things are out of control, that you are forever past the point. You are once again upside down, that is my perpetual plot; I touch the roughness of my father's face, by evening a black beard has already started to grow in, and I smell the familiar scent of soap and cigarette smoke. I look at Olga and she says:

"Well, congratulations! I wish you the best. That's magnificent, sensational news! And what a great birthday present it is for you. So congratulations to you and to the new year, as well."

"When are you going?" I said.

"At the end of the year," said Olga.

"I still want to take you out for dinner. A night out in Prague. That's why I came. Would you have dinner with me? During the holidays, between Christmas and New Year's Eve?"

"I'd love to, Mikuláš," said Olga. "Let's hope there's snow on the rooftops."

"That would be nice," I said. "And if it's on the rooftops, may it also be on the ground."

Trojánka

When I walked with Olga across Charles Bridge to The Green Frog, that wine cellar on Malé Square in the Old Town, we were accompanied by a good, downright festive atmosphere. Olga looked beautiful, truly radiant. It had nothing to do with me, I simply perceived it in the gray draft that came from the pale-blue spectrum's wings. Pigeons were circling above us, several people were looking our way, and the heads of statues turned to look at us, as well. Their wish was that we suit one another. Our wish was that they remain so touchingly handsome. For our occasion it happened that snow had fallen, and the snow was still white.

In front of the entrance to the wine cellar, we ran into Jarmila. She looked funny. She was standing on her tiptoes, studying the menu in its little lit-up case. It could definitely be calculated why this evening of all evenings she was standing on her tiptoes in front of the entrance to the place where I had reserved a table for two, why she wasn't standing firmly rooted in front of the entrance to The Golem, Rudolf, The Three Ostriches, or Waldstein. As if there weren't forty thousand restaurants in Prague, where they post their offer of dishes one hundred and fifty-seven centimeters above the given above-sea level, but why get worked up over it.

The table we'd reserved was not round. On three sides, I precisely recorded, sat: Mikuláš, compound parenthesis/ bracket north close compound parenthesis/bracket; Jarmila, parenthesis south close parenthesis; Olga, bracket west close bracket full stop. The fourth side remained empty, and I thought of Miládka. Prague-Central Station, formerly Masaryk Station, formerly Ferdinand Station, stood just to the east, and on the eastern chair sat a tiny piece of baggage, a little leather zippered bag that belonged to Jarmila, a gift I'd once given her for Christmas, and next to it sat a no less leather bag, this time, for a change, without a shiny zipper, a gift I'd given for Christmas once to Olga.

"Can we really ruin you, without any malice or fore-thought?" said Jarmila, who was now studying the menu sitting down. It suited her. And in the meantime she smoked. She wrapped herself in a nicotine shawl and when no answer was forthcoming she remarked: "Do you know how they say 'quail' in Chinese?"

"Fluently," I said. "Olga, please don't squint at the right side of the menu. Or cover the prices with your napkin. Be a good girl and don't try to save me money!"

Of course, we could have eaten bread, salt, and dry wine, and sat under an olive tree on Crete. But we were sitting in Prague, at The Green Frog, and we hadn't any hunger, just appetite. We're always sufficiently sated, I thought, and I smiled at both of these beautiful ladies, and a fork twisted deep into my heart. Out on the street, automobile horns were snowily honking, but with good willpower and a good imagination you could hear it as the sort of locomotive Béda called a coffee mill and Uncle Boleslav Hunchbacked Amelia. Kormund called it a black washbasin, and me: Sh-sh-sh-sh.

"And the wine, my darlings!" said Jarmila. "A liquid map of southern Moravia."

"The driest there is," said Olga.

"Yes, that goes without saying. Waiter!" I said.

The service was pleasing, and the dishes were perfectly prepared and presented. They poured our wine courteously, with refinement and concern, without any indication of professional servility. Attentively, unobtrusively, they were on the ready, like black-robed sovereign angels. To the two already burning candles they added one more, and we didn't notice when or how. I was happily astonished that one could still, or perhaps once again, be so well, so gloriously served in a Czech establishment. I had so many times been humiliated, insulted, and ridiculed, drenched in sauce, robbed of time, money, and appetite in ghastly, grimy, unventilated pubs by vulgar, choleric idiots and vile flunkies. So what else is new? This too you must know. I was never able to determine whether we were so poorly served because we had such a bad government, or whether the government could not be better because it was so poorly served.

There were, of course, exceptions, and not only this first-class establishment with the beamed ceiling that had been anointed with ox blood, with its reminders of Charles IV, the Czech emperor of the German Holy Roman Empire. Here I was, already reproaching myself again. The cold wine sparkled in dewy glasses. We talked about Charles, the father of our country, who recommended the building of that stone bridge across which I kept going back and forth, and we also talked about President Novotný, whom people referred to as Pop. Jarmila said that at year's end Novák was stepping down, but Olga, who was not so philologically astute regarding the Czech milieu, didn't know who this was, whether a secretary for construction, architecture, or translation, and so we explained to Olga that this was just a nickname for President Novotný. If he actually does step down, then it will be a tiny bit due to my contribution. The high-rise development in Beroun has to be demolished to make way for the new highway to the west, and the housing cells I designed for White Mountain are no longer liveable. If I were to calculate what I did for nearly twenty years, all I'd be accountable for is the clandestine burial of half a billion crowns. With luck it all has crumbled into an infinite number of points, so it mustn't concern me; yet I suffer in silence. The girls weren't happy either.

Hunchbacked Amelia was grinding me in her coffee mill, and Kormund is now carrying on his head, across the Vltava, somewhere near its source, a black washbasin full of sh-sh-sh-shs. You can understand how ashamed I was to be sitting with two women at one table, to be ending the year one thousand nine hundred and sixty-seven, to be turning forty, and to be finding the culinary arts and the well-cultivated Moravian vines corrupting my appetite for the sensation of freedom and for the fleeting sense of abundance we normally felt only when we indulged ourselves at weddings and occasionally at funerals.

We were a bit confused at first, but the wine made us feel elated and soon, under the massive ceiling, we imagined ourselves back in the security of the old days. The heavy velvet curtains were stirred by the brisk breeze, and the twinkling of the candles blurred all of our personal calamities into a tapestry of perfectly harmonized pastels with legendary scenes of grace and heroism, a tapestry we'd never have to see up on any wall.

Olga's long painter's fingers were fiddling with her silver chain, from which nothing hung and which made different sounds when it brushed against glasses filled to different heights. Each of us drank as fast and much as we pleased. Fortunately, the vines didn't ripen for the purpose of apologizes. Jarmila put her head on Olga's shoulder, and why not. They were pretty together. It's too bad that they weren't my sisters or, even better, brothers. Or I could be a Muslim with the prophet-given right to have four wives. It would be clear and unambiguous: Jarmila, Olga, Miládka, and if it's okay with you, Kormund, Kormundová, all so prettily putting down great quantities of geraniums. We shared great quantities of words, as if we were passing among us flower pots to be lovingly watered.

The wine overturned the tiny boxes of our conversation, into which we had placed for safekeeping, even before crossing the threshold of a school, a tiny treasure, a grain of sand we imagined to be a golden linden whirlybird, from which a tree would grow right there in our courtyard. Childhood's shadow play was replaced by the countryside's display, as if we were passing by on a train that kept winding slowly here and there, and with ironic love we told stories on our parents. Between the words, as between the lines, of anecdotes from our past we were rehearsing our personal erotics and politics, which, as we know, always and everywhere are closely intertwined, and we found it very funny indeed.

Thus did we indulge ourselves in free conversation, which we did not, however, strip of its grammatical rules, nor that evening did we dispute how torturous it could be. All we did for this extraordinary, extralinear occasion was to conceal the instruments of torture. It was an *orbis pictus* which we perused with didactic disorder and without any partiality, but with pleasure, the way paintings that touch us can still form themselves into rows in conformity with the Latin, German, and Czech languages, which we of course stirred up, without feeling any sort of duty. It might appear that we were swimming like fish in the ocean, just opening our mouths and reading on each other's lips an ashwood cradle and a crimson scaffold, a building with a roof open to the sky and a grave opened to earth, rain, rainbow, and snow, the tripartite eye of God and the bipartite eye of man, a plowman, a king in his majesty, and a thief whose hand has been cut off as his punishment. Flowers and their colorful appearance in names, sexual characteristics, the symbol of the heart, a soul like a dove and a body like a man or a woman. Conferred on us in our warring lives was a fortunate pause, a truce of ornamental words that sounded musical and, exceptionally, incited us not to judgment but to song.

> On a bridge in Prague
> rosemary grows,
> but nobody waters it,
> not even the fog,
> it grows by itself,
> and nobody waters it,
> it grows by itself in Prague.

Across the restaurant a table was singing this song; they were joined, softly, by the other tables, all but the foreigners, who were, however, keeping the beat. And us, we didn't sing, we just smiled; we didn't have the courage.

"I need to buy an herbarium," said Jarmila. "I know so many flowers and in so many languages, but can you believe that I know most of them just by name? Does anyone know what rosemary looks like? Or kidney vetch? Or monkshood?"

"I don't even know whether 'kazirmut' is the name of a flower or a person," said Olga.

"I'd like a krušník," I said.

"What on earth are they?" said Jarmila.

"They used to bake them at our flat on Trojánka. They're made of black bread," I said. "And here's a question for you: why do you think they call the hill Trojánka?"

While they were trying to answer the question, and failing, I replaced the bill, hidden in a napkin, with some money. In comparison with the loss to one forty-year-old person from one civil divorce and one not so civil separation, the bill for such a plentiful evening, for three adults, seemed to me laughable. Included in the bill were two greenhouse cyclamen, for each woman one flowering plant wrapped in cellophane, for the road.

So I considered this chapter closed. It was done with dignity, solemnly yet festively, and with great spirit. The mortal remains were ambulant. The emotional vessel has been tastefully embalmed, and there was nothing in the way of moral remains. Pay your respects to God, my mother used to say every time we ate, and there were never any problems. Only we haven't taken stock of our inheritance yet, we'll pay a tax on it in the form of memories. If necessary, I'm still ready to sincerely apologize for anything. I think that written correspondence provides just as good an opportunity as seeing someone in person.

The fresh air was a shock. Our lungs rejoiced. Jarmila linked her arms in ours and lifted her feet. We carried her around the State Library like a cherub. A drunk came toward us and protested:

"It takes two of you for one half-pint! You should be ashamed of yourselves, bellboys!"

"Should I prop you against a wall? Yes, I will do it, bossman!" I said.

"Leave him alone!" said Jarmila.

"It's a university wall," said Olga.

"Don't you touch me," said the drunk. "I'm infected."

As we approached Charles Bridge, we were dazzled by the moon, and from the snow on the convex cobblestones, worn smooth in the course of history, it was reflected in a cold, granular glare. The gas lamps buzzed with the restlessness of a fly, and on a sign attached to a red house a golden snake was twisting and turning. Jarmila and I drew twisting lines with our fingers, but we did not succeed in copying the serpent. Olga just took one look at the snake and then closed her eyes and playfully conducted the curve as if it were in a familiar musical key. We applauded. At the Orthodox St. Kliment's I bowed at the waist.

"Everything for the fragrant body," said Olga.

We pressed our foreheads against the window of a toiletries shop with a vaulted ceiling, gothic columns, and a rosette, and we read out the names of the soaps: Sky Blue, Coriolanus, Azela, Emerald, Rosanna, Cleopatra, Azure.

"Milled, top quality," I said.

"So, Mikuláš, you'd like to be king of Bohemia," Jarmila suggested.

"Would you be a good king?" asked Olga.

"Of course," I said.

"We know," said Jarmila.

"What is this Winter King's name? He isn't by any chance a redhead, is he?" said Olga.

"You'd rather elect a foreigner," I said.

We walked across Charles Bridge. In the middle we stopped. Except for the three of us and the crowds of statues along either side, there were no other people on the bridge. For a while we looked and sounded just like the statues. We too had our legends of suffering, love, death, and redemption. What was once alive has already become the past, it already has defining features and petrified gestures, and I was glad that this final view of ours, intended to be retained in our memories, was blanketed with snow.

Not far above us, flying north, was an arrow of wild ducks. It gained height and veered along the arc of the river and into the darkness. Brisk and of the earthtone spectrum was how I, along with the weir foam, felt the water to be, and I think it was all that I felt. At such a moment I wanted to part ways with Olga, and I was glad that Jarmila was still with us, the third wheel whose presence was evidence of the normalcy of the atmosphere and relieved us of any duty to our past intimacy. But before I could manage to say goodbye or goodnight, Jarmila took Olga's hand and rushed off with her in the direction of Malá Strana.

They climbed the stairs onto a platform with iron drainpipes and wooden scaffolding that led over the bridge, which was always, by necessity, being repaired under Arnautov's supervision. I envied him his bridge. By now the bridge is also his, not only Charles's, the father of our country. Was this just a matter of repairs? Or restoration? And wasn't it also construction? Without violating the gothic spirit and the baroque profusion and even a little of the romantic added on top, this man succeeded in probing and accounting for the substance of the sandstone and in directing the work in such a way that the entire bridge of stone after stone and boulder after boulder was completely dismantled and then reassembled and cobbled together exactly the way it had originally looked, but with an entirely new ability to resist further centuries.

My colleague Arnautov, I bow to you from the waist. What you have accomplished, perhaps it isn't real, perhaps it just seems real, as in a painting by Hieronymus Bosch: A river, it might be eternal. Two cities, they might be temporal, one here, old; one there, new. A bridge that, while standing, disintegrates and is reassembled. And while this disintegration and period reassembly goes on, crowds pass by in a variety of plots. Parades, weddings, funerals, festivals, religious processions, the plague, battles, Carnival, people in love, people in despair, dreamers, sleepwalkers, children covered in paint, shop pers, zealots, and one reflective person. That might even be me.

I was seduced and intoxicated by the wine, and this baroque Prague night captivated me like a scene in a play, so that I made my entrance out of the wings at once like an actor and like a spectator. A church tower with gold balls and crosses, and a palace's roofs, bent in several places, were orchestrally harmonized to my inexpressible state of mind. Trees, nearly bare, overhung the bridge and branched into my head, reminding me of bones that in winters long past were buried down to their roots. Above the Čertovka Canal a light was on in a window. Beneath the lamp a man was sitting and reading, although it was late already; he couldn't pull himself away from his story any more than I could from my story on the bridge. The two figures of such different heights engaged me like a page you're just now reading, and as you read, even if you don't realize it, you turn the pages from odd to even; this too you must know. Over Malá Strana, darkly formed of stone, white down was flying. When we used to have big snows, Béda and I would catch ashes on our tongues.

"A night crawler," said Jarmila.

"He's slowing down," said Olga.

"At home I have a whole case of champagne," I said. "You don't believe me?"

When I opened a window, in order to air out the flat, I looked at the bridge, now from a bird's-eye view, and the two rows of statues seemed like black points on a thin line against the backdrop of an even thinner, transparent mist, which rose from the river but didn't do its usual shrouding, it only caught hold, from below, of the bridge tower, the cupola of the Knights of the Cross, and the astrological observatory above the State Library. In the distance stood the Powder Tower. Whoever into it tread was sure to lose his head.

Separated from the light of the street by a wide window ledge, I was able to see through the contending snowflakes a constellation of stars, but I couldn't tell whether the bright and dark shapes I saw were city matter seen against the slumbering map of the sky or a piece of Prague sky seen against the blue spectrum of history once again slumbering deep down in stone.

"So now I'll tell you at last who Kormund really was," I said while popping the cork from the third bottle of champagne.

"That's a ghastly risk you're taking," said Jarmila. "Many good people have lost an eye that way."

"It's pointed at the ceiling."

"When I had an exhibit in Rome," said Olga, "someone stole one of my paintings right out of the show. Did you know that I was incredibly delighted?"

"Don't you have any cigarettes anywhere?" said Jarmila.

"Your soul's made of nicotine," I said. "And now to let you know who Kormund really was. He had such a strong will that he stopped smoking. He smoked fifty cigarettes a day and then brought it to a sudden halt. His wife pleaded with him. She was afraid he'd get cancer."

"That time I was in Rome, I bought a glass dome at a bazaar. That too you must know. Inside the dome were two children on a sled, and when you turned the dome over, it snowed inside."

"I want to tell you that even today Kormund would have been able to build St. Mikuláš'."

"And then the man who sold me the glass dome said..." said Olga.

"You know Italian?" asked Jarmila.

"It's a pure, artistic language. He said, Madam is a Pole? No, Madam is a Czech, I responded. And he said, And you traveled all the way to Rome for a little snow?"

"And so that's Kormund," I said, and Jarmila saved one of my two eyes: while she was popping the cork from a bottle, she shifted the axis of the bottle a small but significant angle, which could not only be precisely calculated, but also drawn.

This was the fourth of the bottles, and I knew that we would not make it through all twelve of them. Kormund, forgive us!

"I am going behind the chimney," I said.

"Won't he fall?" said Olga. "Will he hold on?"

"Don't worry," said Jarmila. "When he drinks, he acts like a lunatic."

"Children, if you'd like a nice view, there's lard floating on the Vltava," I said, and then I closed the window behind me.

I went onto the little terrace behind the chimney, and when with the feeling of sublime relief I aimed for the gutter, it rang out, it thrummed, and steam rose like a ghost. I looked into the sky for a sign of daybreak, which was still a long way off. Yet over on the other side of the courtyard, work had already begun in the bakery. Men in white outfits were taking fresh rolls out of ovens, they're one of those rare group of elects that in a mechanical civilization have the privilege of making things by hand. Handmade rolls are dear to me, I must give you my blessing. Peace be with you!

Ventilation flaps, waving metronomically, discharged into the courtyard clouds of crackling steam redolent of the chimney. The Castle bell rang one of the emergency hours. And within reach of my hand, just beyond the pantile edges of the roof, St. Mikuláš' was looking at me through the pre-morning spectrum like two happy beings in one, clear evidence of the perfection that comes from bringing together the male and female principles. I determined that father and son Dientzenhofer both devised and built very well, a round cupola and a tall, slender tower. Man and woman sailing on a ship in the music of one religion; I could envy them, but why get worked up over it.

The church's two-in-one principle began to turn into a three-in-one, and not before long it adopted the rules of an ambiguous game. I looked at it as an enchantment, something that could certainly not be calculated. One tower remained and I saw two domes, then on its archaic spot sat a single wide vaulting, and to the one slender tower a second slender tower was quickly added, so that there were two towers next to the one cupola, and then once again one tower next to the naturalness of the verdigris two-breasts-in-one.

St. Mikuláš was toying with me. St. Ignaz Dientzenhofer was certainly turning over in his baroque grave. I took care not to fall off the roof. It was slippery, the snow sprinkled on like sugar, or possibly salt, flour even, this too you must know, how to crumble starch from a hollow willow. The shadow church merged, overlapped, and separated, cleaved and unified, and like a fan it opened into vibrating silhouettes that rearranged themselves like a deck of cards. One fateful card, a presentiment of New Year's Eve, pulled itself partly out of the solid block of the church, tumbled the rest of the way out, collapsed onto its side, and took me with it. I lay on the roof like a puppy in hiding, and I looked for the window.

What next? To get you inside, at least inside under a roof. There was bread there, and in the bread a knife. A black ox, no, a black horse, no again, more likely a black mountain, a black forest, black hair, a black pool of water, black earth, but no, once again no; a black mass then? Perhaps a black diamond, graphite, ink, type or lines on white, Father, forgive me, it's just black bread and how wonderful it smells. And how wonderful a pig smells when it's made proper use of. I submerged my hand in a bottle of pickles. The brine was pleasantly cool and on my temporally and eternally bitten hangnails it fizzled like peroxide. The acidity was absorbed into the cuffs of my ceremonial shirt. I ceremonially sucked the acid out of the cuffs with my upper and lower lips, and don't they constitute the mouth that speaks, eats, and kisses? How could they have even more functions? To be silent as snow, quiet as a woman sleeping. Would you like to have breakfast with me? There's bread, pickles, and lard.

Just in case, I made up a sufficiently wide bed. Sometimes you want to sleep with your arms going their independent ways, east to west or north to south, and with a wind rose it could be calculated. Sometimes you don't sleep alone. I put a lambskin bedspread on the floor. Sometimes you're not interested in making a bed and so you go to bed under wool that billows like a sweater Mama washed for you thousands of times, but which she couldn't mend thousands of times, as well.

They lay there in a deep sleep, in a child's embrace, both of them, one big, the other little, Olga and Jarmila, one and the other like an unprecedented comet. It's always destroyed me when a woman lets down her hair, to imagine that on such a stalk grows a natural disaster of a forest and so much wheat. And they pull it from their combs and toss it away, in with indifferent garbage, and each of their hairs, from its root all the way to its end, is named after Olga or Jarmila. They fuse together into a fluffy picture of the crown of one shared, golden black tree whose long, slender trunk, once felled by lightning, has now been peeled by moisture. The trunk is white. At least that's the way it seems to me, in the darkness, but both of them would protest if I were to put it into words. They would say that I must be blind if I can't tell that they still have their summer tans.

Are they dreaming or not? How can one tell from the faces of sleeping women, one of them smiling, the other not? Both have looks that are very close to art. Always baroque sandstone and classic marble. What will I do with them? They're still so pretty. They're still so young, and the freshness of youth still makes their smooth skin taut. They're still in the morning just as they are in the evening.

I leaned down to get a closer look at their faces and I scrutinized their completely dissimilar expressions, which, however, had something in common, as if one talented person had used different techniques. Jarmila is a fragile, sharp engraving made with a steel point pressed into copper, in which a velvet comb is entangled. Olga is a broad, supple spot made with a dripping brush on moderately absorbent, water-marked watercolor paper. She opened her eyes. She lifted her head and touched my chin. She felt my heavy beard, which that night had grown precisely as much as on any night I age. Jarmila woke as well and said, laughing:

"I dreamed that I was slicing an apple, but I couldn't pull the two halves apart. So I unscrewed them. Inside was a golden conical turret."

"It's almost morning. How are you? Would you like some coffee?" I said.

Next to the wall, behind their heads, lay an apple, and I doubted that it had been just left there and forgotten. I broke the apple in two halves and handed one to Jarmila and the other to Olga.

"Rennett," said Olga.

They sat back against the wall, eating the apple and scrutinizing me. Their glossy teeth, none of which life had made them lose, were gnawing at me. Their pearly, chewing reflexes were getting me all worked up. I closed the curtains behind me, and there we were, back in complete darkness. And in the complete darkness I heard the biting of apples, inhaling, the crushing of the core and the whizzing of the stem, which one of them fired at me with her fingernail. I could swear that I saw a blue flash, as when a cube of sugar is broken in half underneath a comforter; do you remember, Béda?

Then silence, nothing stirred. There was just darkness, just the scent of apple, the bipartite fragrance of hair, and from my cuffs the sweet-and-sour fragrance of summer countryside. Before my eyes the dial of my watch ticked greenly. Five twenty-five. By five twenty-six I was naked. I went to put my watch in the little niche with the others, giving myself over to abstract time. Excuse me! I also wound my watch.

Obedient to a will that passed through me like the stroking of fish through the Mediterranean, or like the traces left by an ancient nomadic tribe, I leaned back against an invisible, burning pillar that had thoughtfully been left behind in my domain and whose crimson woofs pulsed through a living mass. So in your plain and simple hand you carry your horn into the darkness and again, as always, like an abandoned totem, you are awed by this thing that has at once so magical and so practical a task, this soft tubing, perfectly adapted for secretion, that also rises up into an invertebrate spine spurting so many surplus cells and ideas. One of these always manages to sink in its claw and its proclivities are absolutely despotic. It wants to live.

A sudden gift of cruel sobriety gave me an unmistakable piece of information, that lying there a step ahead of me was more than just the two women stripped to the waist, that is, the even more naked, bipartite experience of fear: darkness and silence. I do not want to favor them with either light or the slightest of words. This could not be reconciled with the intercourse of my profession. I would like to build both of them a nice house, but I can't, because you can't build a cottage retroactively, but you can always make love, as if for the first time, on a hedgerow still damp from dew, in a passageway whose grating is just about to be shut, in a train, rhythmically, on a hotel bed just before they noisily throw you out.

I knelt at their feet. The darkness was alive and breathing, this too you must know. Auntie is sick and Uncle Boleslav sends you for garlic, down a short corridor to a long larder. Shut the door, there's a draft, he shouts, and you can't see anything anymore. Across your bare foot a chickie scurries, all you feel is its claw and a silken sweeping across your ankle, and you hope it's not a mouse. The door hinge, recently greased, gives a slow, gentle groan. You proceed along the wall by touch. You catch yourself on a nail and your fingers touch dry bast. You trace a fish hook, you toss down a whip, and it falls but doesn't crack, your knees make their impression in a sack of flour. You knock off a dry candle wick and then you see hanging beside the crucifix a bunch of garlic. You remember that hanging on the right are onions, on the left garlic. With your fingers you say that you should find across the knees of the Redeemer first a veil, then a heart that, it is said, eternally burns and bleeds, and across the left arm of both His body and the cross is a bunch of bulbs whose cloves feel like dry mica. And when you return and stumble across some acolyte's bells, you pick the bells up and for a moment you jingle. Then Boleslav strews onto his nut-brown cutting board some garlic and salt, and from an earthen jar, with a tin spoon, you add in bit by bit oval drops of honey translucent as topaz, and even as a child you can already sense that what is coming into existence is a completely crazy but restorative concoction. It will be served with potato pancakes. Then my uncle opens the almanac and puts on his wire-rimmed glasses. He will read about a hunter who goes hunting but never reaches his blind. On the way he meets a maiden who beneath a full moon has gone to bathe in a lily pond.

I discovered hands clasped together in prayer, long and short fingers stacked in a restive heap. I never saw apples being picked from a bough or falling to the ground, but in our dappled corner I saw the bubbling up of earth that's been loosened by a mole. One after the other, I separated the hands' familiar fingers, with nails so short from eternally battering against the keys, from long sharp brushes that buckle like willow rods, as if I had unclenched a staple on parchment paper containing a secret hesitantly resolved to devour me. There were such books at Štěpán's rectory, a whole heap of them.

I was helplessly enveloped by the bilingual perfume, and in the force field of its scent I identified faces. On your lips and on your lips the taste of apple lingered. A kiss is barely material, the touch of a spirit-level bubble, pollen landing on a drum. The women's shoulders abutted, suggesting the sculptural form of a single woman split in half. I am lying as if I've fallen into bracken after tripping over the blade of a saw left out over the winter. I press my ear against a womb whose mouth, according to a certain pulse, articulates teary little voices, then against a breast whose dandelion head wantonly buds. I raise my hand to the larch-colored dune of hair. Its dry cascade crackles. The double-flowing manes merge into the harvested sheaf of a single man-made fountain, which gushes onto my back in the swinging, centrifugal constructions of a spider woken by static electricity. Sparks fly. A full set of limbs – arms, weight-bearing legs, ears, noses for larger and smaller destinations, all that juts out of a torso – starts to dance in a joint, imparted rhythm, like followers of an invoking hand-me-down god who is, in the middle of a circle of invoking incarnations, like an invoked hieratic pole. The figures lose their cohesion. Through the darkness snippets of dreams freely fly, through the framed grasp of a painting that once again stacks the fingers, so that the curve of the chin is also the conception of the entire physique, even of the biphysique, even of the comphysique of the three figures lying here in the conchshell of darkness which is still populated by fabrications of the imagination.

Still we hover, fall, float, still we turn, are moved, embrace, still we care, entwine, wind and unwind, soar, rotate, penetrate, interpenetrate, we withdraw, open and close, and the doors come in all shapes and sizes: eye, mouth, book, river, into which a ring, and still we draw closer, pull away, support each other, we slip and slide, enfold, elapse, elude, we shake off and challenge, permeate and give way, pile up, come apart and tremble, we get stuck, devour and absorb, flicker, adhere and slip and slide, we climb up and fix onto, and never fear, this too you must know, a string of verbs is infinite. We are still jumping over something, a threshold, a brook, burning leaves, and we branch like a small or even a sizeable tree, also like a panicle of caraway. Then we consolidate and break up, toss each other around and disgorge ourselves. We come to and cease to exist. We are forwards and backwards, and what we are still lies in notions of the water, earth, and air, of settled animals decked out in plants and dramatized in the chemical processes of the elements; what we are is still freely anchored in notions of freely flowing memories of one's own experiences and even in notions of the memories of a thousand-year-old culture of conventionalizing personal experiences in galleries of art. Yet to the feelings of bird or fish or flower we designate parables, and on our own likeness we self-importantly confer myths.

And because we are three and not two, putting mortar beneath the last brick of love makes it swing back and forth, and this movement cannot yet be calculated. We are digressing to spheres of interest that have not yet been addressed, that are unfamiliar, blank. In the glass dome it is no longer snowing, the snow is melting and with the snow the colorful children on the sleds are melting as well. The dome has a crystalline emptiness, and as quickly as it expands, that's how quickly it contracts, ad infinitum. No longer can we designate any parables, any records of feelings, any beautiful memories, we exist in the darkness of matter and in a material world of darkness, and this matter is alive and knows and only now, beyond the divide of the imagination, beneath the threshold of pain, and over the roof of deeply immersed passion, does it have the need above all to address mothers and fathers by name.

Mikuláš! Olga! Jarmila!

Then me to you or you to me or us to you or them to me or you two to yourselves or us to somebody else, what we are composed of, but what is not yet shaped, or someone who forms us, speaks, pronounces, addresses, whispers, breathes out a name completely new for us, for the moment, for knowledge and for ignorance, for permanance and for motion, for all of it, and they still have no names. It is like giving a name to an island formed by a volcano that on one particular morning came to exist and in no time at all ceased to exist; it is a record of what never was and will no longer be.

Trojánka!

You would like to convince me, brother Béda, you who are most likely already having for breakfast lukewarm, dingy, decaffeinated coffee there in your institution, that there is a name, title, or designation for this hill that leans out over the countryside, with its particular geological origins and its precise location. But who could convince me that it might have any name other than the word that's been handed down to me? You see, you clung to the land and went mad. I am giving things names again. That is a brick, that is a beam, that is a building. The roof is made of tiles, but again, tiles and roof are words.

So we were conceived like a substance, handled like a story, taken out like the contents of the den by a golden weasel, and we were perfectly rendered, so perfectly we didn't need to ask for whom.

And so we wouldn't wake, we were gently carried down to denser and denser strata of the atmosphere of the soul, to clearer and clearer contours of consciousness, to more and more actual stitches of physiological costumery.

At first, quite motionless, Olga lies in my arms. Cautiously I pull away from her and transfer her head from Jarmila's lap to the pillow. Jarmila is still trembling a bit, as if with excitement she were looking through a bilingual dictionary. I sit down and bring Jarmila toward me, so she is facing me. She thrashes around. Here is a philological leech. She translates me from the devil's tongue into the tongue of angels. Or perhaps the other way round. She opens her mouth, I open mine, but instead of a name, just a mucous membrane. She falls against my chest. There is a symmetry to our bodies, I am in the middle, on the right and on the left of me are two silent women.

I am embracing them. I am embracing their heads. Their hair brushes my forehead like a veil, but standing down in my groin is my other head, bared all the way to the brain. But not yet scalped. Then a hand touches me, to my very roots, and in a moment, when one lightly and the other roughly touches me there in the comically situated portfolio of my paired balls, in the complete silence we hear the rustle of the fragrance of grain and that instant, before unfruitfully littering us, that instant, which might already, a tiny bit, once again suffuse the recovering will, that short instant took me by surprise and I must give it a name without using a word, just a sigh, and for the first time and, I hope, for the last time in my life I will say: oh.

Oh, which belongs to women, escaped from my lips, and in fact it's all I want to be ashamed of now. Both of the women behaved toward me more than compassionately, as if they found it pleasant themselves. The one on the right kissed my fingertips, the one on the left caressed my face. Is it so astounding, is it deservingly proscribed for adult men to long for a tiny bit of tenderness?

"So you see," said Jarmila.

Inside, behind the heavy velvet curtains, there was complete darkness.

"Good," said Olga.

My head started aching and I felt nauseous.

"Yes," is all I said.

We drank some pure, unadulterated water. I suddenly felt much better. We dozed off. Then we talked a bit about the street noises that came in to us from the commonplace morning, or perhaps it was midday, or even afternoon. From the Castle, through the glass and the fabric, came the voice of the bell, sounding scarcely like bronze anymore. It was ringing one hour or the other, we didn't keep count.

When I woke, Olga and Jarmila were still asleep. I dressed quietly and went out to buy some breakfast. When I came out onto Bridge Street, according to the light, which was already in part artificial, I determined that it was dinner I should be buying, but even so I limited my purchases to a light meal. A bag of oranges and flowers. The barber's chair was free, so I decided that while Olga and Jarmila slept, I'd have my hair washed. It was most pleasant. There was nothing but news on the radio. More casualty figures from the world's battlefields. Vietnam, Laos, the Golan Heights. This too is part of my life. What I remember is reported into my consciousness from afar, including the casualties of strangers.

For half an hour I walked along the Kampa and breathed deeply. I opened the door very quietly. I put my bag of eggs, oranges, and rolls down on the doorstep.

"Jesus Christ, I'm so short and yet I smacked my head," said Jarmila. "It's because that idiot has a slanted ceiling!"

"But he didn't build it, he only nailed some boards to it," said Olga.

"My head feels like crumpled carbon paper," said Jarmila.

"And I just got myself a duchess-size period. Do you have any wadding?" said Olga. "I don't even have a handkerchief."

"I could give you a hanky," said Jarmila.

"You're an absolute savior," said Olga.

"Jesus!" said Jarmila. "It's at it again. Like it's doing it on purpose. My head's shredded."

"Come here and I'll blow on it," said Olga.

Olga took Jarmila in her arms and nursed her. Both of them were still quite naked, without any sort of veil. So too, so many times, did I hold Jarmila in my arms. One of Jarmila's hands was holding her aching head, the other was behind Olga's shoulder. Olga was sitting with her legs wide apart. She held and nursed Jarmila like a shepherd boy does a newborn lamb. And above the sculpture of Olga's thigh a spring of dead blood flowed lively. This too you must know. You reached your hand through a blackberry bush for a golden boletus mushroom and on your wrist the vestiges of blood are drying. You're afraid. Was that the hissing of a snake? The wound has two genders, two tracks, certainly two parts to it. I've seen people bleeding from both sides of a single barricade. Screaming in Czech. On the other side of the cobblestones groaning in German. No Latin was to be heard, dear Štěpán, forgive me; in Nomine Patris et Filii et Spiritu Sanctis. Amen. I leaned against the wall.

Having been neither seen nor heard, I descended to the streets of Malá Strana like one of Miládka's baggage receipts, like a barbell that has lost its gravitational pull, Mr. Interim Administrator of my *gymnasium*.

The headmaster of our *gymnasium* was prematurely retired. He was lucky not to have been sent to a concentration camp. The interim administrator took over his position. The *Wehrmacht* gathered before Moscow, lay siege to Leningrad, and took a bite out of Stalingrad, formerly Tsaritsyn, now Volgograd. Whoever made a mistake, and referred to the interim administrator as the headmaster, was severely reprimanded. The new headmaster insisted on this, so that the interim administrator's title always made his provisionality clear.

"Svoboda! Don't you know how to give an Aryan greeting?"

"I'm sorry, but I don't, Mr. Interim Administrator," I said.

"Come here! You will learn! You see? Thrust out the right hand, fingers together, eyelevel. Your turn!"

"Thrust out the right hand, fingers together, eyelevel," I said.

"Do it! Lift it! Don't just say it!"

"The shit with it!" was my response.

Mr. Interim Administrator gave me a first-class smack across the face and took me to the headmaster's office. He took a barbell out of a cabinet. He ordered me to lift the barbell to eyelevel and keep it there until he said it was enough. He sat down at a desk of continental proportions, and sometimes he looked at me and sometimes he spoke:

"As if you didn't know, idiot, that there was an attempt on the life of the representative of the Reich's protectorate. As if you didn't know, blockhead, that there is war and not peace. As if you didn't know, moron, that they could hang us

all, shoot us all, drive us all into the Ukraine, or rub us all out
as they did Lidice. As if you didn't know, hero, that I too can
say 'Shit'!" He smashed his fist against the desk and roared:
"Keep that barbell at eyelevel."

My arms were already shaking, and it hurt especially in
my lower back and knees. I wondered what would happen if
I were to hit him in the head with the barbell. And I was
scared out of my wits when at that very moment he said:

"Now wouldn't you like to hit me in the head with that
barbell, but you'll keep it at eyelevel, until the next bell
rings." He looked at his watch. "Twenty-two minutes to go."
He rose from the table, picked up a pointer, walked over to
a map on the wall, and pointed at it: "Keep it up! Keep it up,
now! This is the Reich. This is Europe on its knees. Only
Russia stands, remember that, Svoboda! And one little Czech
stands in a corner of the room thinking that this has nothing
to do with him. When you are ordered in school to lift your
hand to eyelevel, you lift it! What I must lift is none of your
business. I don't want to be denounced just because of you. I
won't let the *gymnasium* be closed down just because of you.
You see that atlas? You see what Atlas is carrying on his back?
Answer me!"

"A globe, sir," I said, and now my hands were hurting. As
was my back. "May I put it down?"

"Keep it up! Keep it up!" said the interim administrator,
and he said: "We are a small nation, Svoboda! Throughout
history we have always had to defer, calmly, calmly, and most
cautiously. That's why here and now, at this crossroads of
fateful routes from east to west and of historical routes from
north to south, we can still breathe, work, and live. And
teach, you moron! Quietly, quietly, and most tactfully we can
think even of physiologically radical words, but out in the
corridor we are not permitted to do even the most human

things, no, only in the space set aside for such things. Nothing
– the shit with it! Mikuláš Svoboda! Keep it up! And
remember the primary and inexorable rule of our existence
here in this space, this vale! Survive, you idiot! You must
survive, as the poet said, there are too few of us for a
rebellion." He walked right up to me, helped me keep the
barbell up, and suddenly became polite and even addressed
me formally. "Mr. Svoboda, please, this is just between the
four of our eyes, such is the era, believe me, it is possible to
raise a silent protest of conscience, anything more and you've
destroyed yourself and taken with you an entire class of
innocents. Be good, colleague! And keep it up! Keep it up,
Svoboda."

At last the bell rang and the interim administrator took
the barbell from me. It now seemed that everything was rising
up into the air, and although I'd made a point of thrusting my
fist into my pocket, of not lifting it even when he so
vehemently ordered me to, now, delivered of its iron weight,
my hand flew up all by itself, like feathers that had long been
compressed and ingeniously and premeditatedly elongated,
now had been let go and functioned independently, whatever
I wanted, whatever I thought. The interim administrator
smiled.

"So you see. Already things are going easily and well. Even
voluntarily. And that's how it should be. Nice and lightly,
lightly, and most incidentally."

I summarized the situation as follows: I am not dying, but
I am exhausted. My flat is occupied by a harmonious and
rather amorous environment. For the time being, I will not
reclaim that personal space. I will stay at a hotel, whether I
sleep or just lie down. But the category C and category B
hotel rooms were all occupied. The category A rooms were
occupied as well. All that remained were the category A de

Lux with a star. The responses to my questions about price were hard to take, and I told myself that I would be an idiot to pay so much just to take a prone position. At last I stopped going around. I just marked time. I sat on a bench, and I was cold. I couldn't understand why the pigeons weren't cold. They acted like they were right at home, although above them there was nothing but Prague sky. Morons, apparently they have some sort of all-purpose blood circulation, if not sensations in accordance with the Holy Ghost, amen. Forgive me, Štěpán!

Then I thought of Miládka and I marched off to the train station, whose name and title, for simplicity's sake, I prefer not to recall. At the baggage counter, I learned that Miládka was away, that she was working for the railway in Beroun. I wanted to take a train to Beroun, but then I decided that I would travel south to Hrádek, to see Štěpán, but there was no good connection and so I sat down in the waiting room in the Main Station, and when I felt too much like one of the homeless, I went for a stroll on Wenceslas Square.

I don't know whether it's midnight or only nine o'clock, a whole three points away from tomorrow's infinite line, but why get worked up over it. I will not go stay under my drawing board at the institute, I'm on vacation till the end of the year. I'm doing splendid. I gulped down a grilled kielbasa on a paper plate in front of the Luxor, and as I was mopping up the mustard with what was left of the bread, Květa Kormundová came by, with a child holding each of her hands. She too ordered a kielbasa.

"We were visiting grandma, and now we're going back on the night train, but it's been delayed. The boys are beside themselves."

"Petr and Pavel. How can you tell which is Petr and which is Pavel?" I said.

The kielbasa was ready. Květa smiled with those white teeth of hers and said:

"It's simple." When she'd swallowed her first mouthful of meat she added: "It's incredibly hot." She blew on it, gave Petr a bite, then Pavel, or perhaps the other way round, and she said, as if she were ashamed of it: "To be perfectly frank, because I love them."

I went off with Kormund's family. When Květa asked me what I was doing downtown, I said:

"Just bumming around. I was on my way to see Štěpán, I missed the train, and I have to wait until morning. At home they're working on the roof. It's a complete disaster. And you know, an attic is an attic. But it's no big deal."

"Would you like to stay in Kormund's studio?" said Květa.

"Like before? Very much so, if I wouldn't be any trouble to the gentlemen," I said.

"They sleep standing up," Květa said in the elevator.

Kormund had an extra bed behind his drawing board. I fell asleep instantly and happily, if it is happiness to stretch out, to cover yourself with a blanket, to fluff up a pillow for underneath your head. We'll see in the morning.

From the best of all sleeps I was awakened by Kormund. He was a two-dimensional figure, as in a dream, on a piece of tracing paper, still pinned to his drawing board. He tapped me on the face with a ruler. Somewhere in the flat, closed up behind two sets of doors, Květa was crying. Her cries were intermittent but nearly systematic, as when I place line after line on paper, storey after storey, without any regard for the past or the future of the populace. It was pathetic.

"Get up, go, and explain to Květa and the others that I have not betrayed anybody. It's awful, Mikuláš, that with more freedom comes more dependence. So you learn to hate. And I, who can precisely calculate anything, I was supposed to fire out of the darkness at his head, and it was my job to make sure I missed and instead hit the clock hanging above him. Do you understand? In order to stay in his position, he needed to show that people were threatening him. He needed to arrest a few people so that the others would stop trying to be recognized. Can you grasp what I'm saying? Try and explain it to them. I accepted the assignment so that for a long time I could do what I wanted. I was determined to aim at the face of a person, not a clock. I was determined to kill him. Don't ask his name. He wanted the shot to be fired at him, but only with the certainty that the bullet would miss. Are you following me? Power persists only through being threatened. And when we sat like that and old, exhausted Rychta presided, a lower-level plainclothesman came and pulled it all down. He knew everything. He rendered a detailed account of the situation, named the individuals who should be arrested, and yet didn't name any of us, although it was clear that one of us was an agent provocateur. I would actually have been the one, and I would have stayed in my position if I had shot the face of the clock and not the face of the particular person, whom I had long despised. But believe me, if I had fired, I would have shot him right between the eyes. And that plainclothesman said that if one of you would do it, it would just be doing him a favor; defending him is not part of my duty, I just wanted to tell you this. Can you imagine how confused we were? Everyone who was sitting there looked at me, except the plainclothesman, who was looking under the table. Our paternoster was working normally again, and I, when I was already so deeply implicated, I was determined ... to aim, to fire, and to kill. But I would only be doing him a favor. He's already been transferred. Others have power. Perhaps it's better, I don't know. And I should explain to him that I hated him personally, and that when he asked me to fire only for show, that I was determined to put an end to the show. Who'd believe me? It's late, and now you can appreciate why Kormund couldn't live anymore."

Kormund was on the drawing board, on a piece of phosphorescent tracing paper, waiting until I got up and went and delivered Květa from her tears. I stuck to my blanket and pillow, but Kormund kept hitting me in the face with the ruler.

"At least stop torturing me!" I said.

"You can't let her cry all night," said Kormund.

"I can't explain anything to her, she's just a common Czech goose," I said.

"At least wake her when I ask you to," said Kormund, and he stuck the ruler into my mouth.

I got up out of bed and staggered through the familiar enough landscape of the flat, from doorway to doorway, and then I stood at the head of Květa's bed. Intermittently but systematically, she shook and cried in her sleep.

Should I need to wake her, how should I touch her and where? All I knew is that she was suffering, even as she slept, and perhaps I myself was sleeping, sentenced by Kormund to a horrible dream.

Petr came, wearing a nightshirt, or perhaps it was Pavel. He first looked at his pale, suffering mother, then he looked at me, and then he pointed: do this and all will be good! This, this! Don't you see? He tugged at his earlobe and pointed at his mother, who kept crying on and on. Like this! Like this! He smiled and tugged at his ear. A child and on the bed a woman. The way she cried, it pierced my heart.

I knelt down next to the bed and tugged lightly at Květa's earlobe. She cried some more, then sighed, turned over, and fell into a sleep that I myself might never know again.

At the rectory, Štěpán had a little Christmas tree. On the tree were several tapers. It was past Christmas now, but none of the tapers on his tree had yet been lit. He told me that I would light them when we began our dinner. In Hrádek there was snow, from here west all the way to Příbram, south all the way to Šumava, north to Prague, and east most likely all the way to Moscow, and almost certainly all the way to the Pacific Ocean at approximately our geographical latitude. In friendly conversation there is also a substantial amount of confession, not only mutual support and the joy of seeing each other again. I rested my hands on the table and told my story. Did you give me absolution? An apple for me to cut in two? Will there be a star or a cross? In the walnut we cracked late in the evening, there was no carriage, there was no clothing, there wasn't even a single pearl. The inside was solid, fresh, and had a bitter aftertaste, like red wine. We drank from tin cups, and nothing is lost when you sit down once again with someone who loves you, and your night is not complicated by sex.

"So what do you have to say?" I pressed him to talk.

"Me? Nothing," said Štěpán. "Should I tell you to pray? Is six times enough? Our Fathers or Hail Marys? Why don't you just try it. Repeat, keep repeating words, for instance, in heaven as it is on earth; when you've said it seven times, try something new. Full of grace. Repeat it a thousand times. Then try something else."

"Full of grace, full of grace," I said.

Štěpán smiled and said:

"You've got it. For a third of our lives we sleep. And that third has come. Go to sleep!"

"He's still lying in the garden?" I asked.

"In the cemetery now."

"How did you accomplish that?"

"Simple. Just like the first time. Shovel and earth."

"Someone must have helped you," I said.

"A cabinetmaker. Otherwise, there wasn't a single witness."

"And Olga?"

"We write and we will continue to write. I would have thought you two had gone off together."

"I can't."

"I understand. But I would understand even if you went."

"It's all the same to you?"

"Not everything, although everything looks very much like everything else."

"Well?"

"So you would like me to give you some sort of absolution, but I don't have any to give. How have you sinned? All you've confessed to comes from your imagination. And no one can love two people at the same time, not even Olga and Jarmila. You will always love only in succession and with gradations, as in a spectrum."

"So goodnight, my Štěpán," I said.

I don't have any dreams about that time, but it's still not too far off. Yet closer is the New Year. What will you do with your holiday when you no longer want to confess things you've imagined? You will buy a blue tablecloth with white polka dots and go visit Miládka. It's New Year's and everyone's in a good mood, and on trains you feel at home.

At the Beroun train station you're all ready to spread the tablecloth, but they tell you Miládka isn't at the baggage counter. What? She got married. You should have been there. We put a dining car on one of the sidings, it was a wedding like no other before.

"Who did she marry? One of you, in blue, in a railway uniform?"

"What makes you think that? It was a civilian, just like yourself."

I went for a walk, as was my habit, in a forest not far away. I avoided the road to the high-rise development I'd designed, which was already somewhat dilapidated. On the broad foundation of the new highway, tired machines, bull-dozers, and scrapers were lying idle. From my heart I wished them a good repose for New Year's. I walked to a pub for beer and pickled herring. Into the taproom walked Miládka, and she ordered a big earthenware pitcher of beer. I couldn't imagine her taking a glass pitcher to her baggage-handler friends. I rushed over to her. I wanted to give her the table-cloth and I wanted to tell her the story that hadn't a single witness. I thought she'd find it interesting.

"Miládka," I said, "I have something to tell you."

"No! No! Don't say a word, please." In self-defense, she pressed the earthenware pitcher against her chest. "I know, I know, but I forbid you to speak to me!"

"What do you think I want to tell you?"

Now she was holding the big pitcher, with the fine aroma of a beer I well knew, Golden Horse, she was holding the pitcher by its handle, and with the other hand she was intimately handling my ear.

"*I* will tell *you*. I will say it into your ear. May I? But you, Mikuláš, you may not say it. That you love me. And me, I'm married again now," she said festively. "A new year is upon us. Don't you want to drink to it?"

She handed me the pitcher. I drank some beer, and so did Miládka. The foam assaulted our faces and gave our chins splendid white beards. And made us laugh.

"And the luggage?" I asked.

"I'm cultivating mushrooms in the cooperative here. You can't imagine how beautiful it is. It smells like anise. It would be a ghastly bore to spend your entire life moving suitcases here and there, don't you think?"

"Of course," I said. "So have a happy and healthy new year!"

I let her go. From a safe distance I followed her, and she led me to a cottage. There was, of course, a light on in the cottage. Through the kitchen window, whose lace curtains remained open, for me, an unfamiliar man was tenderizing cutlets. I kept watching for a while, to see whether I'd made a mistake and whether he was anything like the plain-clothesman, but I didn't see in him any similar traits. I'd never seen him before. And when the curtains were pulled, I don't know why, all I saw was light with a definite spectrum and in my mind I counted the white polka dots on my blue gift. Once again, I did not make use of the pistol. I had imagined me and Miládka shooting a roll of caps off at midnight.

I repaired to the train station and sat for a while on the platform. The passing locals were full of merriment. Celebrating. People would come up to me and say that when it's New Year's, it's New Year's, with which I heartily agreed, and that Pop isn't Pop anymore, in case you didn't know. I said yes, and they said that I should drink with them, that the new year will be more merry, that it's been a bore under Novák, if you know who we mean by Novák. I said that they are surely referring to the highest representative of the state, President Novotný, and this satisfied them, and they let me sit on my bench and enjoy the solitude of a train station where nothing was traveling, where there was just a glistening track from here to there, and where no train whistled.

But then a train pulled very quietly in and slowly approached the switches and the gravel, which was all over the place, and it was an international express. I went over and tapped on it, as if it were a mailbox. This too you must know. You toss a letter in and tap the mailbox for good luck.

I walked along car after car, it was a longie. Inside, they were making beds, playing cards, and taking naps, and I should have another thousand verbs for what I saw, but I was exhausted. Behind one particular window I saw Olga. Like many of the foreigners and like many of our own who hadn't gone to bed yet, who weren't amusing themselves by playing cards, and who weren't in the mood for a nap, she was looking out the window at the platform. No one was selling frankfurters, because the train was just passing through and, according to the timetable, stopping just for a moment.

I was going with you, Olga, I was going beside you, I was making my escape there by your window, right by your face, and you were looking at me. Why didn't you smile as you do with someone you've known so long, why didn't the blue spectrum of your eye, looking toward the platform and depot, why didn't it recognize me at the closed door of the car as it pulled away, the door that I could still have easily opened? You should know that I have a nice blue tablecloth with white polka dots, the number of which I've not yet had the opportunity to calculate. I also have my papers and even an amusing toy. Do I have to shoot my capgun off in order for you to take note of me? If you were to have taken note of me, I would have gotten on, but the train's already gone and the red squares on its last car are entering the darkness. Snow lowers the curtain. I will walk to Svatá through the forest. I will leave footprints on an untouched surface. You can see even at night. The snow shines. Above Beroun shines a red electric communist star.

I strolled along a shortcut and climbed up above Knížkovice. There I encountered a strong wind and perfect solitude. Tired, I sat down on a log that smelled of pitch, and then I walked further into the forest, in which I did not intend to freeze to death, which I just wanted to pass through, and why not. I no longer indulged myself in such snowy night marches. At least I'll sleep well tomorrow, and it'll be New Year's.

Outside of Svatá I walked along a road. It had stopped snowing. The snow crunched, but it wasn't that icy. There was smoke coming from the houses on the horizon, the moon was setting. In the curve of the road, coming toward me, a few blurry forms emerged. I stopped and counted them. There were six. Why weren't there seven or five? They too stopped and on the road they arranged themselves facing me like a barrier of black points that might appear to be participants in a sufficently long, possibly infinite line that extends right to Hudlice, where there is a celebrated country fair, but in the summer, and extends left all the way to Žebrák and Točník, where there's that royal castle. But best we don't remember.

We stood facing each other in the middle of the road, one and several. Neither me nor them, no one intended to move an inch. All we shared was curiosity.

"Hallo!" one of them called out.

"Ho, ho, ho!" I sang out almost ceremonially, and then I added in a more normal tone of voice: "So, what's up?"

"Tall as you are, you're short!" one of them called. "You just gonna stand there?"

I stood where I was, not a step forward, not a step back. I looked at the group of people and saw that they were all men, most likely young. The first snowball flew past my head, as if fired by a snow soldier. The moon was setting. But the snow and a few stars still sparkled, I couldn't see the fainter stars, snowballs rained, hailed, and struck me, one after the other, and many they were. The men scattered and then came together, they scooped up snow and squeezed it into big and little balls, and with great success they hit me with those big and little balls, which were shattering on contact, breaking into smithereens, marking the immobile target's body and face. They shouted, they laughed, and I could still make out that one voice:

"The communist swine!"

One snowball struck me in the vicinity of my heart. Four sharp needles forced their way through the buttonholes of my wool cardigan and stabbed me in the heart. I might have been dead for a few moments, I don't know, but I did pass out for a long time.

When I opened my eyes, I saw stars above me and I established their position in terms of their constellation. This too you must know. If you fall asleep on a haystack after daybreak, you'll wake up underneath Orion, Cygnus, and Delphinus. I was lying on a toboggan, my head bent back, and other than the sky I could see the toboggan's tracks. They were taking me somewhere, hauling me somewhere; two of them were pulling the toboggan by a rope, the others were hurrying along behind us.

May they haul me, I didn't say to myself, I just felt it, and it was very nice. My heart was still being pierced, but by the time we reached Beroun I'd recovered a little, I got up on my elbows, and by the time we entered the square near the church I was nearly sitting up. This was the end of the road. Voices. Two bands in two pubs opposite one another. Somewhere someone singing. Adults as well as children rolling a snowman in the middle of the square. A window opening. A hand holding a sparkler and waving it around. Someone shouting, you want trotters, you want trotters, captain?

All or nearly all six of them were still standing there in a semicircle around the toboggan. They too were in full voice. They sounded youthful and melodious. I wanted to say something, gentlemen, but the word *patres* flashed in my mind, and it seemed better to say nothing at all. They were examining me with such sentences as:

"He's sitting up."

"If he's sitting up, he's not down for the count."

"One of his shoes is missing."

"I've got it in my bag."

"Then put it on him!

"Rum him or treat him."

"And tie his shoelaces, too!"

"How?"

"He's not down for the count?"

"Gentlemen," I said, "hand me my shoe. Good! Now where are my polka dots?"

"He wants his bag," one of them said, and the bag passed through all their hands. In the bag was my blue tablecloth with white polka dots, and it suddenly occurred to me that if I weren't dead, I could still count the polka dots.

When I got to my feet, I had a good, downright festive feeling. They patted me on my shoulders, as if I had achieved something magnificent. They handed me their bottle of rum and then invited me to join them at one of the pubs. There was music there, but I said I'd rather not.

I stayed out in the square, now practically alone, but lights were on in many of the windows, celebrating New Year's, as a matter of fact the new year one thousand nine hundred and sixty-eight, but other calendars calculate it otherwise. The toboggan stayed outside as well. So I pulled the toboggan across the square to the Blue Star Hotel, but it wasn't open, even though there was music playing there too. Someone was blowing a trumpet solo. Next I walked across the square to the Hotel Bohemia, and like a horse I tied the toboggan up to a stone acorn that was growing on the gate. Here too they weren't asleep, but they too were already closed.

I asked the porter about accommodations. His first impression of me was completely negative, but when he'd looked me over, he smiled and said:

"For you? Of course."

In my room I looked at the mirror in order to understand what was so 'of course' about me. I was completely gray, silver, and white, it was in vain that I tried to shake off the snow that had long ago, while I was sleeping, turned to water. Luckily the room was warm.

It is said: it can turn a man's hair gray.

My aunt didn't call my uncle "Boleslav," she just called him "Hey!"

I would like to know when this happened. It didn't happen long ago, but it did happen very thoroughly. I don't think that even my mama would recognize me at first sight, nor my papa, let alone Jarmila or Miládka, nor even you, my brother, you would have to look me over, look at me for a while.

So actually, at first sight of me, Olga too must not have recognized me from the train, she couldn't have unless I turned gray later, when she and the train left the station and I walked to Svatá, but I don't know precisely when the snow began to fall, whether it was in that one instant when the curtain fell on the red squares of the final car. It could have been a while before that and then, before my hair was covered with snow, I would still have been bareheaded, gray, silver, and white, at most with a reflection in the blue spectrum, something else somewhere between heaven and earth or somewhere on earth or in heaven. And these are the stories, stories of color and of strewn words and a single line that consists of an infinite number of points. I'm looking forward to, after New Year's, being on time for work. I don't think Květa will be angry with me when I show her my gray hair; Kormund's hair was already streaked with gray and Květa's too isn't completely dark anymore. I noticed this when we were eating our kielbasy in Wenceslas Square. Provided she agrees to marry me, Petr and Pavel would have to become architects or designers, but best not keep getting worked up over it. I'm exhausted, but it isn't true that all I want to do is sleep.

With the pleasure that came from its being just a toy, I placed the black pistol against my temple, which was adorned with sparkling frost, like my forest, where I was lucky not to freeze. And without a single thought about Olga or Jarmila or Miládka, even without any more thoughts about Květa, but thinking about Petr and Pavel, for they are boys and boys understand cap guns, I fired once, twice, and then a third time, because good and bad things come in threes. Dryly, sharply, and surely the caps did pop, and there are stories you don't understand, for instance, why you're holding a toy when you should be holding a weapon.

But several stories that seemed to make sense to us or that, as true stories, actually did make sense, but seemed like dreams, these stories are like everything plain and simple: Many things happen between birth and death.

My story is different, and perhaps it isn't a story at all, but just one view. Do you think that I mean that view beyond the wall, of the tow of the blue spectrum of night colors? Certainly. That too. But back when I'm thinking of, no woman had yet entered my field of vision, and no mark of gender had yet been projected onto my retina.

Back when I could not yet tramp around so much, when I couldn't cover so much ground, they'd put me in a carriage, my mama and papa. Together, in concord, they pulled me up a hill. I could see nothing but sharply rising green sides covered with flowers, and Mama's and Papa's hands on the chrome carriage handle. A sky full of clouds. And against the cloudy sky my father's head and my mother's gently blowing hair. They reached the top. They stopped. Father spoke. Mother pointed. But I still couldn't see anything or hear anything, I saw only the tops of the sides and a white cloud, and I heard only my father's flowing voice, but still I am unable to consider the situation logically: they are looking at and describing the wide, wide countryside, and before me is nothing but those green sides, like a green roof. I'd have to scramble up in order to look with them and in order to say with them: Look at that!

Of course, such thoughts could not have occurred to me, I had no more sense than that cottontail hare, or leveret, which not far away was nibbling some clover and phosphorescently announcing with its rear: Hello! Now you see me, now you don't.

Remember: Father and Mother are standing with their backs to me and they're so absorbed, they're so into the view, that I can share this absorption as if their absorption and as if the view itself were flowing through their hands along the chrome handle and down the green sides to me. They've forgotten not only their child, but even about the carriage, or they're mistaken in what they imagine – that the carriage with little Mikuláš in it stands with them on flat ground – and so they let go of the carriage, let their hands drop from the handle and, where the handle was, they take each other's hands. Perhaps they even kissed.

The carriage, with me in it, escapes back down the hill. I skillfully jump out of the carriage, run back to my parents, and say:

"The carriage! The carriage!"

"Never mind! Never mind!" says Father, and he lifts me up in his arms.

"And the sun, look, it's drawing up its last will and testament!" says Mama.

Father keeps me in his arms. I feel the roughness of his face – by dinnertime he's already grown a dark beard – and smell the scent of soap and cigarette smoke. And that is the story, that is the view.

Father holds me in his arms. His heart is beating. Even his watch seems to be beating. Out of the countryside before us comes a light, pleasant breeze. In the valley a river flows forth, perhaps swiftly, perhaps lazily, but certainly blue. And a lazy blue sky. The village is whitening. The great houses, the church, the gathering of lindens, all of them look like toys. Fading, spreading, somewhere a long shadow is drifting off. Here a bell rings. There a stork in flight. I keep looking up at the birds and the birdies and all the members of birddom in flight, but we are as high as the stork and the little swallow points, like pencil points, now glide, now dash and dot themselves below us. The hills are bare of buildings, except for one. That house on the hill is on fire. It burns for a while and then goes out. The sun passes beyond the line and now the phoenix house is sitting there like a gray pigeon.

And here and there are many other, different sorts of hills, which I know from ankles, knees, chin, elbows, from the bow of the canvas cover when hay is pulled on a barrow, the teats of a cow and of the holy Madonna, a loaf of bread. Simple things like this that I have touched. And isn't there also the feel of a straw mattress on which you sleep and which smells of aaronsbeard?

And it's still very near and still very far and still green and still blue, but blue is still just right before the tow of colors of a certain spectrum begins, and along rails that no longer glisten, as if in an arc through a field of lupine and chamomile a choo-choo train is chugging along, and then what seems to be a whistle and the dry clackety-clack of train wheels and the jingling at a railway crossing somewhere, and sheep, and it all resides within the cries of flitting, already nearly invisible martins and swifts.

At an unknown spot, somewhere someone is blowing an instrument, I can't tell which, and like falling asleep to thrumming, like a pebble knocking around in a metal cup, somewhere the murmur of a faraway, enameled sound going somewhere else, a sputtering motorcycle riding off. This too you must know.

"And now I'll show you something," says Papa. "It's really something. Take a deep breath!"

He turned me upside down, held me by my feet, and said, Look now, look, and I opened my eyes, which were just above grass level, and the landscape that used to lie at my feet now lay in the heavens, and as if something had struck me in the chest, as if suddenly, with great force, I passionately took in air, I was flooded by the scent of herbs just beneath grass level and into me rushed a space in which the landscape was reflected upside down, and I was in the countryside and the countryside was in me, and this occurred on Trojánka.

Don't imagine that any name enters into your destiny by chance. It was just as commonplace as the rudiments at school. The way you learned to read, write, and 'rithmetic. And if you never notched up another total love, this one was as three-in-one as our dear Lord God; there was your papa and there was your mama and there is me. And your own life? Partly on earth, partly in hell, partly in heaven.

So try sometimes feeling as if your invisible father were holding you just above your ankles, and you're looking out at the countryside upside down, from any dividing line to any horizon; you will see.

Soon he turned your view back rightside up, but we were forever changed.

So does love arise.

When Papa placed me back on the ground, he said, So you see, and I said, And that's that. Mama smiled and said:

"You are our little countryside boy."

And so I was and forever am characterized, and it happened at the top of a hill that has forever been called Trojánka. My father turned me upside down to the landscape, and the landscape turned upside down to me, this is my world, my destiny, my past, my language, my thought, my project, say what you want; it is and I am part of it.

I am forty years old and I am lying in the Hotel Bohemia on a bed in a room, and the room is a space. It is a space I did not design, I just entered it and now I am once again contemplating, out of a peculiar necessity, a man who is half awake and half asleep, like my country. Period.

Like my own solitude and the solitude of words spoken into the emptiness of the hotel room. I listen. I am huddled, crammed, lodged here on this bed within an infinite number of sounds and words, more and more words and verbal splinters of a love lived transitorily: words whispered, spoken, proclaimed and exclaimed, prayed, cursed, dreamed, vowed, an endless line of words, each of which is divisible into more and more refined shades, ad infinitum, split into more and more distinct kernels of meaning, and which relate to one word alone and which make up one word alone, indivisible as a period. A word that is no longer a word, but just a reminder of a story that was not a story but just a view seen, beheld, examined, as if I were me when Papa turned me upside down to the landscape.

Of course, it could have been a landscape somewhere south of Moscow, near Heidelberg, or in Utah, but what occurred occurred on Trojánka. And so here is where I am.

This book was set in the Adobe Berling Roman typeface and printed by Data Reproductions Corp. in Auburn Hills, MI. The jacket was printed by Strine Printing in York, PA. The book and jacket were designed by Robert Wechsler, and the cover art is based on his photo of Prague.

Living Parallel is the fourteenth volume of Czech literature in translation to be published by Catbird Press since its founding in 1987, including works by Karel Čapek, Vladimír Páral, Jaroslav Seifert, Karel Poláček, Daniela Fischerová, and Jáchym Topol. The Garrigue Books imprint for our Czech literature in translation was named in honor of Charlotte Garrigue Masaryk, the Brooklyn native who was Czechoslovakia's first first lady in 1918, the American who has had the greatest influence on Czech history and culture.

For more information about our Czech literature, as well as our American and British literature and our sophisticated humor, please visit our website, www.catbirdpress.com, or request a catalog from catbird@pipeline.com, 800-360-2391, or Catbird Press, 16 Windsor Road, North Haven, CT 06473.